THE CALM AND THE STORM

THE CALM AND THE STORM

Alan Savage

This first world edition published 2008
in Great Britain and 2009 in the USA by
SEVERN HOUSE PUBLISHERS LTD of
9–15 High Street, Sutton, Surrey, England, SM1 1DF.

British Library Cataloguing in Publication Data

Savage, Alan, 1930-
  The calm and the storm
  1. Torpedo-boats - Fiction 2. Malta - History - Siege,
  1940-1943 - Fiction 3. War stories
  I. Title
  823.9'14[F]

ISBN-13: 978-0-7278-6699-8   (cased)

All Severn House titles are printed on acid-free paper.

Typeset by Palimpsest Book Production Ltd.,
Grangemouth, Stirlingshire, Scotland.
Printed and bound in Great Britain by
MPG Books Ltd., Bodmin, Cornwall.

As you walk through the storm,
Hold your head up high,
And don't be afraid of the dark
At the end of the storm is a golden sky,
And the sweet silver song of the lark.

Oscar Hammerstein II

PART ONE
The Calm

'I have nor peace within nor calm around'
Percy Bysshe Shelley

Business As Usual

S ub-Lieutenant Arnold Cooper's face was flushed as he emerged from the hatch on to the flying bridge of the motor-torpedo boat. 'Plymouth reports convoy under attack by S-boats, thirty-five miles south-west of the Eddystone, sir.' Fresh-faced and eager, he stumbled over the words; he had served with MTBs for more than a year, and under this skipper throughout that time, and, given Lieutenant-Commander Lord Eversham's penchant for seeking trouble, had seen as much action as most men experienced in a lifetime at sea, but the imminent prospect of a fight could still excite him.

'Very good, Mr Cooper. Make to Plymouth that we are on our way to engage but request additional information as to numbers involved. Confirm that to Portsmouth, and then make to all boats: Course two-six-five, two thousand revolutions.' In contrast to his second-in-command, Duncan Eversham's voice was calm. Twenty-seven years old, six feet two inches tall, and with both the build and the somewhat craggy features of the rugby forward and international yachtsman he had been before 1939, he had skippered an MTB from the day war had broken out, and his service record was indicated both by the fact that although on his sleeves were the wavy stripes of an officer in the RNVR, the Royal Naval Volunteer Reserve, in two years he had risen from the rank of sub-lieutenant to lieutenant-commander and flotilla leader, and that on the left breast of his tunic – presently concealed by his oilskin top – he wore the stripes of the Distinguished Service Cross and Bar.

His crews worshipped him, and Cooper, lacking family connections or even a home outside of this little ship, more than most. 'Aye-aye, sir,' he acknowledged, and disappeared below again.

Duncan thumbed the intercom to the engine room. 'We have a situation developing, Jamie,' he said. 'I am increasing speed to two thousand revolutions.'

'Aye-aye, sir,' Engine-Artificer James Goring replied.

'And we will need you up top when we close the enemy.'

'Yes, sir,' Jamie said, enthusiastically.

'Mr Rawlings,' Duncan said, still speaking quietly, 'Have the crew stand by for action, but no one is to come on deck until the bell is rung; we shall be at speed for the next couple of hours.' When it would be a case, on deck, of holding on to avoid being swept overboard by either wind or wave. 'Have Wilson serve an early lunch; there'll be time before we get there.'

'Aye-aye, sir.' The petty officer went down the hatch.

Left to himself on the flying bridge, Duncan eased the throttle forward, listened to the low growl of the Packard three-shaft petrol engine increase to a roar as it developed close to its full four thousand break horsepower, and the streamlined seventy-two-foot-long hull suddenly took off, rising on a plane to skate across the shallow waves; it was a bright November morning, with the sun still low on the eastern horizon behind them, and within seconds they were travelling faster than the light following breeze.

There was no speedometer, but from experience Duncan knew that they were making just short of forty knots, with another few in reserve if he needed them, and even in calm conditions, as the little ship occasionally dipped into a deeper than usual trough, a rattle of spray came aft; the bridge was not roofed and foam splattered across the windshield and settled on his cap and oilskin-clad shoulders. As the flotilla had been cruising south of Portland Bill – just visible to the north – they were some eighty-odd miles from the given position. Much would depend upon how capable the convoy was of protecting itself, and how many of the S-boats were attacking.

He looked left and right at the other five boats in the flotilla, spread out to each side like a naval cavalry charge, each with a huge white bone in its teeth and a bubbling wake spreading away behind it; those waves would eventually break on Chesil Beach. The six little ships were identical, constructed largely of plywood, and displacing forty-three tons when deep loaded, as now. Each was armed with two twenty-one-inch torpedo tubes, mounted in the bows, four machine guns, two heavy and two light, and a single twenty-millimetre cannon, as well as four depth charges on the afterdeck. Each also had a crew of thirteen men.

Schnell-boats, he thought grimly. As the compilers of the Treaty of Versailles had not considered it necessary to legislate for small craft, no restrictions had been placed on the German powers of imaginative inventiveness, thus they had developed a large fleet of the fast motor boats long before the Admiralty had had any idea what to do about them, bound up as they were in a world of battleships and cruisers. Duncan recalled that even after the outbreak of hostilities they had still not formed any idea of what their own boats could be used for; he had been appointed to command one largely because he was a well-known yachtsman, experienced at navigating both sides of the English Channel.

He had not known what he was getting into either, and had in fact been decidedly miffed that he had not been appointed at least to a destroyer. He had put it down mainly to the machinations of his mother. Kristin, Lady Eversham – now the Dowager Lady Eversham – had dominated his life, as, with her remarkable beauty – inherited from her Swedish mother – her enormous wealth – inherited from her Spanish billionaire father – and her ultra-positive personality – inherited from both – she had dominated almost every life with which she had come into contact. This had included, and still did, the admiral who was his commanding officer, who had some ambitions to get to know her better, supposing he ever summoned up the courage to risk it. While accepting that her only son was not only required to fulfil his obligations as a naval reservist but was desperate to do so, Kristin had wanted him in a job where he would be home at least once a week, and she invariably got her own way.

She had also assumed, as had he and everyone else, that skippering a small motor boat operating in the English Channel would be merely a wartime extension of the yachting in which he had spent his peacetime summers, certainly with the war at that time being fought a long way away in Poland.

That perception had been altered abruptly with the successful German invasion of the West, and their consequent control of the French Channel ports that had changed the Channel itself from a domestic piece of water into an unending battle-ground.

And in catapulting the MTB flotillas into the front line it had enabled him to devote his service life not only to what he enjoyed doing most, but what he apparently did better than most, and had earned him both honours and rapid promotion, all without, so far, a scratch. Whereas Father, too old to take an active part in the struggle, but yet determined to play his part the moment he had been given the opportunity, had been blown up, together with his yacht, when engaged in rescuing British soldiers from the beach at Dunkirk, thus propelling his only son into the peerage at the age of twenty-six.

He wondered for how long his good fortune was going to last? And today, of all days, he would have preferred to be at home, with Alison. But even if he could not make it, she would have Mother to shepherd her through the possible traumas of childbirth.

But the German Schnell-boats had to be uppermost in his mind; they remained his chief antagonists and his most serious adversaries, and he had a responsibility to his crew. The enemy were mostly a hundred feet long, displaced twice the tonnage of their British rivals, and were twice as heavily armed. While their size enabled them to be driven by powerful diesel engines, too heavy to be used in the smaller British boats, but yet giving them a fair turn of speed. Lurking in the many ports scattered along the coast only sixty-odd miles away, and alerted by the long-distance Fokke-Wulf Condor reconnaissance aircraft of the Luftwaffe, they could time their forays to catch small convoys just as the skippers were beginning to relax at the sight of the English coast, do the maximum damage, and then dart back to safety before, as a rule, adequate forces could be brought against them.

Today, he was resolved, they were going to be unlucky. Because they could be beaten, by marginally superior speed combined with superior tactics. Duncan had first earned his reputation by destroying one in the rock-strewn waters of the Channel Islands, and since then his flotilla had added another. If he respected the enemy ships, he no longer feared them.

Cooper and Rawlings rejoined him on the bridge. 'All hands standing by, sir,' the petty officer said.

'Thank you, Mr Rawlings. Take a sweep, will you.'

Rawlings had sailed with Duncan since the beginning of the war, and Duncan knew he had the keenest eyesight of anyone on board. Of course, with well over fifty miles to go, there was no possibility of his sighting the engagement as yet, but it was important to make sure what, if any, other ship, whether friend or foe, might be in the vicinity. Rawlings understood what was required, and levelled his binoculars.

'Portsmouth and Plymouth have acknowledged our signal, sir,' Cooper said. 'Plymouth has identified the convoy as a coastal out of Milford Haven. It consists of six small merchantmen and one corvette escort; they are endeavouring to organize some air support, but this may take a little while owing to other commitments.'

'Tell me about it,' Duncan growled. 'Have they any idea of the size of the attacking force?'

'They reckon a dozen S-boats.'

'Shit! And one corvette?'

'Yes, sir. Grub's up. If you'd like to eat now, I'll take her.'

Duncan nodded. 'Probably a good idea. Maintain two-six-five and two thousand.'

He slid down the ladder into what would have been the saloon on a yacht, but here was the mess, where five men were already seated, eating the hot stew provided by Wilson the cook, hanging on to their plates as even in calm conditions, at two thousand revolutions the boat was inclined to bounce.

On a vessel this small, intimacy was inevitable. Duncan and Cooper might each have his own tiny cabin aft, where they shared a heads, but they took their meals with the crew, the only concession to rank being that Duncan sat at the head of the table.

'Any idea what we're taking on, sir?' asked Leading Seaman Morrison, having to shout above the roar of the engine.

'Maybe a dozen S-boats,' Duncan replied. There were a couple of low whistles, and he added, 'There's a corvette already on the scene.'

'Room for one more?' asked Jamie Goring, emerging up the ladder from the engine room, which was situated immediately below the mess deck.

The men obligingly shifted along the bench seat that lined the side of the table to make space for the young man next to Duncan; they all understood and did not resent the fact that the two men, for all the enormous difference in their ranks and their social stations, were friends. Jamie was only an inch shorter than Duncan and slightly built, although he had powerful shoulders and strong hands, with wavy fair hair and fresh features. Just twenty years old and the son of a small garage owner outside the Solent ferry and yachting harbour of Lymington, close to the Eversham estate, Jamie had just become a member of Duncan's sailing crew in the last yacht race before the war. Having sailed the west coast of Europe with his father since he had been a small boy, he knew the waters even better than his friend and commander, for which he had proved more valuable even than as the very capable marine engineer that was his profession. And he also had covered himself with glory over the past two years; on his navy blue jumper he wore the ribbon of the Distinguished Conduct Medal.

Now he asked at large as a plate of stew was placed in front of him, 'Scrap coming up?'

'And how,' Morrison commented.

'All well below?' Duncan asked.

It was a rhetorical question; Jamie Goring was meticulous in his engine room maintenance. Thus it was an indication, as Jamie well knew, that the skipper was not quite as calm as he pretended. Because equally he knew that while Duncan might have been educated at Eton and Pembroke College, Cambridge, as befitted his rank and background, and as opposed to village school and a job in his father's garage at sixteen, he was his intellectual inferior. Where Jamie, an avid reader in his spare time, had spent the last few years studying history and philosophy as well as navigation and motor mechanics, Duncan Morant – as he had then been – had lived the high life, as he felt he was entitled to do, again because of his background and his mother's immense wealth, which had maintained him even after she had been divorced by his now dead father.

Jamie liked the big man as much as he had always envied the Bugatti he drove or the forty-five-foot schooner he had raced in 1939, both of course provided by the fabulous Kristin. But the liking, and the envy, had become submerged beneath the guilt ever since that August day in 1939 when Kristin had elected to sail back with them from St Malo to Lymington following the Cowes–Dinard race. She was of course an experienced yachtswoman. In fact, as she was not averse to confessing, it had been on board the previous Lord Eversham's yacht in the Mediterranean, at the age of fifteen, that she had been seduced by his lordship, who had then been simple Douglas Morant. That event, which had become a sensational scandal when she had been expelled from her Madrid convent as her pregnancy was revealed, had produced the man sitting beside him now.

But that calamitous start to her adult life had not in the least hindered or altered her lifestyle, which was even more hedonistic than that of her son's. When her divorce had been heard, no fewer than ten cases of adultery had been proved against her – not that she had attempted to deny any of them. Thus she was clearly the sort of woman from whom any self-respecting young man should have run a mile. Save that Kristin was not 'a sort of woman'; she was Kristin, who when she elected to impale a man with those huge green eyes always got what she wanted.

And she had wanted him! He had not believed it could be happening. She had been forty-one, he had been eighteen! But she had retained the body, and the ardour, of a Greek goddess, and he had always been a romantic dreamer. What was even more unbelievable was that while he, terrified but eager, had assumed that he was being seduced into a one-night stand by a randy older woman, that had been two years ago, and she still wanted to see him whenever he had shore leave. He would not have been human had he not wondered why, aloud. 'You are what I want,' she had said, adding, 'Now and always.'

So what did he want? Certainly no other woman could possibly ever measure up to Kristin. But could he spend the rest of his life in a whirl of secret trysts . . . and guilt? Because this fun-loving, splendidly bold, and so likeable man beside him, who in real terms had just about become his stepson, knew nothing of it. Jamie had no doubt that Duncan was aware that his mother was totally amoral and sexually voracious, but it would never cross his mind that she would ever take up with a garage mechanic young enough to be her son who was also a member of his crew.

If he were ever to find out . . .

'Purring like a babe, sir,' he said.

'Fuel?'

'Two thirds full.'

Duncan nodded. 'We are going to have to maintain this speed for the next hour at least.'

Fuel consumption was double the normal at virtually maximum revs.

'She'll handle it, sir. And get us home.'

'Good man.' Duncan finished his meal. 'Morrison, I want every man in steel helmet and life jacket when we close the enemy.'

'Aye-aye, sir.'

'Wilson –' the cook had joined them – 'when every man has eaten, have the mess prepared for possible casualties. That will include survivors from any sunken ships.'

'Aye-aye, sir.'

'Jamie, you'll assist Wilson.'

'Aye-aye, sir.'

Duncan drained his coffee, and got up. 'Then good fortune to you all.'

'And to you, sir,' they chorused.

He went up the ladder, and when the last of the crew had finished his meal, Wilson and Jamie started clearing up. 'Reminds me of that time, last Christmas,' Wilson said. 'When we fished that Yankee woman out of the drink. She was some dish, as I recall.'

'Yes,' Jamie agreed, not sure that he wanted to be reminded of that incident. The only rift that had ever arisen between him and Kristin had been when she had discovered that he had been the crew member, as obviously the youngest and most innocent man aboard, deputed by her son to put the glamorous but freezing and only half-conscious Rebecca Strong to bed, a duty that had involved both removing her sopping and equally freezing clothing, and in assisting her to use the heads. Kristin had got over that particular episode, but only a few months later – which was in fact only six months ago – they had been required to rescue Mrs Strong again, this time from the top end of Norway, where she had been to extricate her famous scientist father. On that occasion she had had the support of the British Government, who apparently wanted the old genius working for them instead of the Germans. But as the whole thing had taken a week – and nearly got them embroiled with the super-battleship *Bismarck*, just undertaking her famous if short-lived cruise – once again he had been thrown into what Kristin had considered unacceptable intimacy with the Swedish-American woman.

'She went back to the States after that Norwegian caper, didn't she?' Wilson remarked. 'Cloak and dagger stuff. I wonder what she's doing now?'

Just so long as she's not doing it around me, Jamie thought.

'The skipper's bearing up pretty well,' Wilson continued, in gossipy mood.

'Doesn't he always?'

'Well, yes. But with his wife about to . . . you know about that?'

'Of course I do,' Jamie said. 'But I don't reckon it's any of our business. And I'm damned sure he's not going to let it interfere with his.'

It was past noon, and the Eddystone Light Tower, one of the oldest in existence, was visible to starboard, when Rawlings said, 'Smoke, red ten.'

'At last!' Duncan was back on the helm. 'Make to flotilla, Mr Cooper: Alter course two-five-five. Maintain two thousand revolutions until further orders. Then make to Portsmouth and Plymouth: Am in sight of enemy and will engage within thirty minutes. Give them the exact time of the transmission, and then enter it in the Log.'

'Aye-aye, sir. And not a bloody aircraft in sight,' the sub-lieutenant remarked as he ducked into the hatchway.

Rawlings made a sweep of the sky, but no comment. Duncan concentrated. Now the smoke was visible to the naked eye, and arising from more than one source, and now distant rumbles of gunfire could just be heard.

Cooper reappeared. 'Signals acknowledged sir. They wish us good luck.'

'Very nice. Now make to escorting corvette: Please advise situation. *MTB 41* and support approaching from East. Send that in clear, and use 2182.' This was the international Shipping Channel, on which all ships at sea kept a permanent watch.

'With respect, sir, won't Jerry pick that up? His operators will certainly speak English.'

'I'm sure they do,' Duncan agreed. 'But I'm also pretty sure he can see us by now. And it's our business to discourage him. Carry on, Mr Cooper.'

'Aye-aye, sir.' Cooper disappeared down the hatch.

'What can you see, Mr Rawlings?' Duncan asked.

'Two ships on fire, sir. Another listing. Some boats in the water.'

'Can you make out the corvette?'

'I would say that she is one of the ships on fire, sir.'

'Damnation. And the enemy?'

Rawlings counted. 'I have eleven.'

'Then, if that earlier report was correct, the corvette must have got one of the buggers. What are the rest doing?'

'Circling and using their cannon. I would say they've expended their torpedoes.'

'Very good.'

'I can't raise the corvette, sir,' Cooper said.

'We think she's on fire.'

'Shit!' Cooper muttered.

'They've seen us, sir,' Rawlings said. 'Two, four, six, eight are detaching towards us.'

'Very good. Mr Cooper, make to flotilla: Reduce speed one thousand and prepare for action. Enemy have expended their torpedoes but remember they have two guns to our one. We will follow normal procedure. Aircraft support on way.'

Cooper looked at the empty sky. 'Ah . . .'

'As you say, Mr Cooper, the enemy will be listening. Make that signal and then man the gun.'

'Aye-aye, sir.'

'Mr Rawlings, action stations, if you please. Jettison the depth charges and then take the tubes.'

'Aye-aye, sir.' Rawlings rang the bell violently, and then left the bridge to go aft and get rid of the explosives. The crew swarmed on deck, every man wearing his steel helmet and life vest, as instructed. Two went forward to man the quick-firer, four went, one each, to the machine guns, and the other four, two each, manned the torpedo tubes. They were joined by Rawlings on the tubes and Cooper on the gun. As ordered, Jamie and Wilson remained in the mess to cope with any wounded.

Duncan had already reduced speed to a thousand revolutions, say fifteen knots, and *41* had come off the plane and was gliding gently up and down the low swell, her White Ensign streaming proudly in the breeze; he looked left and right to make sure the other five boats had done the same, then studied the situation. They were now within three miles of the approaching S-boats, with the disarrayed convoy a further couple of miles beyond, still under cannon attack from the remaining enemy boats. But the twenty-millimetre – not quite an inch – shells, while damaging to the superstructures and deck fittings, and lethal to human beings, were going to take a long time to mortally wound the bigger ships.

Duncan raised his hand above his head to indicate that he was about to engage. There was no need to do more than this; he had outlined his tactics from the time the flotilla had come together under his command, and they had drilled and rehearsed and indeed, practised them on innumerable occasions. Thus he knew that his skippers understood his intention was to break through the advancing boats with half the flotilla and gain the convoy, while the remaining three boats engaged their closest enemies. He could also feel sure that none of them was going to get overexcited and fire his torpedoes against an enemy advancing head on, with the minimal chance of hitting anything; they needed to scatter the approaching boats and wait for them to expose a broadside hull. Equally, they had all followed his example and got rid of their depth charges.

'Stand by for speed,' he said into the tannoy. 'Open fire, Mr Cooper.'

Even as he spoke there was a ripple of red from in front of him as the Germans anticipated his command; the range was down to under two miles. But Duncan had already thrust the throttle forward, and the sudden acceleration threw the enemy aims. A quick glance left and right assured him that the other boats were still following his lead. For a brief moment there was a melee as the flotilla threaded its way between the advancing craft. Bullets whistled around Duncan's head and he heard several crunches as they bit into the hull, remembering how, on the early boats such as his first command, a hit low on the thin wooden skin and penetrating could strike one of the fuel tanks and send them all to perdition – he had seen it happen to more than one of his comrades. But a good deal of that vulnerability had been eliminated by the addition of a thin sheet of steel inside the hull and over the tanks, and for the moment *41* seemed to be undamaged, at least sufficiently to impair her fighting capacity, nor did it appear as if any of his crew had been hit.

Equally, however, for all the continued firing of his own guns, the German vessels all seemed still capable of action. But they had scattered to avoid collision, and the bigger boats were slower on the turn. He blew a blast on his siren, and again as previously rehearsed, *43*, *44* and *45* themselves turned to use their torpedoes against any exposed hulls.

The other two continued to follow *41* to the convoy, where the three remaining S-boats, realizing that they were now in some danger, swung away to face them. For a quick moment, one of them was not in line with any of the merchantmen. The range, an estimated two thousand yards, was a little close, but it was only likely to get closer. 'Fire One!' Duncan snapped into the tannoy.

The little ship bucked as with a great hiss the twenty-one-inch missile left its tube.

'Damnation!' For the torpedo, as delineated by the streak

of white foam, was clearly going to miss. But the S-boat was still turning, as was *41*, and her broadside was again exposed. 'Fire Two!'

As he gave the command there was a violent bang from behind him and the wheel spun loosely in his hands. 'Shit!' he shouted. 'Shit, shit, shit!' But at the same time he reflected how fortunate it was that he had dumped the depth charges: the twenty-millimetre bullets had struck exactly where the explosives had been fifteen minutes earlier.

'Fire crew!' Rawlings bellowed, abandoning the now useless torpedo tubes to run aft. He hadn't got there when here was a huge explosion. All heads turned, while several men fell to the deck. Once again the second torpedo had missed its target, but it had maintained its course and struck a second S-boat half a mile behind the first.

The first target was still afloat and uncomfortably close, but Cooper kept peppering it with twenty-millimetre shells and it was again nearly hit by a torpedo from the *42* boat. It turned away and made to the south, followed by its surviving sister, amidst the cheers of the British crew.

Duncan had more important things to worry about, *41*'s steering remained dead, and she was now turning in aimless circles. He put the engine into neutral to avoid ramming either of the other boats or any of the merchantmen, and shouted down the hatch for Jamie.

'Sir?'

'Get aft and see what's happened to our rudders.'

'Aye-aye, sir.'

At that moment Rawlings returned. 'The fire has been extinguished, sir, but I think the rudders have been shot off.'

'Fuck it!'

'I'll take a look below. We could be making water.' Jamie returned down the hatch.

42 was nosing towards them. 'Do you require assistance?' Lieutenant Beattie shouted through his loud hailer.

'Very probably,' Duncan replied. 'But see to the convoy first.'

'Aye-aye. We'll be back.' *42* moved away to join *46* which was already picking up survivors, and being cheered by the crews of the intact ships. Duncan counted five vessels still afloat, although one was burning. The corvette had definitely gone down, as well it seemed as one freighter.

'Fuck it,' he muttered again, and turned his binoculars on the other boats. 'They seem to be off.' The remaining S-boats were following the first two at full speed.

'With good reason.' Cooper pointed at the three Sunderland flying boats dropping from the sky. 'They won't all get home. And . . . glory be! There are only seven of them, sir. That's nine in total, and they started with twelve. We got three of them.'

'There are only two of ours over there,' Duncan said grimly. There was so much to be done, and he was drifting help-lessly. 'Well, Jamie?'

'We're making water, sir. But it's only a trickle. The pump can cope.'

'What about our steering?'

'I'm afraid that's a lifting out job, sir. Sheered right off.'

'What a goddamned mess. Mr Cooper, signal Mr Beattie that when he has picked up everyone he can, we will need a tow into Plymouth.'

'Plymouth, sir?'

'It's a hell of a long way back to Portsmouth.'

'Ah . . . yes, sir.' Cooper paused in the hatchway. 'I reckon we can claim a victory. Don't you? I mean, three of them, all told, for one of ours?'

'And a corvette? And a ship from the convoy? And God knows how many lives? I don't think we can call that a victory, Mr Cooper. Is there any other damage, Jamie?'

'Ah . . . yes, sir.'

'What?'

'Well, sir, there were several hits, all in the stern. Most hit the rudder, but at least five came through the hull.'

'Well, we'd better thank God there are no fuel tanks back there.'

'Yes, sir. But . . . um . . .'

'Oh, Jesus Christ! Both?'

'No, sir. Only yours. The bunk is all shot up and the book-case is in pieces. And that's where we're making the water.'

'Well,' Duncan said. 'You'd better get the bloody pumps working, hadn't you.'

*　　*　　*

'Good evening, milady,' Tim Goring said, as the Bentley pulled to a halt before the petrol pumps, showing, despite the gloom, only side lights in accordance with the blackout restrictions. He then peered into the back seat. 'And how's the little fellow?'

He was rewarded with a deep and somewhat sinister gurgle from the massive chest.

'Please don't bite him, Lucifer,' the Dowager Lady Eversham recommended. 'I'm sure he means well, and you don't know where he's been. He's very sensitive, you know, Mr Goring, and he's feeling upset.'

Tim regarded the enormous Pyrenean Mountain Dog somewhat sceptically. While he accepted that the creature had a right to be insulted – Tim himself, a much smaller man than his son, was no bigger than the dog – he also considered that the monster was well-named, an opinion shared by most people in the neighbourhood. It was not that Lucifer was the least vicious, or even aggressive, unless required to be so by his mistress. On the contrary, it was his love for all humanity that was so often intimidating and even dangerous; Lucifer liked nothing better than to get on his hind legs and embrace the current object of his affection: trying to remain upright with a hundred and fifty pounds of dog wrapped round one's neck was difficult for the strongest of men, although apparently not one woman, his equally larger than life mistress. 'Not well, is he?' he asked, hopefully.

'Of course he's well,' Kristin retorted. 'But he is on his way home from the vet, after getting his shots. He hates going to the vet. Where is Mr Probert?'

'Mr Probert has gone home, milady. It is past six. In fact, I was just shutting down for the night.'

'Then you'll have to do it, Mr Goring.' She thrust the book of coupons through the window.

'Certainly, milady.' Goring fussed. The woman, and her dog, might be menaces, but servicing the Eversham cars was a sizeable part of his business. 'Her . . . ah . . . well, Lady Eversham . . . I mean . . .' Having two Ladies Eversham living in the same house was embarrassingly confusing.

Kristin opened her door and got out to stretch her legs. They were very long legs, matching her height, and although presently encased in trousers were, Goring knew, well worth looking at whenever she deigned to wear a skirt – the Dowager Lady Eversham cared nothing for fashion. But she didn't have to. Apart from her legs, her white cashmere jumper seemed close to bursting, and Goring also knew that her auburn hair, presently concealed by a bandanna tied beneath her chin, was long and lustrous. To possess all this, and be obscenely wealthy – he could not imagine the value of the three rings she was wearing, revealed as she pulled off her gloves – as well, not to mention being only forty-three years old and possessing an overwhelming personality, set her apart from any other woman he had ever met. He often wondered how her daughter-in-law, a really sweet young woman, coped with being shut up with her all day.

'Lady Eversham,' Kristin announced, 'is as well as can be expected for someone in her condition.'

'Ah . . .' He was again embarrassed, bent over the filler cap to screw it tight.

'Any minute now,' Kristin said. 'Which is why I should be at home.'

'Of course, milady. Do give her my best wishes. His Lordship . . .?'

'I imagine he's already there. But you know what men are like, at least the first time. My first husband,' she added reminiscently, 'fainted.'

'Well, milady, it's a big business. Especially when you're just standing there, unable to help.'

'The late Lord Eversham,' Kristin pointed out, 'did not faint at my delivery, because he was not there. I think he was playing polo or something. He fainted when I told him I was pregnant. We weren't married at the time, you see.'

Goring gulped.

'And,' Kristin added, 'I was only fifteen. He was very upset. He had the choice of marrying me or being charged with the rape of a minor. They were very big on rape in Spain in 1913. Still are. Not that I would have charged him. It was such fun. But he didn't know that.'

Goring licked his lips.

'And it has all turned out for the best hasn't it? Did you faint when Jamie was born?'

'Well . . . no, milady.'

'Because you are made of sterner stuff.'

'Ah . . . I wouldn't care to say. I'll just tear out the coupons.' He headed for the office, but to his alarm she followed him.

'Anyway, you have Jamie home for the weekend.'

'Ah . . .' He opened the door, allowed her in, and hastily closed it again to stop the light showing.

'He is home?' A slight note of anxiety entered Kristin's voice.

'Well, no, milady.'

'What do you mean? They were supposed to complete the patrol by lunchtime. And Lord Eversham had especially arranged to be off duty for the weekend.'

'I know, milady. Jamie told me. But he's not home yet. They must have been late getting in.'

'Yes,' Kristin said. 'Put that on the account, will you, Mr Goring.'

'Of course, milady. And I do hope all goes well with her Ladyship.'

'Why shouldn't it? Good night, Mr Goring.'

She pulled on her gloves and got behind the wheel, but did not immediately drive away. This was partly to allow Lucifer to welcome her back; he regarded even a ten-minute separation as a reason for a lot of heavy breathing and a cold wet nose pressed into the back of her neck, which could be disconcerting when driving. But it was also partly to get her emotions under control.

An only child, since the death of both her parents she had loved only four living creatures. One was at this moment subsiding in the back seat behind her. Another was her only son. A third was that delicious boy Jamie, the culmination of a long search for the ideal sexual partner – that he happened to be twenty-three years younger than her and a motor mechanic was a typical example of Sod's Law, but she had long ago resolved never to allow Sod's Laws to interfere with her life. And the fourth was that delightful girl who now shared her home and her life.

The problem was that the three humans stood or fell together, almost literally. Alison Brunel had been a second officer in the Wrens when Duncan had met her during a tour of duty at

Scapa Flow. She had not, on the surface, been the ideal wife for the future Lord Eversham, but as far as Kristin was concerned she had been a vast improvement on that ghastly prig Lucinda Browning, to whom Duncan had happened to be engaged at the time, and in addition, she had taken to Lucifer, something Lucinda had never been able to do.

The breaking of the engagement so that Duncan could marry a junior officer in the service, someone who had no background, either financial or social, had been a hugely delicious scandal, as far as Kristin was concerned. But there remained that potentially catastrophic link.

She had worked it, through Rear-Admiral Jimmy Lonsdale, that Jamie had been posted to Duncan's boat as engineer; she wanted them both where she could watch over them, just as she had immediately worked it that Alison had been transferred to Portsmouth so that she could be near her future family.

But she could only control things when all three were on dry land. When the two men were at sea, and always together . . . she had actually been at sea with Duncan and Jamie, three times, and been under fire with them, too, on two of those occasions. The first had been when she and Alison had inadvertently got involved in the Dunkirk Evacuation in June 1940, and had watched her ex-husband's launch blown out of the water, with him in it, while Alison had been struck by a stray bullet. The second had been just over a year ago, when they had rescued her from the Channel Island of Guernsey following its capture by the Germans. It was on that occasion that Duncan had fought his famous battle with an S-boat. She had found it all tremendously stimulating, but she had been left in no doubt how vulnerable those tiny plywood boats were. As long as she was on it with them, it hadn't mattered; she had no desire to live if they died, anyway. But when she wasn't with them, she was perpetually aware that if one went the other would too. And not yet to have returned from a morning patrol . . .

Alison had become an added responsibility. Having fallen in love with the girl at first sight, pulling strings to have Jimmy Lonsdale, one of the very few men able and willing to overlook her reputation and meet her on her own ground – obviously he knew nothing of her relationship with Jamie, but then the only person in the world who did know about that was Alison herself – transfer her from Signals to be one of his secretaries at Portsmouth had been an obvious step. Thus she had shared in all the traumas involving the MTB flotillas; it had been even worse for her because her sharing, like her mother-in-law's, had to be at second hand, waiting for the little boats to come back. Or not.

That had been slightly relieved when she had been obliged to leave the service on becoming pregnant. But the waiting was still there. And now they were several hours overdue.

With Lucifer's greeting complete, she engaged gear and hurtled down the three miles to the Eversham mansion, parked in a flurry of flying gravel, opened the back door for the dog and hurried to the front door of the house. This was opened for her by Harry, who was officially Duncan's valet, but as there was no room for a valet in a small warship and he was too old for active service, had become her butler. With the exception of Lucia, her Spanish maid, all her pre-war staff, including her original butler, had been called up; Lucia now doubled as cook.

'Give him something nice for dinner,' Kristin instructed. 'You know how he hates being jabbed.'

'Yes, milady.' Harry's hand was being vigorously licked; Lucifer was well aware of where his food came from.

'Lady Eversham upstairs?'

'Ah . . . yes, milady.' More than anyone else, Harry found having two Ladies Eversham in the house a confusing business; they were both his mistress.

Kristin nodded and climbed the small staircase to her private sitting room, taking off her gloves and bandanna as she did so to shake out her hair. 'Darling!'

'I'm so glad you're back.' Alison Eversham was a small, slight young woman who wore her straight black hair cut just below her ears. Her beauty lay partly in her piquant features, but even more in her bubbling personality. But at this moment she was looking unusually pensive, and sitting very straight on the settee. 'Lucifer all right?'

'He didn't actually bite the vet, which has got to be a plus.' Kristin frowned. 'There haven't been any calls?'

'Why, no. Were you expecting one?'

Kristin gave a sigh of relief.

'Do you know what's happened to Duncan?' Alison asked. 'He said he'd be home this afternoon.'

'I know he's going to be late,' Kristin said carelessly. 'I think we both need a drink.' She went to the sideboard and poured two glasses of sherry.

She had forgotten how well her daughter-in-law had got to know her over the past year. 'You don't know at all,' Alison said. 'Something's happened.'

'Of course nothing's happened,' Kristin asserted. 'It's just –' the telephone jangled – 'I'll get it.' She ran to the table. Alison, starting to rise, subsided. 'Yes?'

'Kristin!'

'Jimmy! Tell me.'

'There was an action this morning, off the Eddystone.'

'And?'

'Duncan covered himself in glory, as always. Sank an S-boat.'

'And?'

'Oh, he's all right. But he lost one of his own, and *41* is all shot up. Rudder gone, and a few dozen bullet holes. It seems to have been some scrap.'

Kristin drew a deep breath. 'Any casualties amongst the crew?'

'Only minor.'

Kristin's breath rushed through her nostrils. 'So when are they coming home?'

'Ah. They had to be towed into Plymouth for repairs. These will take a couple of weeks.'

'Shit! The crew don't have to stay with the boat, surely.'

'No. They should be back here tomorrow. How's the little lady?'

Kristin looked at Alison's stomach. 'I don't think she's going to wait that much longer.'

'Well, as I said, he'll be home tomorrow. If I get a moment, I'll come across myself. I love you.'

The phone went dead. 'As you will have gathered,' Kristin said. 'They've had a scrap. Everyone is all right, but the boat is in Plymouth, under repair. Duncan will be home tomorrow.' She held out the sherry glass. 'I think we both need this.'

'I don't think I should,' Alison said.

'Oh, come now.'

'Because –' Alison's face twisted as she had another cramp – 'I don't think Duncan is going to make it.'

Relationships – 1

'Is all well?' inquired Rear-Admiral James Lonsdale. A somewhat stocky man with bristling, short, iron-grey hair and pugnacious features, he was universally feared by his staff and subordinates, but Duncan was always sure of a welcome.

'Mother and child are doing well, as they say, sir.'

The admiral had known the young man a long time. 'But there's a but?'

'The birth occurred six hours before I got there.'

'Surely Alison understands that the blame lies with Jerry rather than you?'

'Of course she does, sir. But that doesn't make any difference to my feelings. The arrival of a first son has to be one of the most important moments of a man's life.'

'The important thing is that the little chap did arrive.' Lonsdale had never married, however much in recent years his thoughts might have roamed in that direction. 'Sit down.'

Duncan lowered himself into the chair before the desk, placing his cap on his lap.

'What's the damage report?'

'*41* will be out of action for a fortnight, sir. And we lost *44*. And three men.'

'But you picked up the other ten. And sank three S-boats. That's a considerable victory.'

'One of the enemy was sunk by the corvette before they got her, sir. The corvette was also lost.'

'Damned shame. But the Sunderlands are claiming two more. I think we can say that is was a pretty successful operation. And, by God, we needed one. *Ark Royal* has gone.'

'*Ark Royal?*' Duncan was horrified. 'But . . .'

'I know. Jerry has claimed to have sunk her on God knows

how many occasions. Unfortunately this time it's true. She was torpedoed only a few miles east of Gibraltar, and crippled, but the hit did not seem to be immediately mortal. So she was taken in tow, and was actually in sight of the breakwaters when something happened internally and she went down. Presumably a bulkhead gave way. Anyway, we've lost our number one aircraft carrier. It happened a couple of weeks ago but has been kept under wraps, for obvious reasons.' He brooded for a few moments while Duncan was still trying to assimilate the news. Then he said, 'However, onwards, and hopefully, upwards.' He paused, clearly choosing his words. Duncan had equally known him long enough to realize that he was about to say something important. But he could only wait. 'Come to the window,' the admiral invited, getting up.

Duncan stood beside him.

'What do you think of her?' Lonsdale asked.

Duncan frowned. 'That looks a big gun.'

'It is, for an MTB. A six-pounder.'

'Good lord!'

'She's our newest design, straight from the yard. *412*. She's the usual seventy-two feet, but displaces forty-six tons, fifty-three full load. That's because of her heavier armament and increased accommodation. You'll see there are no depth charges, but apart from that she has the usual complement of machine guns and two tubes. These are eighteen-inch. She's designed purely for aggressive action against the enemy. I had hoped she could be equipped with this new radar thing that apparently allows you to see through fog, but it seems there aren't enough available yet, and the big ships have priority.'

'She still sounds tremendous. But that weight . . . aren't we giving away our biggest advantage: superior speed?'

'She's done forty knots on trials.'

'With what machinery?' Duncan was sceptical.

'The same Packard three-shaft.'

'With respect, sir, I don't think that can be mathematically possible.'

'Hull design, Duncan. Hull design.'

'Well, sir, if that is true, it should certainly put the wind up Jerry.'

'Ah . . . yes. I should think it would. Sit down.'

Duncan obeyed, frowning at the choice of words. 'May I ask—?'

'Yes. She's yours. By the end of January you'll have a flotilla of six.'

'That's tremendous news, sir. Thank you. Will my present crew be able to transfer?'

'If you wish them, certainly. There will have to be an additional four.'

'I understand that. Well, with your permission . . . may I take a closer look?'

Lonsdale cleared his throat. 'There is a caveat.'

Isn't there always? Duncan thought. 'Sir?'

'Ah . . . I don't suppose, in your yachting days, that you ever cruised the Med?'

Again Duncan frowned. 'No, sir. I did not.'

'Hm. Well, I served in that theatre before the war. Not in a yacht, of course. But I can tell you that navigation is a lot simpler down there than it is up here. Virtually no tidal movement, and almost always good vis.'

'Yes, sir. Mother has spoken of it.'

'Of course she would have,' Lonsdale agreed, not anxious to get drawn into the experiences of Kristin's youth, even if he had to assume that Duncan knew of them, as had they not happened, he would not be here at all.

'And that is where I am being sent?'

'Believe me, Duncan, I feel a shit about this, at such a time. But you see, you have become a high profile figure, and their lordships want you for this job. Apart from the catastrophe of losing the *Ark*, things are not going well down there. As you know, we took a hammering during that Crete fiasco, and the losses were particularly heavy in destroyers and light cruisers. God knows we're stretched thin enough trying to protect our Atlantic convoys, but the convoys to Malta are hardly less important. Now that we're short a carrier, and with Germany pouring men and munitions as well as oil into Libya, holding Malta, bang in the middle of their supply route, is essential. But every convoy takes a pounding.'

'You are sending a flotilla of MTBs for escort duty, sir?' Duncan could not believe his ears.

'No, no. That would be an absurdity. But we cannot fight a war purely on the defensive. That is the surest way to lose it. The Italians have been using their MTBs very effectively; they have quite a few of them. Relatively big ships, ninety-odd feet long, sixty-two tons full load. Because of the small distances they are virtually in the same situation as the S-boats here in the Channel. They can dart out of the Italian ports, shoot up their targets, and nip back again in a matter of hours. Their lordships want us to be able to do the same. These Bagliettos or whatever can't match boats like *412*, for two reasons. They're not as heavily armed, just two twenty-millimetre guns together with the usual machine guns and torpedo tubes. And they're not as fast. They're using an Isotta-Fraschini engine that only develops about three and a half thousand horsepower. That gives them thirty-two knots maximum. But they're not your main target. I'm just indicating what they have been doing successfully with craft far inferior to yours. You'll be based on Malta, that is, within spitting distance of the Italian coast. In and out, eh? In and out. Shoot up everything that moves. If you encounter the Italian boats, shoot them up as well. It's morale boosting we want.' He paused for breath, having whipped himself into a spate of enthusiasm.

Duncan was more inclined to concentrate on essentials. 'My commanders, sir?'

'They will be assigned as the new boats become available. I know you'd like to take all of your present people with you, but we need men with their experience up here as well. You'll have approval of the list.'

'Thank you, sir. Would I be right in assuming that their lordships do not wish the Italians to expect us?'

'Oh, indeed not. This has to be top secret.'

Duncan gazed at him, and he flushed. 'Well, of course, your wife will have to know. She is still covered by the Official Secrets Act.'

'And Mother?'

Lonsdale sighed. 'I know. There's no way we can keep it a secret from her. But she doesn't mix much with other people. Does she?'

'Certainly not Italians. But . . . she's liable to blow her top.'

'I know,' Lonsdale said again, even more sadly. 'But there happens to be a war on, and you are a serving officer. Not even Kristin can take on their lords of the Admiralty. Do point this out to her.'

'Ay-aye, sir.' Duncan stood up, hesitated. 'Do you have any idea how long this tour will last?'

'I'm afraid not. As I said, I really am sorry that this has come up, at such a time. But . . .'

Duncan put on his cap and saluted.

For visits to the boatyard Kristin drove the Sunbeam; it was less conspicuous than the Bentley. And if she supposed that any car going to the yard at this time was conspicuous, she had every reason to be there, legitimately; it was the present home of *Kristin* the forty-five-foot schooner named after her, and paid for with her money. With Duncan's time committed to his motor boat, she had made sure that everyone under-stood it was her business to keep an eye on his yacht, in order that she would be ready to take to the water when the war was over. And it was where she most enjoyed being, even if today was on spec.

The yard was deserted – the entire work force had joined up – and looked utterly forlorn in the November drizzle. Thus the gate was padlocked. But she had a key. She braked the car, pulled the hood of her oilskin top over her hair, got out, unlocked the gates, pushed them open, and drove in, stopping again to close them behind her and restore the padlock; she had no wish for some curious passer-by to wonder why they were open and investigate.

She felt a pleasant, building sense of anticipation, as she always did on these occasions. This was heightened by the venue. She was surrounded by yachts of all shapes and sizes, sitting up on their legs, cocooned in their canvas covers. Their masts were stacked to one side. But in front of her was the large open shed in which *Kristin* waited. With both her masts out and also covered in canvas sheeting, she looked just as forlorn as every other craft, but at least she was dry.

Kristin parked on the edge of the overhang, got out, and looked at the bicycle leaning against the wall, feeling a great sense of relief spreading through her body. Then she walked round the hull, as she always did, looking up at the timbers, and at the forward end of the keel, where there was a deep nick in the lead. That had happened on the yacht's last voyage, on the Cowes–Dinard Race in 1939, and could not be repaired until after hostilities had ended – there was no lead to spare. But it was a constant reminder of those now far-off and halcyon days. She had not been on the race, but she had sailed home with them afterwards, and discovered Jamie.

She had of course known him, vaguely, for a long time, but only as a young boy who worked in his father's garage. On that gale-driven voyage she had found what she had always wanted. In every way. Even the fact that he would never use her name, always referred to her as milady even when she was lying naked in his arms, was an essential part of the ambience of their relationship. Of course she would not have been human had she not occasionally wondered where it was going to end, where it could possibly end. But in time of war that applied to almost every aspect of life, and as she did not want it ever to end, it was not worth thinking about.

'Milady?' He had heard the car engine, and now came down the ladder from the deck. She went towards him, shrugging the hood from her head, took him in her arms for a long, slow, deep kiss.

'Now,' she said, when they paused for breath, and fondling his jumper. 'You're as wet as I am.'

'I'm going to take it off anyway.'

'Let's get up there.'

He climbed behind her, looking up at the long legs above him. These were presently encased in trousers, but he knew what lay beneath the damp cloth, and that in a matter of minutes they would be all his. 'I came yesterday,' he said. 'As soon as I could get away.'

'And I wasn't here. I'm sorry. Something came up.'

'Oh!'

She reached the top of the ladder, swung her leg over the rail. 'Silly boy. I was playing the midwife.'

'Milady? You mean, her Ladyship—?'

'A bouncing baby boy.'

The hatch was open, and she slid down the ladder into the saloon, a stark place at the moment, with all the books, the crockery and cutlery, the charts, stowed ashore, together with the cushions and curtains. It smelt dank and unloved. But there was a mattress and two blankets on the starboard settee berth; she had seen to that over a year ago.

'Wow!' Jamie commented, following her down the ladder.

'You mean you didn't know? It was in this morning's *Times*.'

'We don't take *The Times*, milady.'

'Good lord! What paper do you take?'

'*The News of the World*.'

'That's a weekly, isn't it?'

'Yes. So—'

'And it's a bit, well . . .'

'Gossipy?'

Kristin regarded him. Clearly that was not the word she had intended to use, so he hurried on. 'And actually, I'm not sure if they do personal announcements. But you mean you . . .?'

Kristin took off her oilskin top and hung it in the cupboard where it could drip through to the bilge. 'I didn't deliver it. I was speaking figuratively. But I had to get her to the hospital, and as Duncan wasn't there, I had to stay with her. I mean, he's my first grandchild. He's the sweetest thing. But a grandchild! My God!'

Jamie stood behind her and put his arms round her, holding her breasts; as she never wore a bra, he could feel the chill-hardened nipples through the cloth; nuzzling her neck he could inhale her perfume. Everything about her was perfection. 'Was it very grim?' he asked, as he kissed her ear.

'Grim? Good lord, no. Just time-consuming. Giving birth is about the most sublime moment of a woman's life.'

'Oh! I thought . . .'

She turned in his arms, and his hands slipped down to hold her buttocks. 'You've read too many books written either by men, who know nothing about it anyway, or silly women who get hysterical over a cut finger. Of course it can be very painful. But so can a hangover. The point is, any pain is bearable, as long as you know it's going to end.'

'Um.' He was not convinced, as he released the belt for her slacks and let them slide down about her ankles.

She did the same for his pants, then pulled her head back. 'And all the time you were being shot to pieces.'

'Do I look as if I'm in pieces, milady?'

'No. But one day they're going to stop missing. It keeps me awake at night. How long are you going to be home?'

'Well, the boat really was shot to pieces. And it's stuck down in Plymouth. Unless they give his lordship another command immediately, it could be a fortnight.'

'Stupendous.' She kissed him. 'Would you like me to have your child, Jamie?'

'Milady? What? I mean . . .'

She gave a delicious gurgle of laughter, and slid his drawers down as well, to caress him. 'I'm still capable, you know. And this chap is definitely up to it. Did you really think I was past it?'

'Well . . .' He hid his embarrassment by lifting his shirt over his head.

'It's a matter of taking care,' she explained, and let her knickers follow her pants. 'Technically, there is only one day in every month that a woman can conceive. It's quite simple to work out. It's the method practised by Roman Catholics for centuries, as we're forbidden to use contraceptives. Did you know I was a Roman Catholic?'

'Well, no, milady.'

'Born, bred and educated. But I soon got over that sort of thing.'

'And this date-watching really works?'

'Don't you have proof of that? Actually, to be safe, one shouldn't have sex for perhaps two days on either side. But I could easily make a mistake.' She lifted her sweater over her head, and, naked, lay on the berth and pulled the blanket over her.

He sat beside her, moved the blanket sufficiently to caress her breasts; her nipples were still chill-hardened. 'And what would happen then?'

She giggled. 'I imagine everyone would suppose that Jimmy Lonsdale was the father.'

'Do you sleep with him?'

'Once. It wasn't very exciting.'

'But would you like to again?'

She lifted the blanket to allow him to lie beside her. 'I like sleeping with you. I wish I could, properly. I would like to spend a night with you more than anything else in the world. Would you like that, Jamie?'

'Of course I would, milady. But—'

'There is no problem that cannot be overcome, if you want it badly enough. And if you really do have a fortnight off . . . Stroke me, Jamie. Stroke me.' She gave several sighs, subsided, and then stirred again. 'I want you in me.'

Now they sighed together, until he lay still, his cheek against hers. Then she giggled again. He raised his head. 'Milady?'

'I was just thinking. If I were to become pregnant, it would put Jimmy in an impossible position. Everyone thinks we're an item. If he were to stick to the truth and deny responsibility, people would think he was the most utter cad. But if he didn't deny it, he could be held up for conduct unbecoming an officer and a gentleman. Especially an admiral and a gentleman.'

'He'd have to marry you,' Jamie said, absently.

'Good lord!'

He rolled off her, and rose on his elbow. 'And we'd have to stop seeing each other.'

'Never.'

'Milady, I couldn't possibly . . . well, I mean, the wife of an admiral.'

'The fact that I'm Duncan's mother doesn't bother you.'

'It does bother me. Very much. But you're not Duncan's wife.'

'I think you're a little too moral for your own good. Certainly for my good. And a little bit of guilt is good for the soul. It keeps us humble.' She reached down to hold him. 'I think you are almost ready for round two. I know I am.'

Kristin was soaking in her bath when the sound of Lucifer barking alerted her to a car in the yard. She got out of the water, dried herself, put on her dressing gown, untied her hair, and went through her bedroom into her sitting room just as Duncan reached the top of the little staircase, looking almost as tousled as she was, and he was in uniform.

'You have just got to put that dog on a diet,' he said.

'He does love his food so.' Kristin looked at her Cartier lapel watch, which was lying on the coffee table. 'Six o'clock. Time for a sherry.' She sat on the settee while Duncan poured. 'I assume you've been to the hospital.'

'Of course.'

'And all is well?'

He handed her a glass, and sat beside her. 'All is very well. At the hospital.'

He was her son. Kristin turned her head to look at him, even as she sipped. 'I don't think you've finished.'

He drank more deeply. 'They're giving me a new boat.' He gazed at her, then finished his drink, and got up. 'I think I feel more like scotch than sherry. You?'

'No, thank you. I understood that *41* is going to be out of action for some time. Aren't you being given any time off?'

Duncan chose to ignore the sudden coldness of her tone. 'This is the very latest thing in MTBs. It has a six-pounder gun! Think of that, Mother, compared with the twenty-millimetre. We could blow an enemy out of the water at a couple of miles range. I'm going to take her out tomorrow. That reminds me, I must get hold of young Goring to come with me. I suppose he is home?'

'How am I supposed to know where Goring is?' Kristin inquired. 'Anyway, the whole idea is outrageous. When are you supposed to take command of this boat?'

'As I said, tomorrow. We should be operational by the end of the week, as soon as I get my crew together.'

'I never heard such rubbish. I must have a word with Jimmy.'

'Mother!'

'You have been on duty virtually non-stop for the past two months. Now you've had your boat shot out from under you. You're entitled to a break. And you're a father!'

Duncan again sat beside her, glass in hand. 'We happen to be at war.'

'We have been at war for the past two years. Are you

going to tell me that if you have a couple of weeks leave we are going to have to surrender?'

'You must know that we're not doing very well.'

'We're doing a whole hell of a lot better than at the beginning. We've beaten the Luftwaffe, and now that Hitler has got himself embroiled in Russia, he has surely abandoned any idea of trying to invade us.'

'Unfortunately, it doesn't look as if the war with Russia is going to last too much longer; the Germans will be in Moscow any day now. And our position in North Africa is precarious.'

'What, against Mussolini's lot? We've just finished smashing them.'

'Yes. So Hitler has sent a German army to his support. Well, a panzer division, anyway.'

Kristin blew a raspberry.

'Believe me,' Duncan said. 'With the Germans taking a big interest in the Med, our position there could be seriously compromised. It is already. *Ark Royal* has been sunk.'

'Oh, rubbish. That's another piece of Nazi propaganda.'

'Not this time. Several of our ships apparently saw her go down while they were trying to save her. I had a long chat with Admiral Lonsdale today, and he told me that the Admiralty are very worried. If we were to lose control of the Med it would be disastrous.'

He paused, because his mother was looking at him with her 'I am not amused' expression, and he realized that he might have got ahead of himself.

'So,' she said. 'Jimmy has taken up discussing grand strategy with one of his lieutenant-commanders.'

'Well . . .'

'And he is giving you command of a brand new boat with a big gun. I assume there are going to be others?'

'I'm to have a flotilla, yes.'

'I regard sons who lie to their mothers as the lowest form of humanity.'

'I have never lied to you in my life,' Duncan protested, stretching a point.

'Not telling the whole truth is the same thing as lying.' She held out her glass. 'I will have a whisky, and you can tell me what really is going on. He is sending you to the Mediterranean.'

He took both glasses to the sideboard, replaced her sherry glass with a tumbler, poured. 'He isn't sending me anywhere. He's as upset about it as anyone. The Admiralty is sending a flotilla of MTBs to the Mediterranean, yes. They have to do something, and they don't have that many big ships to spare.'

'But they can spare a man who has just become a father.'

'Now you know they can't take things like that into consideration. They happen to think I'm about the best they have. At least, in MTBs.' He gave her her glass, remained standing in front of her.

She drank. 'And of course, they're right. Have you told Alison?'

'I thought I should tell you first.'

'You mean you didn't feel up to fighting her and me at the same time. Shit!'

'Mother?'

'How long are you going for?'

'I have absolutely no idea. But it could be a while. Everything depends on how things develop.'

'Shit, shit, shit.'

'If I were in a battleship or something, I could be away for months at a time. Even years.'

'Will you be taking your current crew?'

'I certainly hope to. I mean, I wouldn't feel right without Jamie down in the engine room.'

Kristin appeared to be blowing into her whisky.

'And Cooper is coming along very well.' Duncan was becoming enthusiastic again as he reckoned he had surmounted his first hurdle. 'While Rawlings is as good a petty officer as any I've had. The complement is going up to seventeen, but I should think anyone would be happy to serve in the Med. Warm seas, sunny skies. I bet you remember those, Mother.'

'I remember them very well,' Kristin said, thoughtfully.

Duncan frowned.

'When I think of the houses,' Kristin mused. 'Gandia! The beach! Madrid! Do you know it is six years since I last saw them. Lived in them.'

'They'll still be there, after the War.'

'Will they?'

'Doesn't Carlos write you every month? Isn't everything being looked after?'

'He does say that,' Kristin conceded. 'But you know what lawyers are like.' She gave a heavy, and totally unrealistic, sigh. 'I suppose, one of these days, I am going to have to get down there and see for myself.'

'Mother, you are being absurd. How are you going to get there?'

Kristin sipped her drink. 'I don't suppose you'd like to drop me off on your way down?'

'That is quite out of the question, and you know it.'

'Oh, what a fierce naval officer you are. Well, then, I'll have to chance my arm, by steamer.' She held out her glass. 'I'll have another of those.'

'Mother,' he said. 'I would not like you to misunderstand the situation. We are not being based on Gibraltar. Our base is to be Valetta. That is in Malta.'

'I know where Valetta is. I have been there. And of course you will not be based on Gibraltar. Oh, by the way, when will you be leaving?'

'The end of January.'

'Ah!' Kristin commented.

'I am damned sure,' Duncan growled, absently eating a grape from the bowl on the bedside table, 'that she is planning something.'

'Your mother is always planning something,' Alison pointed out. 'Plans are her life.' Even if, she thought, it is simply when next to get together with her toy boy. She remembered how shocked she had been when she had realized what was going on, as had had to happen once she had moved into the house. But as she had quickly realized that it was ridiculous to be shocked by anything Kristin said or did, she had accepted the situation. The only aspect of it that she disliked was that it involved keeping a secret from her husband, something she had never intended to do. But again, she had reflected, it was Kristin's secret, not hers, and she was not sure that she had not grown to love her over the top mother-in-law as much as she loved Duncan. 'If she did decide to go to Spain,' she said. 'Would she be in any danger?'

'Not once she got there. She's Spanish.'

'And her dad fought for Franco? You mean he was a Fascist?'

'She's always been a bit vague about that. I suppose because Franco is a dirty word over here. But I damned well know that he didn't fight for the Communists: he died before the civil war started. And you must admit that, deep down, Mother is a bit of a Fascist herself, even if she'd brain anyone who accused her of that. Or who attempted to impose any governmental restrictions on her lifestyle.'

Alison preferred not to comment. 'Well, then . . .'

'But getting there, through the U-boats . . . and even that's not the real point. She'd be abandoning you.'

'Won't you be abandoning me?'

'Well, yes. But I'm not going. I'm being sent. And I was leaving you in her care.'

'Duncan Morant, I am twenty-six years old. I am quite capable of living by myself for a couple of months.'

'With Baby?'

'Baby will keep me occupied. And Harry and Lucia run the place like clockwork. Anyway, Kristin is getting me a nanny.'

'How on earth can she get a nanny? Isn't every woman capable of it in war work?'

'Not every woman. And she seems to know a Spanish family who she thinks have a daughter who would do very well. Actually, I rather like the sound of that. I'd prefer someone about my own age.'

'Do you speak Spanish?'

'Well . . . no. But if this girl lives in England, I'm sure she'll speak English.'

'Hm. What about Lucifer.'

'Lucifer and I have always got on very well.'

'He knocks you over.'

'He did that once, on the occasion of our first meeting.' When, she recalled, she had been a bundle of nerves, as she had just also met Kristin for the first time, and realized that while, as Second Officer Alison Brunel, from a comfortable

but by no means wealthy background, she might have fallen
for plain Lieutenant Duncan Morant, RNVR, who had not
seemed very different, only nicer, than most of the other
naval officers who has squired her since she got her commission, she had actually fallen into a whirlpool of extreme
wealth with all the eccentricity that was inclined to produce.
And she had grown to love every moment of it. 'Since then,'
she said, 'he has been a perfect gentleman. Just tell me one
thing. You *are* coming back?'

'That is actually my intention, yes.'

'I'm glad of that.'

'But . . . Holy smoke!'

Alison raised her eyebrows.

'What about the christening?'

'I wondered if you'd remembered that. I have it in mind.
We'll organize it for January, before you leave. I know it's
a bit short notice, but that's the way the cookie crumbles.'

'It'll have to be a small affair.'

'And Kristin won't like that, either. But there's a war on.'
She smiled at him. 'It won't be as small as our wedding,
right here in this hospital, with my arm still in a sling.'

'God, when I think of you getting hit by that bullet . . .
and you shouldn't have been there at all! Does it still hurt?'

'Only when it rains.' She watched the door of the private
ward opening. 'Here's Baby. You've never seen him have lunch.'

'Do you think I should? I mean . . .'

'Silly boy.' She unbuttoned the bodice of her nursing gown.
'He won't mind. In fact, I'll bet he doesn't even notice.'

'What do you reckon?' Duncan asked, as he closed the throttle
and *412* lost way and came off the plane. In front of them
was the Needles Channel into the sheltered waters of the
Solent, the red-and-white light tower rising on its rock
pinnacle to starboard, the solid bulk of Hurst Castle looming
to port, while the wake created by their recent speed rippled
into Christchurch Bay.

'Oh, she's a dream, sir,' Cooper said enthusiastically. 'And
that gun . . . I can hardly wait to line up an S-boat.'

'Hm,' Duncan said. 'Would you like to skipper one?'

'Me? You mean there's another?'

'There are going to be quite a few, given time. But I am to have the first six.'

'But—'

'You're to get another stripe.'

Cooper stared at him with his mouth open.

'Don't you think you deserve it?' Duncan asked. 'You've better than a year in MTBs, and you know as much about handling one as anyone.'

'Well, not really, sir. And to be given a brand new boat . . . Would I, ah . . .?'

'You would still be serving under my command, yes. But I must tell you that we will be going overseas. Does that bother you?'

It was a rhetorical question, as he knew that since his parents' early deaths Cooper's only living relative was the elderly uncle who had paid for his schooling and for Dartmouth.

'No, sir. May I ask—?'

'No, you may not. You may not even speculate, at least in public. You'll be told when the time comes. For the present, my instructions are to get the new flotilla into top working order by the end of January.'

'Aye-aye, sir.'

'So?'

'Will it be held against me, sir, if I say that I would rather remain with you?'

'Well, obviously it will not be held against you by me; I'm flattered. As regards your record, all I have to do is not recommend you for a separate command at this time. Then the brass will grumble that I am deliberately holding you back, but they'll have nothing against you. And you'll get that extra stripe anyway.'

'I wouldn't like to—'

'Forget it. You're a career officer. I'm only in it for the duration.' The Isle of Wight was now blocking the southern horizon, as the mainland of England was blocking the north. In here the seas were always calm, and the channel buoys and markers were always in place. 'By the way,' he said. 'Have you any plans for Christmas?'

'Not really, sir.' Cooper held his breath, remembering the

previous Christmas, when he had been invited to lunch with
the Evershams and found himself spending the afternoon tête-
à-tête with that fabulous woman who was Duncan's mother.
Looking back on it, he had almost felt that if he played his
cards right . . . but he understood that had been the amount of
wine he had drunk exciting his libido; not only was she light
years above him socially, she was old enough to be his mother.

'In that case,' Duncan said. 'Why don't you lunch with
us again? If you won't be bored.'

'Oh, good lord, no, sir. Thank you very much. If you're
sure Lady Eversham . . .'

'Lady Eversham,' Duncan said, 'will be delighted. That's
settled, then. Take her in, Mr Cooper.' He stepped away from
the helm. 'Keep her on one thousand.'

'Aye-aye, sir.'

Cooper wrapped his hands round the spokes, and Duncan
slid down the ladder to the mess, then down the next ladder
into the after companion, turning forward to open the door
to the engine room. Here the noise was less than usual, with
the revolutions cut down, but he still had to shout. 'How's
it going, Jamie?'

'She's a dream, sir.' Jamie tapped the starboard tank. 'And
this extra fuel . . . two thousand seven hundred gallons . . .
wow! We could go a long way in this boat.'

'That is what we are going to do.'

'Sir?'

'That bother you?' Duncan knew that, like Cooper, Jamie
was an only child. Unlike Cooper, he still had both his
parents, with whom he seemed to be very close.

'No, sir,' the boy said without hesitation. 'Will it . . .?'

'We'll be gone a minimum of six months.' He studied
Jamie's expression. 'Does *that* bother you?'

'Ah . . . no, sir.' Crikey, he thought. What is Kristin going
to say? Or worse, do?

Duncan had noticed the slight hesitation. 'I'm afraid orders
are orders. Will your parents be upset?'

'Only a little, sir. They know we've been pretty lucky, so
far, with me being able to get home so regular. But you, sir,
with your baby . . . is Lady Eversham . . .?'

'As you know, Jamie, down to six months ago Lady

Eversham was a Wren officer. She understands the requirements of the service.'

'Of course, sir.' Jamie understood that Duncan had mis-
interpreted the question.

But now he said, 'My mother, now, you remember my
mother, Jamie.'

'Yes, I do, sir.'

'Of course, she's sailed with us a few times. One would
have supposed she'd have accepted by now that wars are no
respecters of preconceived points of view. But she is
absolutely livid. Mothers, eh? I'll leave you to it.'

'Duncan!' Rear-Admiral Lonsdale cried ebulliently. 'Come
in, come in. Have you heard the news?'

'No, sir. I've been at sea.'

'Ah, yes. How are they coming?'

'Very well, sir. As long as the new boats are ready by the
end of January, we will be.'

'Excellent. And you're happy with your commanders?'

'Oh, indeed, sir. The entire MTB fleet wants to volunteer.'

'You'll have the pick of them. But the news, eh?'

'Yes, sir,' Duncan said, patiently.

'Last evening, our time, the Japanese attacked the American
Pacific Fleet at Pearl Harbor!'

'My God! You mean there was a battle?'

'Hardly a battle,' Lonsdale said. 'It was a massacre! The
Japs attacked with carrier-borne aircraft. How in the name
of God the Yanks allowed a Japanese fleet to get within
striking distance of Hawaii without doing something about
it is incomprehensible, but there it is. Tokyo is claiming that
the entire US Pacific fleet has been wiped out. That is to
say, eight battleships.'

Duncan stared at him. 'Eight? That's not possible.'

'Washington isn't actually denying it. And don't let's forget
that the Japanese gained a similar scale of victory over the
Russians at Tsushima in 1905.'

'All without a declaration of war?'

'Oh, there was a declaration of war. But it only got to
Washington after the attack had started. Apparently the
Americans are spitting blood.'

'So what happens now?'

'Well, obviously, we are at war with Japan.'

'We? Have they attacked us?'

'There is some talk that Singapore has been bombed. And reports of troop movements against Hong Kong. I mean, they've obviously gone to war to get hold of the oil and tin and rubber of South-East Asia. That means Malaysia and the Dutch East Indies. This strike is to make sure the US can't interfere. Anyway, we're committed to backing America. By the PM, anyway.'

'Can we possibly fight Japan and Germany and Italy?'

'With America on our side, we can fight, and beat anybody. This is what the old boy has been waiting for. It changes the whole strategic situation. In our favour.'

'Even if the Yanks don't have a fleet any more?'

'They'll get a fleet,' Lonsdale asserted. 'There is no way the Japanese can carry the war on to the American mainland. That would mean sustaining an army over seven thousand miles of open water. I'm not saying the next year or so isn't going to be tough. But in the long run, we can't lose. And don't forget that Hitler is wholly committed to Russia, right now.'

'For the next two weeks, or so.'

'For a lot longer than that, Duncan. Even if Stalin packs it in tomorrow, it's going to take an awful lot of troops a hell of a long time completely to subjugate a country the size of even European Russia, and then keep it subjugated.'

'Well, sir, I hope you're right. Does this development affect my orders?'

'Not in the least. We still have a war to fight over here.'

'Aye-aye, sir.' Duncan stood up.

'Oh, by the way,' Lonsdale said. 'Your mother has very kindly invited me to Christmas lunch.'

'Has she?' Duncan asked, without thinking.

Lonsdale raised his eyebrows. 'Did I so blot my copy-book last year?'

'Good Lord, no, sir. I'm delighted. It's just that Mother, well . . . she's not very pleased with this new posting.'

'And of course, she blames me.'

'Well, sir, you know Mother.'

'Yes,' Lonsdale agreed, drily.

'But actually, I would like you to have a chat with her.'

'I can't change the orders, Duncan.'

'Of course I understand that, sir. It's just that, well, as I said, she was furious when I told her I was going to the Med for an indefinite period, and then, when she realized that it was going to happen no matter what, she became rather thoughtful, and began muttering about the houses in Spain, about how long it is since she's seen them.'

'Your mother has a house in Spain?'

'Two, sir. There is the mansion in Madrid, and the villa in Gandia. That's on the East coast. They were her father's you see, and she inherited them.'

'But . . . what about the estate here?'

'Oh, she bought that off Father after the divorce.'

Lonsdale scratched his head. 'Doesn't she also have a house in Guernsey?'

'Well, I suppose technically, the house on Guernsey is mine. It also belonged to Dad, you see. He used it as a holiday home. He left it to me in his will, but I couldn't meet the death duties.'

'So your mother paid up. And now she's lost it to the Germans.'

'Well, for the duration.'

'Is she very upset about that?'

'She takes these things in her stride. Like the house in Bordeaux.'

'What did you say?'

'Well, that's gone as well,' Duncan said. 'For the duration.'

Lonsdale was obviously wrestling with his mental arithmetic. 'Your mother has five houses?'

'Well, yes.' Duncan's tone suggested, doesn't everyone?

'And having lost two of them, she's worried about the three that are left.'

'It's not quite like that, sir. As I said, she doesn't worry about things like houses, *per se*. Although, well, she was born in the Madrid mansion. And the house in Gandia was a holiday home, and one always remembers one's childhood holidays with nostalgia. I still remember my summers in

Guernsey. And of course, during his yachting days as a young man, Father kept his boat in Gandia.'

'Ah, yes. Quite. Well, obviously, one can understand her point of view.'

'But you see, it's not really the houses. She wants to be near to me. I suppose I'm all she has. In human terms, I mean.'

'Duncan,' the admiral said, speaking as reasonably as he could, 'it is eight hundred and fifty miles from the east coast of Spain to Malta. That is as the crow flies. That is eight hundred and fifty miles of water, infested with enemy submarines, surface craft and aircraft, not to mention torpedo boats. Does she seriously suppose that you are going to be able to come home every weekend? Or every fortnight? Or every month? Or at all, for Christ's sake, throughout your tour of duty?'

'That is what I'd like you to explain to her, sir. She doesn't take much notice of anything I say.'

'And you think she'll be interested in anything I might have to say?'

'Well, sir . . . I wondered if you might not be able to give her some reason for wishing to stay here.'

Lonsdale regarded him for several seconds. 'That is the damnedest proposition I have ever heard.'

'Just an idea, sir.' Duncan put on his cap, saluted, and left the office.

Relationships – 2

Duncan left the command building and went to the officers' mess, where he had the use of a private telephone, called Eversham House. 'Hello, Harry. Is Lady Eversham about?'

'Ah . . .'

'My wife, Harry.'

'Oh. Right, sir. She's in the garden with the baby. I'll just ask her to come in.'

'Hold on. Is my mother with her?'

'No, sir. Lady Eversham is out with the dog.'

'Fine. Ask Lady Eversham to come to the phone.'

He waited, and then Alison said. 'Duncan? Don't tell me you're not coming home.'

'I'm not, tonight, I'm afraid. We're out at the crack of dawn; it's a business of getting our new crews familiar with the boat.'

'Oh! Baby will be so disappointed.'

'Will he?'

'Well . . . I'll be disappointed. And your mother.'

'Listen. We have a small problem.'

'Oh, yes.'

'I have just come from the admiral's office.'

'And?'

'He tells me Mother has invited him to Christmas lunch. Again.'

'Well, yes. I think it's a good thing. Don't you?'

'In the circumstances, yes. However, as I didn't know this was happening, I invited Cooper.'

'Oh!'

'You remember Cooper. When he first joined he came upon us trying out the master's bunk.'

'I remember Mr Cooper very well,' Alison said. 'I also remember that his presence at lunch last year didn't go down very well with the admiral.'

'That's what I'm calling about. We have to find a woman to partner Cooper, then Mother won't have anyone to flirt with save the admiral.'

'Who did you have in mind?'

'I don't have anyone in mind. I don't know any young girls.'

'Oh, shit! When you say young . . . how old is Cooper anyway?'

'Well, he was eighteen when he joined the ship last year. So I imagine he's nineteen now.'

'For God's sake, Duncan. Hasn't it occurred to you that most eighteen and nineteen-year-old girls like to spend Christmas Day with their families?'

'Even if that means passing up an invitation from the fabulous Dowager Lady Eversham?'

'With the deepest possible respect, Duncan, that is the one thing I would not mention. She'd run a mile; her parents would insist on it.'

'Hm. I suppose you're right. So . . . we have to risk another irate admiral.' Just when I really want him to get together with Mother, he thought.

'Wait a mo,' Alison said. 'I have an idea. An admiral. That might make a difference.'

'You think you can find someone to give up her Christmas lunch with her family to have lunch with an admiral, who will be old enough to be her father?'

'Yes,' Alison said. 'If she happened to work for him.'

'What?'

'Barbara Parsons. She's not eighteen, or even nineteen. But I don't think she's much over twenty. She's a pretty little thing.'

'And she works for Lonsdale?'

'Not directly. But she's a member of the Command Structure, and works in the same building. She was in Personnel when I left in May, and I know she hopes to go places.'

'She'd be scared stiff.'

'I don't think so. She struck me as being quite a tough little character. And as I said, ambitious. Would you like me to give her a call?'

'My darling, you are an absolute treasure.'

'You remember that,' Alison suggested.

'I suppose,' Kristin remarked, 'that you are wildly excited at the prospect of spending the next few years in the Mediterranean.'

Jamie stopped kissing the back of her neck. He had been concerned by her apparent preoccupation throughout the afternoon, nor was it her usual habit to lie with her back to him, although he was not going to complain about that; with his arms round her so that his hands could hold her breasts, and his genitals pressed against her buttocks, her most exciting features were all available at the same time. 'We're only going for a couple of months.'

'Oh. really, Jamie. Surely you've been in the Navy long enough not to believe that twaddle.'

He nibbled her ear. 'Well, milady, however long it is, we have to go. Orders.'

'You don't have to do anything. If you don't want to. You could desert. Ow!'

His sudden squeeze had been inadvertent. 'Milady!'

'I'd look after you. Hide you. Go away with you. Anywhere in the world.'

'Milady, we're at war.'

'South America isn't at war. Brazil! We could go to Brazil. Brazil does not have an extradition treaty with Britain. Or with anyone, I don't think. So they could never get you back. Rio de Janeiro is the most exciting city in the world. Copacabana is the greatest beach in the world. I'd buy us a house. I'd buy us a sugar estate, and you could be manager. Oh, we'd have such *fun*.'

'Milady—'

'But you don't want to do it.'

'Milady, I swore an oath. Anyway, being at sea is the only life I want to have. I mean, fighting for one's country is the greatest honour any man can receive.'

Kristin moved his hands and rolled out of the bunk. 'I have

bestowed on you the greatest honour any man can have: the love and trust of a woman.'

'Milady . . .'

Kristin pulled on her knickers. 'But as some man said, I could not love thee half so well loved I not honour more. Or words to that effect.'

'I could not love thee, Dear, so much, loved I not honour more. Lovelace.'

'What?'

'That is the exact quotation, milady. It was written by the Cavalier poet, Richard Lovelace, in a poem to his lady friend, called *Lucasta, On Going To The Wars*. I suppose it's very apt.'

'My God!' Kristin said. 'You frighten me. Do you carry all that stuff in your head?'

'Only things that interest me.'

'Well, as you say, it's very apt. As that is just what you are doing. Going to the wars.'

'But I'll see you again.'

'I don't see how you can, if you're going to be in the Mediterranean and I'm here.'

'But we don't go for another six weeks.'

Kristin finished dressing. 'It may be possible to arrange something.'

'What do you think of the news?' Duncan asked his mother, sitting beside her on the settee in her boudoir.

'What news?'

'Oh, Mother! The news from Singapore.'

'I don't think I know anyone in Singapore.'

'Mother, I'm talking about *Prince of Wales* and *Repulse*.'

Kristin frowned. 'Aren't they battleships?'

'*Repulse* is actually a battlecruiser. Was. *Prince of Wales* is, was, one of our very newest battleships, yes.'

'I wish you'd try talking English instead of gobbledegook. Is, was, was, is? Wasn't *Prince of Wales* involved in that fight with *Bismarck*?'

'Yes, she was. But they, I mean the two British capital ships, were both sunk, a couple of days ago. Off the coast of Malaya.'

'Good heavens! It must have been quite a battle. How many Japs did they take with them?'

'They did not take any Japanese ships with them, because they did not see any Japanese ships. It wasn't actually a battle.'

'Don't tell me they collided or something?'

'They were attacked by Japanese aircraft, and sunk in an hour.'

Kristin regarded him for several seconds, then got up and poured herself a whisky. As an afterthought she poured one for him as well. 'Aren't we talking about ships of more than thirty thousand tons?'

'*Prince of Wales* was nearer forty.'

'And they were sunk by a couple of aircraft? That has got to be ridiculous.'

'But true. Don't forget that we sank a couple of Italian battleships in Taranto last year, with aircraft. Or that the Japs sank, or put out of action, eight US battleships at Pearl Harbor only a week ago.'

'All those were at anchor or moored. Not at sea and under way, able to take evasive action.'

'I don't think being able to take evasive action does a lot of good, if there are enough aircraft in the attacking force. Anyway, this sort of thing was predicted long ago. That Italian fellow, Douhet, prophesied at the end of the Great War that the time was coming when battleships would be overwhelmed by air attack. Nobody believed him. And when that American fellow Mitchell said the same thing a few years later, he was cashiered.'

'Are you saying that the battleship is an extinct species?'

'It may well become so. What is certain is that from here on any battle squadron has to be covered by an adequate air screen.'

'And you are saying that the Admiralty did not understand this?'

'I think they did, but not quite sufficiently. Apparently there was an aircraft carrier detached to accompany the battle-ships, and form a proper task force. But she hit a rock or something on her way to the rendezvous, and they decided to press on without her.'

'What a fuck-up.' Kristin handed him his glass and sat down again. '*Ark Royal* and now this. Tell me, what exactly does this mean, Duncan?'

'In the short term, it means that neither we nor the Yanks have any major naval units left in the Pacific, save for a couple of US aircraft carriers. That may well be important. Trouble is, the Japs have at least seven carriers. So right now they hold every high card. In the long term, well . . . it is going to completely revolutionize naval warfare. I think it has already done that.'

'Shit,' she said. 'Shit, shit, shit. If an armoured battleship can be sunk by air attack, what chance do you have in a small piece of plywood?'

'I think more than a battleship. Because we are fast enough to take evasive action. Don't forget that our flotilla was attacked on our way up to Scapa, last year.'

'And one of you was blown up.'

'But the other two got away.'

'Hooray, hooray, hooray. So what do you do? Put all your names in a hat every morning, and draw one, and say, right, it's your turn to get blown to bits today?'

Duncan sighed. 'Crudely put, but that is the nature of the beast. And you know that it doesn't only apply to us. It applies to anyone and everyone engaged in the shooting end of a war. You know that it applies every time we go to sea.'

'In home waters,' Kristin pointed out, 'you can call for support. From what you have told me, you may not be able to do that in the Mediterranean. Just as those two battleships apparently couldn't do it in the South Seas, or wherever. Does Alison know about this?'

'I'm about to tell her. But I thought I should tell you first. I don't want her getting scared. What you have to do is project a combination of stiff upper lip, gung-ho, and yo-ho-ho, let's get at 'em.'

'Who'd be a mother,' Kristin remarked.

'And you are?' she inquired, surveying the short, somewhat plump young woman, with the pert features and the wavy yellow hair, standing in front of her, and clearly in a state of abject terror.

'This is Barbara Parsons,' Alison explained. 'I told you about her.'

'You told me that she was a Wren.'

'She is. You are still a Wren, aren't you, Barbara?'

'Oh, yes, milady.'

'You're a second officer, aren't you?'

'Yes, I am.'

'I was second officer when I met my husband,' Alison reminisced, dreamily.

'But you're not in uniform,' Kristin pointed out, surveying the dress with some disfavour.

'Well . . . ah . . .' Barbara looked at Alison for direction as regards etiquette.

'Oh, she's milady too. No, that's wrong. I should have said, she's milady also. Actually, she's Milady One, and I'm Milady Two.'

Barbara began to look more terrified than ever.

'You still haven't told us why you are not in uniform,' Kristin reminded her.

Barbara gathered her wits. 'Well, milady, as it's Christmas, and I am not on duty . . .'

'Of course,' Alison said sympathetically. 'Why should you be in uniform? It's a lovely dress.'

'Where is Lucifer?' Kristin inquired. He was the ultimate test of strangers coming into her world.

'He's locked up. He knocks people over,' Alison explained to Barbara. 'And is very good at tearing dresses. Now come into the drawing room and have a glass of champagne.'

Barbara cast Kristin a nervous glance to make sure that Alison was not exceeding her prerogatives, and then followed her through the doorway.

'Harry!' Kristin shouted. 'Do let the poor boy out. Next thing he'll be biting holes in the wall.' She followed Barbara into the drawing room, where Alison was dispensing champagne. 'Do sit down. That chair would be best.'

She indicated a very solid armchair. But she was too late. Glass in hand, Barbara had inadvertently sunk on to the settee. Now there was a rushing sound and a huge volume of white fur charged past Kristin and landed on the couch beside the unfortunate young woman.

'Aargh!' Barbara screamed, drawing up her legs and throwing the glass over her shoulder as Lucifer started to lick her face.

'Lucifer! Really!' Alison said. She had already poured another glass.

'He loves you,' Kristin pointed out, reassuringly. 'With him, it's always love at first sight. Unless he hates you. That's always at first sight too.'

It was difficult to determine who was panting more loudly, Barbara or Lucifer, but at least he had subsided, although his huge head remained in her lap.

Alison held out the fresh glass.

'I'm sorry,' ' Barbara said. 'I . . .'

'Forget it. Par for the course.' Alison stooped and picked up the discarded glass. 'See? Not even broken. And champagne is good for the carpet.'

Kristin had heard the roar of the Bugatti. 'The boys are here.' She went into the hall, and to Barbara's great relief, Lucifer got off the settee to accompany her.

Duncan came in first, and accepted the charge. He always embarrassed Lucifer by being big enough and strong enough to lift the dog from the ground, and deliver a bear hug of his own. 'Sorry we're late.'

'Don't tell me there's been another disaster,' Kristin commented, replacing the stymied Lucifer for a hug.

'Just came in. Hong Kong has surrendered.'

'Oh, good Lord! Jimmy!'

'Kristin!' He embraced her in turn, while Lucifer endeavoured to climb up his back.

'What does that mean?'

'Well, to us, the Navy, not a lot. There was precious little chance of us being able to defend it, anyway. But first reports are suggesting it was pretty much a massacre.'

'You said it surrendered.'

'I don't think the Japanese understand the meaning of the word. They never surrender themselves.'

'Good Lord!' She said again, and stepped past him. 'Lucifer, please behave. Mr Cooper. Arnold! How nice to see you again. Do you remember me?'

Cooper was still fending off Lucifer. 'How could I forget, milady.'

She moved Lucifer's paw and tapped the young man on the chest. 'I invited you to dinner once, and you never came.'

'Well, milady, I wanted to. I intended to. But—'

'I know. Duncan took you off on that wild trip up the Gironde and nearly got you killed.'

'I never knew about this,' Lonsdale remarked, frostily.

Kristin raised her eyebrows. 'I thought you ordered the operation.'

'I ordered the Gironde raid, yes. But I didn't know, well . . '

'You're a busy man. We can't expect you to know everything. Come and meet Barbara.'

The men followed her into the drawing room, where Barbara had got to her feet, desperately trying to straighten her dress.

'You'll have to excuse her appearance,' Kristin suggested. 'She's been cuddling Lucifer.'

Barbara shot her a glance but was distracted by the admiral. 'Don't I know you?'

'Yes, sir.' She looked about to curtsy. 'Second Officer Barbara Parsons. I'm in Personnel.'

'Good heavens!'

'Barbara is Arnold's date,' Alison explained.

'Ah!' The admiral looked greatly relieved.

'Oh, I say!' Cooper commented.

'Of course, you haven't met,' Alison said. 'Lieutenant Arnold Cooper, Second Officer Barbara Parsons.'

'Champagne,' Duncan suggested, passing round full glasses.

'That was a magnificent lunch,' Lonsdale said, finishing his port.

'And now,' Kristin remarked, 'I suppose you are rushing off, leaving me alone.' They actually were alone, as the young people had elected to take Lucifer for a digestive walk; after the sticky beginning Cooper and Barbara had seemed to warm to each other.

The admiral fiddled with his glass. 'I came out with Duncan, so I have to wait for him to take me back in. Actually, I wondered if we might have a chat.'

'Oh, splendid. I do like having chats. But isn't that what we're doing now? Having a chat?'

'This is a matter I would like to discuss with you in private, without risk of interruption.'

Kristin regarded him for several seconds; his cheeks were crimson, and he had not actually drunk all that much. 'Well, then,' she said. 'You'd better come upstairs.'

'Eh?'

'To my private sitting room. You've been there before.'

'Ah. Yes.' He recalled two previous occasions, one when Duncan had been reported missing at sea, and he had called to make sure she was all right. She had just left her bath and was wearing only a towel, and that she had very rapidly discarded, whether by accident or design he had never been sure. It was not an occasion he would ever forget. But then he had been protected by the additional presence of a carefully calm Alison. The second time had been the night before he and Duncan had left for Norway to rescue Rebecca Strong and her father. Kristin had assumed she would never see either of them again, and one thing had led to another. That also was not an occasion he would ever forget, even if Kristin had not up to now shown any wish to repeat it. That had always been something of a relief.

'So, come along.' Kristin got up and led him into the hall, from where the small staircase mounted, opposite the huge main staircase. This was quite steep, and he found himself staring at her buttocks moving beneath her skirt, and her ankles emerging from below it. Why am I doing this? he wondered. The idea of again being able to get close to Kristin was enchanting. But after that first occasion he could have no doubt that should one get close to Kristin, on a permanent basis, one was finished as a separate entity.

She opened the door and led him into the so comfortable room. 'Some more port?'

'I think I've had enough.'

'That is very responsible of you. Now, I just have to check Baby. I'm in charge, you see, when Alison is out.'

'Oh! May I come with you? I haven't seen the little chap yet.'

'Of course you may, as long as you don't make a racket.' She led him along the corridor into the main part of the house, and to the nursery. 'We have a nanny on the way, but she hasn't arrived yet.' She stood above the cot. 'Voila!'

Lonsdale peered. 'He's fast asleep.'

'And I sincerely hope he stays that way until his mother comes in. When he wakes up he is going to want to be changed and fed. Changing I can cope with, food, his sort of food, I'm a little short of right now.'

'But you're enjoying being a grandmother?'

'Really, Jimmy, is there a woman alive, at least under the age of fifty, who can put her hand on her heart and say, I enjoy being a grandmother? And when she's only forty-three . . . Even if he is cute, and the future of the family, he's also a constant reminder that the past is gone for ever. Although you know, it would be a hoot if I were to have a child of my own, now. This little chap would have an uncle younger than himself, and Duncan a brother younger than his son. Wouldn't that be deliciously complicated?'

'Ah! Well, yes, I suppose it would.'

'I'm still capable, you know.'

'Oh, quite. Absolutely.' He bent over the cot. 'He's . . . well . . .'

'As ugly as sin.'

'Of course he isn't.'

'Jimmy, if you and I are going to remain friends, you simply have to learn to cut out the cant. All babies of one month old are as ugly as sin, in real terms. One has to hope they grow out of it.'

'You are incorrigible.'

'I always have been. Come along.'

He followed her back down the corridor. 'What are you going to call him?'

'Duncan. I think it will be Duncan John. John is the name of Alison's father. Now, you had something to say to me.' She sat on the settee, and crossed her knees. 'The floor is yours.'

'Oh! Ah! I would hate you to think that I am trying to interfere in your life.'

'My dear Jimmy, you are welcome to interfere in my life whenever you get the urge. Just so long as you don't ever attempt to change it.'

'We . . . I . . . we . . . are concerned about this idea of yours of going off to Spain.'

Once again Kristin regarded him for some seconds. Then she asked, 'We?'

'We're thinking only of your well-being. Of the dangers of undertaking such a journey at this time.'

'We?' Kristin repeated, her voice now taking on the menace of a distant thunderstorm.

'Well . . . Duncan and I.'

'You and Duncan have been discussing me?'

'We're thinking only of your safety.'

'That is very sweet of you. However, that definitely does come under the heading of trying to tell me what to do, and what not to do. Do you know, I thought you wanted to be alone with me to make me a proposition.'

'Eh? What?'

'Don't you want to make me a proposition?'

'Well . . . I mean . . .'

'Do you remember,' Kristin said, 'that in June 1940, I went to Guernsey, and got caught there by the Germans?'

'I do indeed.'

'Of course. You very gallantly sent Duncan to get me out.'

'Well, it wasn't quite like that. I was told to provide an MTB to carry a troop of Commandos to raid the island, and obviously the skipper had to be familiar with Channel Island waters. So Duncan was an obvious choice. And, as you were stuck there, it seemed obvious that he should pick you up at the same time.'

'It was in the nick of time. I was about to be sent off to a concentration camp.'

'I know. But I really hadn't intended you to get mixed up in a naval battle.'

'It was tremendous fun. But you never asked me why I went back to Guernsey in the first place, with the Germans running riot all over France.'

Lonsdale looked somewhat uneasy. 'Well, I knew you, or rather, the late Lord Eversham, had a holiday home there, and there was some talk about retrieving a valuable painting.'

Kristin raised her eyebrows. 'You mean you don't remember it? I showed it to you.'

'Ah. Yes. Well . . .'

'You mean you felt it was improper to look at it?' She smiled. 'I don't know how valuable it would be, offered for sale at Sotheby's, but it was valuable to me. Did you ever meet my husband?'

'Yes, I did. Once or twice.'

'And I'll bet you found him a colossal bore. Well, he was, in recent years. But, you may not believe this, in his youth he was a real go-getter. And he was madly in love with me. Or at least with my body. So he had me painted. It was just after the end of the Great War. I was twenty, and my figure had entirely recovered from having Duncan.'

'And that painting was in the Guernsey house. Yes, I remember. What I never understood was why you didn't reclaim it when you divorced Eversham. I mean, that was several years ago? Before this war started.'

'He divorced me,' Kristin said, darkly. 'And as you have gathered, the painting was in the Guernsey house. Which belonged to him. I asked for it back, and the bastard refused to give it to me. What is more, he had the locks on the Guernsey house changed, so that I couldn't sneak across and get in. I was livid but there was nothing I could do about it; legally, the painting belonged to him. Then the poor old sod got himself blown up at Dunkirk, and his entire estate, such as it was, went to Duncan. So I was able to get hold of the keys at last, and naturally the first thing I did was nip across to Guernsey to collect the painting.'

'Two days before the Germans arrived! That was an incredibly risky thing to do. I mean, I can appreciate that the painting had some sentimental value . . .'

'I had no idea the Germans were going to pounce so soon. Anyway, Jimmy, you're missing the point. Now I know you never looked at it properly, or at all. Sentiment didn't really come into it. I told you, I was twenty years old when it was painted, and Douglas wanted a memoir of me at my beautiful best.' She paused to gaze at him.

'You mean . . . gosh! But even so, well, I mean, there are lots of famous nudes about.'

'Jimmy, Douglas didn't just want a nude of me. He wanted

a sexy nude. In fact, he wanted the sexiest nude the artist could devise.'

The admiral realized that his mouth was open, and hastily closed it.

'The thought of a bunch of Nazis wanking themselves before my portrait, or worse, taking it back to Germany for public display . . . I simply had to get it.'

'Of course, I understand now. What a story. But at least it turned out well. But why, if you're that concerned about it, haven't you had it destroyed? Or have you?'

'Have it destroyed? Don't be absurd.' She got up, held out her hand. 'It is still hanging above my bed. Come along, and I'll show it to you, again. And this time I want you to *look* at it.'

'I think it may be going to snow,' Duncan remarked. 'Do you suppose they'll get chilblains?'

'That depends on how much they take off,' Alison suggested. 'Or if they take off anything. They've only just met. Lucifer, do leave that poor little bunny in peace. He's at least six feet down by now. You'll have to dig up half the county to get him.'

Lucifer took his nose out of the rabbit warren to look at her reproachfully, then realized she was right and went bounding past them; where there was one rabbit there would surely be others.

'Well, I think you made an inspired choice,' Duncan said, 'They seemed to take to each other.'

'I think she's in a state of shock.'

'Eh? He's a very personable lad.'

'Not with him. With us. I think she feels she has got herself mixed up in a madhouse. Well, she could be right. Especially with Kristin in a very odd mood.'

'Is she in an odd mood?'

'Yes, she is. You haven't been home for a week. I don't really blame her. With you, and . . . well, with you going off to the Med . . .'

He squeezed her hand. 'Are you not in an odd mood?'

'Yes, I am. But I suppose I conceal it better than Kristin. And I suppose having been in the Navy myself helps. But . . . oh, Duncan . . .'

She stopped walking and turned into his arms. He kissed her forehead, then her nose before getting to her lips. 'Nothing is going to happen to me. I have spent two years at war, and I have never received even a scratch.'

'That is the last thing you should say. Think of the law of averages.'

Lucifer having returned, boisterously, they resumed walking, hand in hand.

'Are you going to rejoin, when Baby Duncan is a bit older?' Duncan asked.

'I don't think it's a good idea to look that far ahead, with a war on. Would you like me to?'

'I would like you to do exactly as you choose. But it was rather fun having you in Jimmy's office, knowing that you were watching us come and go.'

'Yes,' she agreed thoughtfully. 'Do you think she really will go rushing off to Spain, just to be within a thousand miles of you?'

'Why do you think we are taking this walk in the freezing air? Jimmy has promised to talk some sense into her.'

'Do you think he can?' They left the trees and the house was in front of them. Alison checked to look over her shoulder. 'You don't suppose they're lost?'

'Cooper is a seaman. How can he be lost?'

She looked up at the sky, which was totally overcast. 'What's he supposed to navigate by?'

'Well . . . the wind direction.'

'There is no wind. And it's going to be dark in an hour.'

'That's a fact. Perhaps we should send Lucifer to find them?'

'I do not think that would be a good idea; he's liable to bring them back one at a time by one leg.'

'Well, we'll give them another half an hour. I need to get some of Lucia's mulled wine inside me before I freeze. And Baby will be waking up any moment now.'

They were approaching from the rear of the property, and Lucifer had already charged across the croquet lawn, barking. Harry heard the noise and opened the door for him and them; the dog shot past the butler to get to his bowl just in case it was supper time.

'Brass monkeys,' Duncan explained as they took off their coats. 'Always makes him hungry. Lady Eversham in the drawing room?'

'No, sir. She went upstairs.'

'And Baby?' Alison asked. 'Oh! There he is. I hear him.'

They had reached the front hall while talking, and she ran up the grand staircase to reach the nursery. There was no sign of the admiral. Duncan went to the foot of the small staircase, considered.

'I don't think we should interrupt them,' Alison said, returning down the stairs with Baby Duncan in her arms, and allowing her feminine instincts to take control. 'Lucia,' she called. 'We are dying for some of your mulled wine.'

'Of course, donna,' the maid agreed. 'I will just heat it up.'

Duncan was still standing at the foot of the stairs; the door at the top, into Kristin's sitting room, was ajar, and there was not a sound to be heard.

'Come on,' Alison said, taking off her sweater and opening her shirt to release her nursing bra. 'She's your mother, not your daughter.'

He sat beside her and Lucia served the wine, as Baby got to work, noisily. They looked at each other as they heard a door close above them. 'Maybe you'd better button up.'

'Oh, come now. He's a grown man, even if he is an admiral. And if I cut the boy off in midstream he'll make a lot of noise.'

They looked at the drawing room doorway, and a moment later Kristin appeared, with Lonsdale beside her. Kristin looked as radiant as ever, the admiral suggested a strange mixture of guilt and the cat who has just swallowed the canary. And they were holding hands.

But Lonsdale checked at the sight of mother plus child. 'Oh, I say . . .'

'A feeding mother is the most beautiful of sights,' Kristin pointed out. 'Where are Mr Cooper and Miss Parsons?'

'We don't know,' Alison confessed. 'They wandered off. I think we are going to have to go back and look for them.'

'Must have been love at first sight,' Duncan suggested.

'How romantic. Well, we won't wait for them. Harry, we'll have a bottle of Bollinger, and when you bring it, ask Lucia to come in as well, will you. Duncan, Admiral Lonsdale has something to say to you. Jimmy!'

'Ah. Well. Yes. Your mother . . . well . . . with your consent Lord Eversham, Lady Eversham, I mean, the Dowager Lady Eversham, has consented to be my wife.'

When Cooper and Barbara finally returned, after dark, they had to be warmed up with mulled wine, following which more celebratory champagne had to be drunk. By the time the party finally got around to dinner it was obvious that Duncan was not driving anywhere that night, and they all had to be put to bed, while Lucia sorted out things like new toothbrushes and spare razors.

Alison did not inquire into the various arrangements, but let them get on with it, again under the general supervision of Lucia; there were six double bedrooms in the house apart from Kristin's suite. As they were all on duty the next day, breakfast had to be very early. Then there were tearful and loving farewells, although Barbara, having arrived by bus, was going with the men in the Bugatti. It should, Alison supposed as she waved them out of sight, be an eventful trip; the Bugatti was a two-seater with only a narrow rumble seat behind, and with its roof up was very intimate, even for the two in front.

But they all seemed happy; she could only hope that there would be no naval emergency for the next few hours.

She wished she could feel the same on the domestic front, went up to Kristin's sitting room. Her mother-in-law had not come down to breakfast – Lonsdale had gone up to say goodbye – and was sitting up in bed drinking black coffee. 'Well,' she remarked. 'I think that went off very well. Did that girl and Cooper share a bed?'

'I think it's a very strong possibility. I'll have to ask Lucia. And you?'

'I'm engaged,' Kristin reminded her, primly.

'Of course. Am I allowed to ask . . .?'

'Is it important to you?'

'As a matter of fact, it is. Does he know?'

'Does who know what?'

'I'm not supposing that Jimmy knows about Jamie. But does Jamie know about Jimmy?'

'I don't see how he can, as it only happened yesterday, and I haven't seen Jamie for three days.'

'But . . . well . . .'

'We decided that we had run our course.'

'You mean you had already made up your mind to marry the admiral. Three days ago.'

'No, I had not,' Kristin said, a trifle brusquely. 'I told you, I just realized that there was no future for either of us. I mean, Jamie and me.'

'Does Jamie realize that too?'

'Oh, for God's sake, Alison, don't you have a head? I do. No, Jamie did not realize that. You know what men are like; they always think they can maintain the status quo for as long as they want.'

'So,' Alison said. 'As far as he knows, you had a lover's tiff. Are you going to tell him it's more than that, or are you going to go on seeing him?'

'I can't go on seeing him if he's in the Mediterranean, can I?'

'Was it as cold-blooded as that?'

They stared at each other, and to her consternation, Alison saw tears emerge from Kristin's eyes and roll down her cheeks. 'He probably went to the boatyard yesterday morning,' she muttered. 'That was our Christmas present to each other, last year. He would have waited . . . and I never turned up. Oh, Alison –' she grasped her hand – 'I feel so *wretched.*'

'And Jimmy?'

'I just wanted to *do* something. Can you understand that?'

Alison squeezed the fingers. 'I'm glad you're human. Tell you what. Get dressed and we'll take Lucifer for a walk with Baby.'

'Isn't that something?' Mary Goring asked.

'He's a lucky man,' Tim agreed. 'Do you know him, Jamie?'

'The likes of me don't get to know admirals,' Jamie pointed out.

'I suppose that's true. I wonder if we'll be invited to the wedding?'

'Us?' his wife asked.

'Well, we look after their cars. Have done for donkey's years.'

'I wouldn't hold your breath,' Jamie advised. 'I'll be going out for a while.'

'You'll freeze.'

'It's not that cold.'

His father watched the door close behind him. 'He's in a funny mood. You don't suppose he's worried about this new hush-hush assignment?'

'Jamie?' Mary asked. 'Not him. He's worried about leaving his girl.'

'Jamie has a girl?'

'You never notice anything, Tim Goring. Whenever he has a furlough, he always takes off in the middle of the afternoon. Now, why should he do that, if he's not meeting someone?'

'Could be a pal.'

'If it is, we may have a problem. He's been doing it now for over a year.'

'But if it's a girl, how come he's never bought her home?' Mary shrugged.

'You don't think she's, well . . .'

'Maybe she isn't ideal. But that's his business. He's fighting a war, risking his life every time he goes to sea on that little boat. He's entitled to have some fun, even if she's the village tart.'

Tim scratched his head, as he realized he had perhaps never known his wife as well as he had thought he did.

Jamie dismounted, wheeled his bike up to the gate, and unlocked it. In the middle of a cold December afternoon the streets of Lymington were deserted. In any event, if anyone questioned what he was doing, he was looking at Lord Eversham's boat, which he did regularly; everyone knew he had been part of the racing crew before the war and was now part of the MTB crew as well.

He closed and relocked the gate behind him, walked the bike across the yard, and leaned it against the shed wall, as he always did. The ladder was in place, and he stared at it for a few moments, remembering the last time he had climbed it, behind Kristin, looking up at all that beauty which had so strangely come into his keeping. Temporarily.

He climbed up, unlocked the hatch, and sat in it, looking

down at the bunk, with the mattress and blankets, waiting. All history, he thought. Just because he would not become a criminal for her. That had to make her a very wicked woman. But hadn't he always known that she was a very wicked woman?

But of course she wasn't. She had been blessed with both the looks and the money to live her life as she chose, regardless of anyone else, and for the most part regardless of man-made laws and conventions. Had she not been like that, she would never have looked twice at him in the first place.

And in real terms, was Duncan any different? Yes he was. Simply because he possessed an overwhelming sense of responsibility, of duty, which led him always to do, or attempt to do, the right thing. Kristin had never had to cultivate that. Because of what most people would regard as the catastrophic start to her adult life, she had been faced with two choices, either to curl up in shame and live the rest of that life under a shadow, or to square her shoulders and say fuck you to the world. She had chosen the latter course. In that sense she had revealed a courage beyond the reach of so many people.

He ought to wish her every joy at this stab at respectability, save that he did not feel that she would find any joy with a man like Jimmy Lonsdale. He knew nothing about the admiral at all, about his personal qualities, his ambitions, or his faults, but he did know that one did not become an admiral in an institution like the Royal Navy without subordinating one's basic or even critical instincts to the requirements of the service and of the country. It followed that one's wife had to do the same.

He sighed, and turned his head to look at the gate. He thought that he would give ten years of his life to see the Sunbeam drawing to a halt beyond them, watch that superb figure getting out to unlock them, knowing that within minutes she would be in his arms.

But it was not going to happen. He realized there was a tear rolling down his cheek.

PART TWO
A Change in the Weather

'Jolly boating weather'
                    Eton Boat Song

Life on the Ocean Wave

'**G**entlemen!' Rear-Admiral Lonsdale surveyed the seven officers standing on the pontoon before him, surrounded by the office buildings and gun emplacements of Portsmouth Harbour. Immediately behind them the six motor boats lay moored, in pairs, bobbing gently to the slight swell that came in through the pier heads, and on the decks of which the various crews also stood to attention.

The admiral knew all of the officers, even if a couple only slightly. Now he passed slowly down their ranks, Duncan at his side. 'Lieutenant Beattie.'

Lonsdale shook hands. Beattie had served with Duncan most of the past year.

'Lieutenant Linton.'

Linton was another of Duncan's experienced commanders, who had in fact lost his boat during the famous raid up the Gironde the previous year.

'Sub-Lieutenant Matthews. Sub-Lieutenant Wilcox. Sub-Lieutenant Partridge. And Lieutenant Cooper, my executive officer.'

Lonsdale smiled at the young man, who he had last seen cuddled in the back seat of the Bugatti with Second Officer Parsons on Boxing Day. But now was not the time to inquire into how that romance was going, supposing, in these circumstances, that it was going at all.

He stepped back to survey the expectant faces. 'I am sorry to have kept you in the dark for so long, but I know you all understand how essential it is that we keep our plans close to our chests. I can now tell you that you are going to the Mediterranean.' Another smile. 'I have a suspicion that you have already worked that out for yourselves, if only because of the issue of tropical whites. You will be based, at least in the first instance on Malta, and your exact role will be outlined to you when you get there. However, I can tell you that it will be an aggressive one, in that you will, whenever the opportunity presents itself, initiate action instead of merely reacting to the enemy, as has so often been our role here. In this I have every confidence that you will cover yourself with credit as you have always done under my command. I need hardly say that I am sorry to lose you, but I look forward to getting you back again. Now I know that Lieutenant-Commander Eversham wishes to have a tactical discussion before you cast off, so I won't keep you. Stand down. And God's speed.'

'Three cheers for the admiral,' Duncan called. Both officers and men responded with a will. 'Now,' Duncan went on, 'If you gentlemen will assemble in the Mess on board *412* I will join you in a few minutes.'

He walked back along the pontoon beside the admiral. 'That's a lovely ring you've given Mother.'

'She seemed to appreciate it. It was bloody difficult coming even close to the stuff she has already.'

'It's the thought that counts. And when I see you again . . .'

'I don't think anything will have changed,' Lonsdale said. 'We have decided to wait a while.'

'Ah!'

'Yes,' Lonsdale agreed. 'One should not begin a relationship with one's prospective son-in-law by stringing a line. Your mother made the decision.'

'Excuse me, sir, but did you say, prospective?'

'That is exactly it, Duncan.'

'But I thought . . . the ring . . .'

'Oh, we are officially engaged. But . . . I am going to be frank with you, Duncan. I don't suppose sons ever take the time to analyse their mothers very carefully, but it cannot have escaped your notice that Kristin is a woman of moods and impulses. On Christmas Day she was very definitely in the grip of both a mood and an impulse. I have no idea what inspires these, certainly in her case, but I cannot feel confident that it had anything at all to do with me. On the other hand, I had had a lot to drink, and I have always, as I am sure you have observed, been very fond of her. So, one thing led to another, and, well . . .'

'You felt obliged to do the decent thing.'

'Don't get me wrong,' Lonsdale said. 'There is no woman I would rather marry than your mother. In fact, she is the only woman I have ever considered marrying. And I still have every hope, and indeed, intention, of bringing it off. But I am becoming increasingly aware that whether I make it or not is entirely dependent on her.'

'And you feel that she's gone off the boil.'

'I'm not sure she ever was on the boil, as regards me. As I said, I wish to be entirely frank with you.'

'Thank you, sir. I appreciate it. But . . . do you mean you feel there is somebody else?'

'I really can't say.'

'She's never shown any interest in anyone else,' Duncan said, thoughtfully. 'To my knowledge. I mean, not recently. And we have always been quite close. Anyway, I would have observed him coming or going, or there would have been telephone calls . . .'

'But you're not there all the time, are you?'

'No, sir. But Alison is. Or has been certainly for the past year.'

'And of course you have no secrets from each other. So I am just being a silly old man with cold feet. I have absolutely no business raising the matter when you are off on a dangerous assignment. Please forgive me and forget it. Obviously the reason your mother doesn't want to discuss wedding plans right now is that she wants you to be present. Which is as it should be. So, come back safely. I assume the christening went off all right?'

'Oh, splendidly. Well, up to a point.'

'Oh, no! What happened?'

'When we went back to the house for a drink after the ceremony, Lucifer fell madly in love with the vicar.'

'My God! Is he out of hospital yet?'

'Mother is buying him a new cassock. But he has developed a nervous twitch. May I ask, sir? This hesitance Mother is showing about naming the date . . . it couldn't possibly have anything to do with that crazy idea of her visiting Spain?'

'I'm afraid I simply do not know.'

'But . . . you're not going to let her go?'

'If she decides to go, the only way I can see of stopping her would be to lock her up. I do not have the jurisdiction to do that. Our best bet is that there are no berths available for non-essential personnel. So –' he held out his hand – 'good luck! I think we are both going to need it.'

Duncan had been at war long enough to know that the gravest mistake a man could make was to become distracted by domestic problems before going into action, and actually it was a relief to be able to shut his mind to them – which included having said farewell to Alison and Baby Duncan, not to mention Lucifer, and of course, his mother. By the time he saw them again, if he saw them again, he had no doubt that the current difficulties would have been overcome, or at least faded away.

'Gentlemen!' he said, to the officers, who had assembled in the Mess on *412*. 'I am sorry to have kept you waiting.' He unrolled the large-scale chart of the coastal waters of Western Europe, extending from Land's End to Morocco, and spread it on the long table. 'As has been made very plain to you, their lordships wish our mission to be secret, at least until we actually get there. This means that our first business is to reach Gibraltar without being noticed. That is to say, without putting into port, or even approaching land close enough to be spotted.

'We will therefore leave at dusk tonight and proceed down-Channel as if on ordinary patrol. Speed will be maintained at fifteen hundred revolutions, twenty knots, so that we should be off the Scillies at dawn tomorrow. Once we are past the Scillies, we alter course south-west, maintaining twenty knots. This will take us a couple of hundred miles west of Ushant. By 1600 we should be in a position approximately ten degrees West Longitude, forty-seven North Latitude; when we will alter course south-west by south. This will enable us to pass Finisterre at a distance again of a couple of hundred miles. By 0900 on day three we should be thirteen West and forty-three degrees thirty seconds North. Course will then be south by west, to give St Vincent an equally wide berth. We will maintain this course for twenty-five hours, that is, until 1000 on day four. Once we are two hundred miles south-west of St Vincent, that will be thirty-five North and twelve West, we will alter course due east, and make for Gib, ETA dawn on day five. I am giving you these coordinates now, so that you will know what to do in the event of the flotilla having to scatter either because of enemy action, or forced by the weather. Should this happen, you will proceed on your own in line with these instructions. It must be clearly understood that there is to be no radio communication, either between us, or between us and any shore station, until we reach our destination, although of course you will maintain a radio watch to monitor weather and any shipping movements close to us. As long as we are in visual contact, we will communicate by lamp. If you get into trouble, outside of visual contact, you will have to get yourselves back out. I am sorry, but there it is.

'Now, this route involves just over seventeen hundred nautical miles. At twenty knots, that is, half-speed, this is well within our range. But it also involves nearly four days at sea. We could go faster, of course and get there in half the time. And thus, you might say, halve the risk of being detected. However, we would also be burning twice as much fuel, and risk arriving at the Straits of Gibraltar with virtually empty tanks, and no room for manoeuvre if we run into an enemy. I have given the matter a lot of thought, and I have decided that the longer journey, with the certainty of arriving at our destination with fuel in hand and thus the option of high speed action if need be, is a safer course than going flat out and allowing ourselves no margin for error.

'Now, weather. Of one thing we may be fairly certain: we are not likely to run into any fog once we are into the Bay. However, tomorrow is February the first, and although it appears settled at the moment, it is a time of year when both Biscay and the Atlantic can be boisterous. Mr Beattie and Mr Linton, who were both with me in a Biscay gale last year, will be able to reassure you that the seas are not dangerous as long as they are headed, and at this time of the year the weather, at least down there, is most likely to be from the south-west. An easterly gale should not present a problem; there is insufficient fetch for really big seas to build. Should it be from the north-west or north, you will have to turn and head the seas for as long as they are high enough to be dangerous; that is likely to involve the forced scattering I have mentioned. In those circumstances, your prime responsibility is the safety of your ship and your crew. Once the weather abates, you will resume your journey. You will have been blown off course, but you have your sextants and your chronometers, and you will regain the designated track as quickly as possible. Operating at half speed, you should have ample fuel reserves for this purpose. Any questions?'

He surveyed their tense faces. 'Very good. Return to your boats, and prepare to cast off at 1800. I shall wish you good luck and we shall have dinner together at The Rock Hotel on Wednesday evening.'

They saluted and filed from the cabin. 'Will we all make it, sir?' Cooper asked.

'I'll be damned annoyed if we don't. We aren't likely to get any replacements for a while.'

'Yes, sir. Permission to go ashore for half an hour.'

Duncan regarded him. 'You reckon she'll still be there?'

'Yes, sir. They're all working late tonight.'

'Then half an hour, Mr Cooper.'

The boy hurried off, while Duncan scratched his head. He hadn't realized things had progressed so far so quickly. Mother the matchmaker. Or was it Alison, inadvertently? Or even more inadvertently, himself? In more ways than one. He had set out merely to make sure the admiral had the opportunity for a serious chat with Mother, to talk her out of the absurd idea of visiting Spain.

Now Cooper was clearly wildly in love, at an age and in a rank when he could not possibly contemplate marriage, and the admiral . . . he had always supposed that one day Lonsdale might pluck up the courage to propose, but he had never really expected Mother to accept. Duncan was not as lacking in perception as many people supposed, and he adored his mother. He adored his wife as well, but in a totally different way. Alison, and now Baby Duncan, were there to be cherished and protected. Mother was there to worship and obey, and certainly to accept for what she was. She would never change. She would never wish to change. She knew that as well as anyone, just as she had to know that Jimmy

Lonsdale would require that change, to a way of life he could understand, and control, which to her was anathema.

Yet she had said yes! So she had had a lot to drink; he had never seen his mother either drunk or not in full control of her faculties. Something far more destructive than alcohol had been at work. Something of which he could not imagine. And Jimmy Lonsdale was now trying to come to terms with that. Could it really be another man, who had let her down? Mother, who boasted of what in other people would be considered frailties? He had to have been quite a guy.

He sighed, and went down the ladders to the engine room, where Jamie was contemplating his kingdom. 'All set?'

'Aye-aye, sir.'

'We shall be under way for something more than eighty hours, non-stop.'

'That shouldn't be a problem, sir. I changed the oil this morning.'

Duncan nodded; he had expected nothing different. 'Parents all right?'

'They're not shouting for joy. I wouldn't expect them to be. Any more than . . . well . . .'

'Yes,' Duncan said. 'Navy wives, and Navy mothers, eh? You're lucky, Jamie, in not being married. Not even a girl, eh?' He paused to frown at the shadow that had flickered across the young man's face. 'Or do you have a girl, tucked away in darkest Lymington?'

'No, sir,' Jamie said, emphatically. 'I do not have a girl, anywhere.'

'Very wise, while there's a war on. So, what are you looking forward to most, in the Med? Blue skies and warm water?'

'I am looking forward to killing as many Germans as possible, sir.'

'Ah . . . right.'

'That's what we're being sent there to do, isn't it, sir?'

'That's true. Only I suspect we are going to encounter more Italians than Germans.'

'They're all enemies, sir.'

'Quite. I'll leave you to it. We'll be casting off at 1800.'

'Aye-aye, sir.'

Duncan closed the door. Another bloke in a very odd mood,

he thought. In their two years of serving together, he had never heard Jamie express a desire to kill anyone. Indeed, on the couple of occasions he had been required to do so, personally, he had been quite upset. So, he thought: he does have a girl he's leaving behind.

At 1800 all hands were in their places. It was already dark, and there was only a light south-westerly breeze, but it was still very cold on the water; every man wore a greatcoat under his oilskins. Duncan turned the ignition key, and the Packard growled into life. Instantly the other five boats did the same. He looked to his right; *413* was moored outside him. 'Whenever you are ready, Mr Beattie,' he called.

'Aye-aye. Take in those lines,' Beattie said.

The crew of *412* were waiting to pass the mooring lines across to their mates, and *413* moved quietly away, her deck hands taking in the fenders.

'Stand by, Mr Rawlings,' Duncan said.

'Aye, aye, sir.' Rawlings left the bridge. 'Stand by the deck.'

The crew took up their positions on the pontoon side of the hull.

'Cast off aft,' Duncan said.

'Aft away, sir.'

'Cast off, forward.'

'Forward away, sir.'

'Bear away.'

Two boathooks pushed the hull away from the floating dock. Duncan cast a last glance up at the Command Building. This was blacked out, but he had no doubt that quite a few eyes were watching them leave. Certainly Lonsdale would be there. And Barbara Parsons? This time last year Alison would have been with them. Instead of which she was home with Baby and Mother and Lucifer. The two women would be having a drink. But they would also be watching the clock; they knew what time the flotilla was leaving.

Now it was necessary to concentrate. Inside the crowded inner harbour the boats had to operate at the lowest possible speed, and with only just over three feet in the water the MTBs took a lot of steering. He spun the helm to and fro to bring her round and then straighten her up, following Beattie between the breakwaters and into the more open waters of the Solent. Speed was increased to a thousand revolutions, but Beattie waited for Duncan, as Flotilla Leader, to pass him before doing the same.

Duncan looked over his shoulder. They were carrying no lights, but from the white wakes he could see that all the boats were in line behind him.

Rawlings rejoined him. 'All fenders inboard, sir.'

'Thank you, Mr Rawlings.' Duncan thumbed the intercom. 'All correct, Jamie?'

'Purring like a babe, sir,' was Jamie's inevitable response.

'We'll be moving up to fifteen hundred once we're through the Needles.'

'Aye-aye, sir.'

Cooper arrived. 'Weather report, sir. There's a front out in the Atlantic, moving this way. Not very fast, though.'

'But we're going towards it,' Duncan reminded him. 'What can we expect?'

'South-westerly Six, occasionally Eight in gusts. Sea state moderate to rough.'

'Not too bad.'

'No, sir. But . . . ah . . .'

'Yes?'

'As the front goes through, the wind will veer north-west to north, and may increase for a while.'

'A while being?'

'Perhaps four hours. Then it will move east and decrease by Tuesday morning. While it has a northerly component there may be snow showers.'

'In other words, a bloody blizzard. Thank you, Mr Cooper. Mr Rawlings, use the lamp and signal Mr Beattie to check his forecast. Request him to pass the message down the line.'

'Aye-aye, sir.'

Rawlings got to work with the Morse lamp, while Duncan reflected that it was probably a good idea to get the heavy weather out of the way at the start of the voyage.

Once they were through the Narrows and out into the Channel they adopted normal watch-keeping procedures. As skipper,

Duncan did not have an allotted watch; like Jamie in the
engine room and Wilson in the galley he was technically on
call at all times. The other fourteen crew were divided into
two watches, the Starboard, under Cooper, and the Port, under
Rawlings. These operated in four-hour shifts, except for the
two Dog Watches of two hours each, from 1600 to 1800,
and from 1800 to 2000. This was necessary as, because four
goes evenly into twenty-four, without the Dog Watches to
create seven instead of six spells, the same men would be
on the same watch throughout the voyage, which would
include a nightly stint on the least popular watch, the Middle,
from 2400 to 0400, a period that bisected the night.

However, at the start of a voyage, Duncan always took the
helm for a complete watch, and although they had cast off
at 1800, he remained on the bridge until midnight, by which
time, despite endless cups of hot coffee, he was thoroughly
chilled.

By then they were halfway down the English south coast,
and when he awoke at 0600 it was to a freshening south-
westerly wind and a lumpy sea, dotted with whitecaps which,
as the boat was going into it, sent a continual rattle of spray
aft. But the Scilly Isles were visible to starboard

Cooper was sharing the helm with Morrison. 'Good
morning, gentlemen,' Duncan said, and used his binoculars
to look behind them. It was still dark, but both *413* and *414*
could be identified, so presumably the other boats were in
line astern. 'Morrison, make to *413*: Alter course as per
instructions. Inform following boats. Acknowledge.'

'Aye-aye, sir.' Morrison got busy with the lamp.

'Any problems?' Duncan asked.

'None, sir,' Cooper replied. 'It's getting up, though.'

'Spot on time. Low cloud will be good for us.'

He went down to the Mess and was served breakfast by
Wilson, together with the other members of the Watch, then
visited the engine room as he heard the sound of the pump,
which indicated that Jamie was up. He knew the bilges were
dry save for some condensation, but Jamie pumped every
morning. This was necessary because the petrol gave off
vapour as it was fed into the engine, and this gathered in the
bilge. Unless it was regularly removed, it would build into

a highly inflammable and therefore explosive gas which could be ignited by the slightest spark and blow the boat and everyone in it to Kingdom come.

'All well?' he asked.

'Aye-aye, sir.'

'Fuel consumption?'

Jamie indicated the sight gauges, which were still showing virtually full. 'Maybe fifty gallons.'

Duncan nodded. 'There will be a bit of a bobble later on. We may have to turn up into it. I will maintain fifteen hundred for as long as possible, but it may be necessary to come down to a thousand.'

'Aye-aye, sir.'

Nothing seems to bother that boy, Duncan thought, as he returned to the bridge. At least at sea.

The wind continued to rise as the day wore on, and with it the sea. Coming out of the ocean, the swell was long, and the crests, if now breaking regularly, were more of a nuisance than a hindrance, although the alteration in course meant that the seas were on the starboard bow and this threw the little boats about. Duncan kept an eye on the flotilla behind him, and they all seemed to be coping.

But throughout the afternoon conditions worsened, and as projected, the wind veered. As the seas were now quite big, it was not only uncomfortable but even dangerous for the relatively small craft to take them on the beam. 'Make to all boats, Mr Rawlings,' Duncan said. 'Reduce speed and head the wind. Resume track at discretion when conditions improve.'

As dusk approached, the clouds became increasingly low and threatening, delivering a succession of rain squalls, which did indeed occasionally contain sleet and hail, driven by winds of close on forty knots. Heading them at relatively low speed, the boats responded very well, but it was uncomfortable, compounded by the knowledge, understood by all hands, that they were now steadily heading the wrong way. The only comfort lay in the knowledge that in these conditions, and with the clouds so thick and low, they were at no risk of being spotted by any patrolling German aircraft.

And around midnight, again as forecast, the wind veered some more and began to abate. It was an utterly black night, and with still a lot of breaking water about it was impossible to discern any wakes. 'Make to north-west, Mr Rawlings,' was the best Duncan could do. 'Am resuming track. They must be out there somewhere.' There was no response from the darkness, but he had left the decision as to when to resume the course up to the individual commanders, and he had to have confidence in their professional judgements.

Once *412* was back on course – Duncan did not reckon they were more than fifty miles north-west of their track, and if the clouds lifted he would be able to get a sextant reading tomorrow – he increased speed again, toured the ship to make sure everything remained watertight, and then turned in for a few hours.

At dawn he was back on the bridge, to find conditions greatly improved. There was still a lot of cloud, but it was fast moving and there were patches of blue, while the sea was no more than moderate. It was even reasonably warm, at least compared with the previous day. But . . . 'Where is everybody?' he inquired.

'I thought I saw something just now, sir,' Cooper remarked. 'But it's gone again.'

Duncan swept the northern horizon, but could see nothing but heaving whitecaps. Then he tried the southern; it was quite possible that *412* could have been passed in the night. But there was nothing there, either.

'Should we turn back and make a sweep, sir?' Cooper asked.

'Certainly not, Mr Cooper. They have their orders. Maintain course and speed.'

But it was disconcerting to feel that he might have lost his entire command. Of course that was impossible. He had always known they would be separated by the gale, but the storm had been very brief and thus they could not have been scattered very far. Nor had the weather ever been severe enough to endanger a properly handled seventy-two foot boat; his skippers were all experienced seamen.

Yet he, and Cooper and Rawlings, spent most of the day

on the bridge with their binoculars. Throughout the morning the skies cleared, the wind dropped, and the seas subsided. While it steadily warmed up as they motored south. By noon they were basking in unbroken sunlight, and his sextant reading was reassuring.

The swell, out of the south-west, remained high, some thirty feet, Duncan estimated, but the crests were three hundred feet apart, and *412* slipped gently down and then up in an almost soporific motion. In the troughs, the horizon disappeared altogether and it was just blue water all around them, but on the crests visibility seemed endless. And at 1400 Rawlings suddenly said, 'I have a boat. No, two. Bearing ten degrees on the port quarter.'

Duncan's noon sight combined with his chronometer timing had enabled him to estimate that they were at least two hundred miles from the Portuguese coast, therefore any small vessels out here were extremely unlikely to belong to the Portuguese fishing fleet, which, with the Atlantic having developed into a vast battleground, had become strictly inshore. Nor was any Portuguese fishing boat, or any U-boat on the surface, capable of matching an MTB for speed even at cruising revolutions. 'Signal them to identify themselves,' he said.

It was a slow business, as the lamps could only be used when all the little ships were on the crests at the same time. But gradually the identification came through. '*413*. *416*, sir.'

'It's a start,' Duncan said.

By dusk, two other boats had joined. 'That leaves *414*, Linton, unaccounted for,' Cooper remarked.

'Damnation,' Duncan commented. He could not stop himself recalling Napoleon's maxim, that a lucky general was more valuable than a good one. Linton was an excellent seaman, and with Beattie he had been part of the flotilla that had carried out that spectacular raid up the Gironde the previous year. But his had been the only boat to run aground on the way upriver, and worse, it had been the only boat to be sunk on the way back. He had done nothing wrong; they had all had to run a gauntlet of hostile fire when passing the little river port of Paulliac, but the fact remained that his had been the one to take a fatal hit.

'Signal all boats to reduce speed and close up for a chat,' he commanded.

The five boats came together in a vast raft, fenders scraping against each other in the swell. The skippers accumulated on board *412* to report, but none of them had any useful information. *414* had been third in the line, behind Beattie's *413* and in front of Matthews' *415*. When the wind had shifted, they had all obeyed orders and turned up to head the seas. Both Beattie and Matthews had seen Linton turn with them, but then, in the darkness and the wild conditions, they had lost sight of him as all the boats had lost sight of each other.

'He had given no previous indication of any problems?' Duncan asked.

'No, sir,' Matthews said. 'As he was the boat in front of me, I had my eyes on him throughout yesterday, and he seemed perfectly happy.'

'Hm. Well there is nothing we can do about it now, save hope that whatever his problem was he manages to sort it out and rejoin in due course.'

'You don't suppose he . . . well . . .' Wilcox looked embarrassed.

'No, Mr Wilcox, I do not,' Duncan said. 'There are only three possible scenarios. One is an engine failure that would leave his boat without power. However, in those circumstances he would have rigged a sea anchor and ridden the gale out. Now it is certainly possible that repairing any engine damage may take some time, but that is no reason for supposing he may have foundered. The second possibility is that he hit something and holed the hull. Out here in the open sea that would be a million to one misfortune, and certainly at reduced speed he is not likely to have sustained fatal damage. The third possibility is fire and perhaps an explosion. But visibility last night was never poor enough for us not to see a ship on fire at a distance of a couple of miles, and none of us saw even a glow. For those reasons I consider that we may assume that Lieutenant Linton and his crew are merely delayed. You may resume course and speed to our next way point, south-west of Cape St Vincent. I estimate that blow cost us about six hours, we should therefore reach the point at 1600 tomorrow instead of 1000 as I had intended. However, we shall still be in Gibraltar for dinner on Day Five. Thank you, gentlemen.'

'Do you really think Linton is all right?' Cooper asked, as they got under way, Douglas on the helm.

'If he is, he'll join us. If not . . .'

'You sounded so sure.'

'That is a necessary part of being in command, Mr Cooper. The men you expect to follow you into battle must never doubt your certainty. But I did not lie to them. The odds on Linton's survival are far greater than any on his being lost. Therefore, until we have definite news to the contrary, we must believe, and we will believe, that *414* is afloat and making every effort to rejoin us. Hello, Jamie. Problems?'

Jamie took deep breaths. 'No, sir. Save that it gets a bit stuffy down there.'

'I'm sure it does. And it's going to get stuffier as the weather warms. Once we're in Gibraltar, I have instructions to issue every man with a salt tablet every day.'

'Salt, sir?' Cooper asked. 'Isn't too much salt bad for you?'

'Too much of anything is bad for you, Mr Cooper. But too little salt in the system can be catastrophic. And your sweat is virtually pure salt. When you're sweating heavily, as we will be in the Med, it has to be replaced, or we'll have people falling about with heat stroke. I don't suppose you've ever sailed the Med, Jamie? You seem to have sailed pretty well everywhere else in Europe.'

'Not the Med, sir. It's a bit far away for even a couple of months' summer cruise. My Dad's old Bristol Pilot Cutter only made seven knots with a fair breeze.'

'So we'll all be tyros. I've at least been told about it, often enough. My mother did a great deal of sailing down there, before and immediately after the Great War.'

'Did she, sir?' Cooper asked enthusiastically. 'Did her parents live in the Mediterranean?'

'Well, of course. Her father was Spanish.'

'Her maiden name was Ojeda de Santos Lopez,' Jamie said, absently.

'What?'

'I beg your pardon, sir. It just slipped out.'

'How did you know that?' Duncan asked.

'Her Ladyship told me, on that voyage home from St Malo in 1939.'

'And you've remembered it, all this time? She must have made quite an impression.'

'She is quite an impressive lady, sir.'

'She is indeed. Well. I'll tell her that you still remember that trip, when we get home. She'll be tickled pink.' He looked at his watch. 'I'm turning in. Good night, gentlemen.'

Cooper waited for him to disappear down the ladder, then remarked, 'I had no idea you knew the Evershams that well, Goring.'

'I don't know them at all, sir,' Jamie said. 'I only work for them. Good night, sir.'

A glorious sunrise promised another glorious day, but there was no sign of *414*. Duncan lowered the binoculars he had been using to survey the horizon. The other boats were all there, in line astern, ensigns flying proudly, for all the world as if they were at a revue off Spithead. In another few hours they would be in position to alter course for the temporary haven of Gibraltar. He wondered if by any chance Linton would be there to greet them?

'Begging your pardon, sir.' Petty Officer Rawlings had also been using his glasses. 'What do you make of that fellow?'

Duncan had been only interested in the sea horizon. Now he raised his binoculars to study the approaching aircraft, at this moment no more than a dot, but certainly coming towards them. And out of the south. Where the flotilla was, two hundred miles off the coast of southern Portugal, the next English or allied controlled territory in that direction was St Helena, and that was a very long way away.

'Hm,' he commented

'Could be Spanish,' Rawlings suggested. 'From the Canaries or Azores. Or Portuguese, out of Madeira.'

'Either way,' Duncan pointed out, 'he should surely by flying north-east. Not due north.'

'I would say, sir, that he's spotted us, and is coming for a closer look.'

'Yes,' Duncan agreed, thoughtfully. 'Mr Rawlings, make to flotilla: Furl ensigns to prevent immediate identification and then prepare for dispersal in the event of air attack.'

'Aye-aye, sir. You reckon that an enemy bomber would be this far out? Do they have the range?'

'The Fokke-Wulf Condor does. It's a reconnaissance machine, used for convoy-spotting rather than combat, but we know that it carries bombs. It looks to me as if he's going home from patrol, but he's still capable of signalling our presence, if he identifies us as an enemy. Make that signal, Mr Rawlings. And then call all hands to action stations. Steel helmets and life jackets.'

'Aye-aye, sir.' Rawlings' lamp started clacking.

Duncan thumbed the intercom. 'I may be using full speed very shortly, Jamie. We have company.'

'Aye-aye, sir.'

'When you hear the bell, if everything down there is satisfactory, put on your life jacket and steel helmet and get up top.'

'Sir?'

'We may be going to be bombed, Jamie. You know as well as I that if we take a hit she'll be gone in a flash.'

There was a brief hesitation, then Jamie acknowledged. 'Aye-aye, sir.'

Duncan maintained course and speed while watching the approaching plane. The sea being calm save for the undulating swell, he could steer with one hand and use the glasses with the other. The stranger certainly had the wide wingspan associated with the Condor, and it was descending all the time. At the very least it intended to have an uncomfortably close look at the five little ships.

Rawlings completed his signal and received the necessary acknowledgement. Then he looked at his captain. Duncan nodded, and the petty officer lowered the ensign and rang the bell, violently. Men immediately appeared on deck, and Cooper on the bridge, pulling on his life jacket. 'Problems?'

Duncan pointed.

'Shit! Do you think he means business?'

'I'm very much afraid he does. There's still a chance he may mistake us for Spanish or Portuguese, but I suspect that we're too far offshore to be innocent. In fact . . .' The aircraft was dropping lower by the moment. 'Mr Rawlings, signal flotilla to disperse and defend. Then man the machine guns.' He picked up the intercom. 'Jamie, we are scattering at full speed.'

The Condor, now definitely identifiable, was coming straight at them; he could imagine its radio crackling away. He used the tannoy; Rawlings was already on the deck beneath him with his gun crew. 'Fire as she bears, Mr Rawlings. All hands stand by for full speed.'

He thrust the throttle forward and *412* seemed to leap out of the water. The Condor soared overhead and at the same time he put the helm to starboard, taking the little ship out of its line ahead position. Just in time! Behind them there was a plume of spray where a bomb had been dropped. The machine guns chattered but owing to the speed and violence of the manoeuvre there was little chance of hitting the attacker.

Duncan brought the boat round in a tight circle. The rest of the flotilla had also scattered, and were racing to and fro, so far unscathed, although he could make out a couple more plumes of water. But the attack was over; the enemy plane was disappearing to the north. 'Stand down,' Duncan said into the tannoy as he reduced speed. 'Mr Rawlings, make to flotilla: Resume course and speed.'

'Bit abortive,' Cooper commented.

'That was a gesture. What really matters is what kind of a message he got off. And what is in the vicinity.'

'Like over there, sir.' Jamie had come up to the bridge.

Both officers turned sharply, stared at the low silhouette of the U-boat, perhaps three miles away.

'That was quick,' Cooper said.

'I think she's been there all the time,' Duncan said.

'How come we didn't spot him?'

'Because he only had his conning tower above the surface, so that he could be in contact with the plane. That attack was a distraction.'

As he spoke there was a flash of light, followed by a much bigger plume of water from about a hundred yards away.

'Permission to reply, sir,' Cooper said.

'Certainly. But that's a four point seven. We can't get close enough.'

'And she's submerging, sir,' Jamie complained.

'Shit!' Cooper said. 'And we've no depth charges.'

'We need to get him back up, at close range,' Duncan decided. 'Mr Cooper, as the whole world seems to know where we are, radio silence ends now. Signal flotilla to close up to attack U-boat. Then signal Gibraltar that we are attacking; they may have a spare aircraft or two standing by. Use 2182 and send in clear.'

'Aye-aye, sir. But . . . what are we going to attack with, lacking depth charges?'

'He doesn't know that, Mr Cooper.'

'Aye-aye, sir.' Cooper slid down the ladder.

The other boats had by now closed up. Duncan pointed at the disturbed water where the submarine had dived, but he didn't think she was merely taking evasive action; her skipper had shown that he meant to sink them if he could.

'Mr Rawlings,' he said; the petty officer had stood down his machine-gun crews and rejoined them on the bridge. 'Signal flotilla: Prepare to receive torpedo attack. Keep right up to him to shorten the range.'

'Aye-aye, sir.'

Duncan increased speed to close the gap; at anything under a thousand yards any torpedoes would be largely ineffective. He kept gazing at the swirl of water where the submarine had now disappeared. But . . . the periscope was still carving a thin white wake through the calm sea.

'I don't think he's taking us seriously, Mr Cooper. Man the gun and see if you can put a shell close to that stick.'

'Aye-aye, sir!' Cooper slid down the ladder to the deck, summoning his gun crew as he did so.

'Jamie,' Duncan said. 'Use the radio. Make to flotilla: Target periscope.'

'Aye-aye, sir.' Jamie disappeared through the hatch.

They were within five hundred yards of the marker. Cooper had depressed the six-pounder and now it exploded. The shell plunged into the sea in the midst of the confused water, and was immediately joined by one from *413*.

'That should make him think a bit,' Duncan growled.

'The bastard is sounding, sir,' Rawlings said in disgust.

The periscope had disappeared. But the water was still disturbed. Cooper was looking back at the bridge. 'Hold your fire, Mr Cooper,' Duncan shouted, and put the engine into neutral; the boat skated to a stop in the centre of the eddy. 'Jamie!' he shouted down the hatch. 'Make to flotilla: Join me and stop.'

The other boats were all around him. Now they closed right up and stopped, the other skippers clearly mystified.

'Now, Jamie. Signal: Gun your engines in neutral.'

'Sir?!' He obviously found the idea of racing his precious engine without load disturbing.

'Do it, boy.'

The signal was made, and all five engines roared together. The racket on the surface was tremendous, but Duncan reckoned it would be even louder beneath. He counted to ten and then reduced the revolutions. 'All right, Jamie. Signal: Reduce revs, scatter, but stand by your guns for enemy action. We want the periscope.'

He put his engine slow ahead, and turned away; the disturbance on the surface had all but disappeared.

'You think that'll bring him up, sir?' Rawlings asked.

'That depends on his nerve. I think he'll want to have a look at just what is up here. And if, as I think was the case, he's been on the surface for some time before we saw him, he'll have been listening on the open channel and before he dived would have heard our signal to Gibraltar and have to expect more trouble on the way.'

'If I were him I'd get the hell out of here.'

'Like I said, Mr Rawlings, all depends on his nerve and his temperament. Is he going to crawl away from a bunch of little motor boats when if he can get a clear strike he can sink one or maybe even all of us? And I'll bet he has no idea that we have six-pounder guns. Mr Cooper,' he shouted. 'Your target is the periscope, the moment it breaks the surface.'

'Aye-aye, sir.'

'Jamie, make that signal to all boats.'

'Aye-aye, sir.'

The engines were muted now, as the boats slowly circled.

Duncan was reminded of the scene from *Moby Dick*, when Captain Ahab and the crew of the *Pequod* were waiting for the white whale to blow. Moby Dick had sunk the whaler!

Five minutes passed, then ten.

'Keep your eyes peeled, Mr Rawlings,' Duncan said.

'Aye-aye, sir. But I think he's gone.'

'Yes,' Duncan said sadly. 'Well . . .'

Jamie was standing in the hatch, using binoculars. 'Over there, sir.'

They all swung their glasses, and made out, about half a mile to their south, the tell-tale swathe of white water.

'Mr Cooper, south by west,' Duncan shouted. 'Five cables, open fire. Jamie!'

'Aye-aye, sir.' Jamie was already descending the ladder to remit the orders to the flotilla, but Beattie had also seen the periscope, and *413*'s gun was already firing. The others immediately commenced, and the sea around the periscope was turned into a maelstrom by exploding six-pounder shells.

'She's gone again,' Rawlings commented.

Duncan couldn't believe they hadn't at least blinded the beast, but he had to allow for that possibility. 'Jamie!' he called. 'Signal flotilla to stand by for possible torpedo attack.'

'But if we damaged his eyes, and he can't see us . . .' Rawlings ventured.

'Then he can't attack us,' Duncan agreed. 'But in that case, he won't be able to attack anybody else, either, except on the surface. So he'll either have to pack it in and go home or be vulnerable to escort fire. Or lose his rag altogether, and . . .'

'Movement, sir.' Jamie was back in the hatch.

'Signal: Close up to point blank range. Mr Cooper, open fire the moment anything shows.'

He put the engine slow ahead, and *412* crept towards the disturbed water. And saw the conning tower emerging. As it did so, the hatch was thrown open and men poured out to man the gun. But already they were shrouded in six-pounder shells. One burst on the deck beside the gun, another ploughed into the tower itself. The rest burst in the water around the U-boat, but one or two certainly hit the hull.

The gun crew gallantly manned their weapon, but for a

fatal second failed to select a target from the five little boats around them, and in that time the U-boat was hit several more times, one shell bursting immediately behind the gun and sending men sprawling.

'Torpedo!' Rawlings shouted.

Whoever had given the order to fire had clearly not lined up his target, but even so Duncan's heart seemed to climb into his throat as he saw the white streak, well away from *412* but . . . the other boats had seen it too, and only *416* found it necessary to take evasive action, then the streak disappeared into the Atlantic.

The guns were still firing, and there came a puff of smoke, out of the conning tower, followed by a booming explosion. Almost Duncan thought he could see the hull splitting into two, and she went down in seconds. 'Make to flotilla,' he told Jamie. 'Good shooting! Mr Rawlings, will you stand by to pick up survivors.'

Old Friends

'Lieutenant-Commander Lord Eversham, sir,' said the Wren.

'My dear fellow! Come in, come in.' Captain Brownlow returned Duncan's salute, given somewhat hesitantly as this was the first time he had worn his whites, and in his shorts and white stockings and bare knees he felt a trifle exposed; reassuringly, the captain was also wearing shorts. Now he shook Duncan's hand. 'Welcome to Gibraltar. We expected you this morning.'

'I had hoped to be here this morning, sir. But we were delayed, first of all by bad weather, and then by a U-boat.'

'Ah, yes. I received a copy of your signal. I'm sorry we couldn't provide any assistance; things are a little tight around here at the moment. And I see the blighter got one of you.'

'Sir?'

Brownlow returned to the window, from which he had apparently watched the flotilla come past the breakwaters. 'We were told there would be six.'

'Yes, sir. But one went missing in the storm we had on Sunday. I'm still hoping he'll show up.'

'I see. So the sub turned out to be a damp squib.'

'Well, I suppose it did, for him. We sank him.'

'What?' The captain returned to the window and levelled his binoculars. 'You've no depth charges.'

'No, sir. We enticed him to the surface and used gunfire.'

'Gunfire? You're sure he went down?'

'He went down, sir. There were five survivors, who we have handed over to the Shore Patrol.'

'Good heavens! Well, congratulations. You'll bring your officers ashore for a drink in the club.'

'Thank you, sir. I am taking my officers to dinner at The Rock.'

'But you'll have a drink with us first, I hope. You understand that you're en route for Malta?'

'Yes, sir.'

'But you'll have a week or so off, here, first, eh? The next convoy isn't out until then.'

'You wish us to be part of a convoy, sir?'

'Well, of course. You can't go on your own. You'd never get there.'

'Ah . . . may I ask, sir, what will be the average speed of this convoy?'

'That depends on the speed of the slowest vessel. The ships are more carefully selected than in the Atlantic, of course; out there they take anything that's going. I think we can guarantee ten knots.'

'Ten knots. To cover about eight hundred nautical miles. That's better than three days. We can do it in one.'

'One what?'

'One day, sir.'

Brownlow looked at him for several seconds, then sat behind his desk. 'And enemy attack?'

'Well, sir, we're not too easy to catch. I understand that the most dangerous part of the journey is in the approaches to the Sicilian Channel. If we left here at noon, we'd be in Malta for breakfast. That is to say, our approach to the island, and the Channel, would be in darkness.'

Once again Brownlow regarded him for some seconds. This was clearly an aspect of naval warfare with which he had not previously come into contact. 'What do you require?'

'Food and water, sir. And ten thousand gallons of fuel. That's two thousand for each boat. Our tanks are pretty dry.'

'Ten thousand. I think we can manage that. Fuel oil is always a problem.'

'Not fuel oil, sir. High octane petrol.'

'You require ten thousand gallons of aviation fuel?'

'Yes, sir.'

'Hm. I'll have to get on to the RAF and see what they have.'

'Without the fuel to operate at high speed, sir, we may as well not be here.'

'Oh, quite. I take your point. When would you wish to leave?'

'Well, sir, we've had a pretty exhausting trip down. I'd like to give my men a couple of days rest. And if we're taking another long trip at full speed, I need to give my engineers some time to check their machinery, carry out an oil change, and that sort of thing. Say three days.'

'Three days. And one day to get there, you say. Well, I suppose, Lieutenant-Commander, that Malta can survive for another four days without your assistance. I look forward to meeting your officers. Shall we say, the club at 2000? There'll be time for dinner afterwards.'

'Am I allowed to give my crews shore leave, sir?'

'Of course. I'd say they deserve it. But do ask them not to break the place up.'

'You're new,' said the girl behind the bar.

She was an attractive little thing, with pleasantly pinched features, shoulder-length yellow hair – clearly dyed judging by the dark roots – and a full figure.

She was addressing Jamie, but Morrison was the senior member of the foursome doing the town, and now occupying a corner of the somewhat crowded room; two other young women and a man were further along the counter, also serving drinks. Like their captain, the men were rather embarrassed by their new uniforms; if, for evening wear, they were allowed long trousers, it was still the first time that they had ever appeared in public in white. 'We're all new,' he announced. 'As regards Gibraltar.'

She turned her gaze on him. 'I didn't think you were familiar. What'll it be?'

'Do you have beer?' Able Seaman Jackman inquired.

'Of course we have beer.'

'Then pull four pints.'

She got busy on the pump.

'You're a Gibraltarian, right?' asked Able Seaman Lowndes.

'Of course.'

'But you're on our side.'

'Of course I'm on your side, stupid. I'm British.'

'How come you're British, if you're a Gibraltarian?'

She raised her eyes to the ceiling. 'Because Gibraltar is a part of Britain.'

'I never knew that.'

'I don't think it's technically correct,' Jackman argued; he had a reputation as an intellectual.

'Can it,' Morrison recommended. 'We're here to drink beer, not get involved in a political discussion.'

'That'll be one and four pence.' She pushed the four pints across the counter.

'Where'd it come from, a gold mine?' Morrison inquired, but he laid the coins before her.

'Maybe you hadn't noticed there's a war on. My name is Pamela,' said the barmaid, scraping the money into the drawer and fluttering her eyelashes at Jamie. 'What's yours?'

'Jamie.'

'Ooh, that's romantic.'

'Is it?'

'I'm off duty at midnight. You could walk me home.'

'Tell you what, darling,' Lowndes said. 'We'll all walk you home.'

Before Pamela could reply, they were interrupted by a large man in an indeterminate khaki uniform. 'This is an Army bar.'

'Oh, shit!' Pamela muttered. 'Drink up, Jamie boy.'

'You mean the Army owns it?' Jackman asked, interested.

'I mean only Tommies come in here.'

'Well, then,' Lowndes said. 'This is your lucky night.'

'You're new around here,' the man said, magnanimously. 'What ship?'

'*412.*'

'What the fuck is that?'

'Mind your language in front of a lady,' Morrison recommended.

'Well!' remarked a delighted Pamela, fluffing out her hair.

'It's a motor-torpedo boat,' Jamie explained, trying to keep the peace.

'You mean one of those plywood jobs that came in this afternoon?'

'That's right,' Morrison said, draining his mug and putting it on the counter, somewhat heavily.

'Another?' Pamela asked, hopefully.

'Later, darling.'

'What're you doing here?' the soldier asked. 'Running messages from one side of the harbour to the other?'

'Listen, friend,' Jackman inquired. 'When did you last see action?'

'I'm on garrison duty. If an enemy shows up, I shoot him.'

'And if he doesn't, you hang about bars and drink beers.'

'Why, you little runt . . .'

'Mr Bertrand!' Pamela called, urgently.

'Yesterday,' Lowndes announced, 'we sank a U-boat.'

'You mean you frightened him to death?'

'Are you calling us liars?' Morrison inquired.

'Mr Bertrand!' Pamela shouted, more urgently yet.

'All sailors are liars,' the soldier pointed out. 'It's because they spend all their time fishing. Haw, haw, haw.'

'Bugger that!' Lowndes bawled, and threw a punch.

The soldier caught his fist and his arm and threw him instead, across the room. Then he turned back with an air of self-satisfaction, and ran into Morrison's fist, and Morrison was at least as big a man.

'Mr Bertrand!' Pamela screamed, with some reason, for all the other soldiers in the bar were now converging on the four sailors. This time the proprietor apparently heard her, and he clearly had experienced a brawl before, because his reaction was instantaneous: the lights went out at the same time as he blew a very loud blast on a police whistle.

This had no immediate effect, and the entire bar became an indecipherable mass of men, oaths, breaking furniture and shattering glass. Jamie, at the very back end of the bar, was out of the thick of it, but when someone barged into him he threw a punch of his own and connected with something, although whether it was one of his pals or a soldier he had no idea.

Then there came several more blasts on whistles. These were outside the building, and like the first had no immediate effect on the fighting, but they were followed by shouts and the hacking sounds of nightsticks being used indiscriminately. Jamie felt someone else against him and inhaled a rather cheap perfume. 'Let's get out of here,' Pamela whispered.

'I can't desert my mates.'

'Listen, they're all going to the jug for the night, and they'll all be on a charge tomorrow morning. You'll be better off with me.'

He felt a traitor, but he had no desire either to spend the night in jail or face an irate Duncan, so he let her take his hand and lead him through a hatch in the bar and out of a door into a starlit night.

'It isn't midnight yet,' he pointed out.

'Oh, the bar will be closed. Maybe put off limits for a while. It's happened before. This way.'

He followed her through several alleys, clustering at the foot of the mountain that gave the colony its name, without any idea where they were going. 'Does that mean you'll be out of a job?'

She giggled. 'There's lots of jobs, with all this military activity about. Anyway, you were going to make me a present, weren't you?'

'Was I?'

They had reached a house, and she stopped at the foot of the steps. 'Just how old are you?'

'Twenty.'

'Shit! Don't tell me you've never been with a girl before?'

'Of course I have.' If you only knew, he thought.

'There's a relief. So what's the going rate, in England?'

'Eh?'

'Oh, for God's sake. You only had one pint. Or were you boozing up somewhere else before coming to us?'

'No, no. We only left the ship an hour ago. We were late getting in, you see, and the ship had to be put to bed first.'

'Did you really sink a U-boat?'

'Of course we did.'

'Happens every day, does it? But that makes you a fucking hero. How much money do you have?'

He felt in his pocket, brought out the two notes he found there. 'Two pounds.'

'God Almighty! My lucky night!' She extracted the notes from his fingers, tucked them into her bodice. 'Come along, sailor. Let me give you something to remember.'

She unlocked the door, while Jamie tried to get his thoughts together. Do I want to do this? he asked himself. While I'm still dreaming of Kristin? Then he realized that he did want to do it, had wanted to do it, desperately, ever since his last, sterile visit to the boatyard. Besides, it might help to exorcise Kristin.

In any event, Pamela had made off with his money.

'Now really,' Duncan commented, surveying the three men standing before him; each had visible bruises and strips of plaster draped across their faces and knuckles, while Lowndes' right arm was in a sling. Beside them Rawlings looked grimly disapproving. 'We are regarded with suspicion in any event at the moment, as no one seems prepared to accept that we are worth a damn. In addition, I promised the port captain that we would behave ourselves. And you go breaking up a pub, and putting a soldier in hospital.' He surveyed the bandaged wrist and arm. 'I suppose that happened hitting somebody?'

'It's a sprain, sir,' Lowndes said.

'That is not an explanation. How soon will you be fit for duty?'

'I can manage now, sir. The blighter took me by surprise.'

'With respect, sir,' Morrison said. 'That soldier insulted us. He insulted the flotilla. That means he insulted you, sir.'

'And so you laid him out. I am sure you should be commended. Unfortunately, that is not how he tells it. They want me to take away your stripes.'

'Well, sir . . .'

He paused as Jamie entered the Mess, which had been barred to all hands while the hearing was going on.

'You are not allowed in here, Goring,' Duncan said, formally. This was an official matter.

'With respect, sir. I was in the bar last night.'

'Keep out of it, boy,' Morrison muttered.

Duncan was looking at the charge sheet. 'Your name isn't here.'

'They overlooked me in the dark and the fuss, sir. And I was able to get out the back.' And stack up some more guilt, he thought. Apart from deserting his pals, he had had a thoroughly miserable night. Not that Pamela had been unwilling, but compared with Kristin she had been a carthorse. In every possible way, clothes, perfume, mannerisms . . . even cleanliness. The result was that he had been unable to make it, and had had to endure her very obvious contempt, even if she had done her best to conceal it. He had sometimes wondered if the past two years of intimacy with Kristin would mean that every other woman would be a disaster. Now he knew. The sailors exchanged glances; they had a pretty good idea with whom he had got out. And where he had spent the night.

'Then you were fortunate,' Duncan pointed out. 'I strongly recommend that you take Leading Seaman Morrison's advice, and dissociate yourself from these proceedings.'

'But I was there, sir. And I heard that soldier call us liars for claiming to have sunk a U-boat.'

'Did he, now,' Duncan commented. And turned his head again as another figure descended the ladder. 'Oh, really, Mr Cooper, this is a military tribunal.'

'I apologize, sir. But I thought you would like to know . . . *414* has just entered the harbour.'

'What?' Duncan got up, then looked at the men standing on the other side of the mess table. 'Oh . . . charges dismissed. I'll sort it out.' He climbed the ladder.

'This really is a bad show,' Captain Brownlow remarked.

'I have great news, sir, ' Duncan said.

'What?'

'*414* has turned up.'

'What?'

'My missing boat. Seems she had an engine breakdown in that storm we went through, and it took several hours to repair. But apparently she was only about a hundred miles behind us the whole way.'

'You must be very pleased. Now, about this fracas, which has made the newspapers . . .'

'With respect, sir, that soldier called me a liar.'

'Did he? But you weren't there. You were having dinner at The Rock. Weren't you?'

'I was, sir, yes. This character was talking to some of my men, who took deep offence.'

'And caused a brawl which involved several hundred pounds worth of damage and at least one hospitalization.'

'When the bill is presented to my ship, sir, it will be paid.'

'And that's it?'

'Well, sir, an MTB is a very small boat and thus a very small world. There is no room for any dead wood. Every man has his part to play, and that part has to be learned through weeks of training; we cannot just pick up replacements at the snap of a finger; every trained man is vital to the security of the ship. Just as every man has to rely on the man beside him, which means that they have to know each other very well and trust each other absolutely. It stands to reason that I cannot go to sea if any of my people, much less three of them, are under arrest or restrained in any way. Nor, as I have explained, is it possible for me to pick up three replacements. My orders are to get to Malta as rapidly as possible, ready for instant action, and with your permission that is what I intend to do. I will take my boats out of here the moment I receive the fuel I need.'

Brownlow considered for several moments, then sighed, and nodded. 'That is probably the best solution. Ten thousand gallons of high octane petrol. Yes. The RAF aren't very happy about it, but I think I can sort it out.'

'With respect, sir.'

'What?'

'We need a bit more than that, now.'

'Why? Wasn't your original estimate calculated?'

'Oh, indeed, sir. But it was based on the five boats I then had with me. Now that *414* has joined, we need another two thousand. That is, twelve thousand gallons in total.' He didn't want there to be any mistake about that.

Brownlow held his head in his hands.

'Kristin!' Lonsdale said into the telephone 'Great news! Gibraltar has signalled that the flotilla has arrived.'

'Are they all right?' Kristin asked, waggling her eyebrows at Alison, on the far side of the room.

'Oh, indeed. Mind you, they had a bit of a rough ride. Bad weather to begin with and then they actually managed to run into a U-boat.'

'You said they were undamaged!' Kristin's voice was suddenly sharp.

'According to the signal, they are. And they managed to sink the U-boat, believe it or not. Seems he made the mistake of engaging them on the surface. He probably felt they were not worth wasting a torpedo on, and he obviously didn't realize they had the new six-pounders.'

'And they suffered no casualties themselves?'

'None have been reported.'

'Well, that *is* good news. Thank you so much for calling. I'll open a bottle of champagne. Will you be coming out to drink it with me?'

'Ah . . . I'm afraid I can't make it, tonight. Tomorrow all right?'

'Of course. I can open another bottle then. So you say they're in Gibraltar. How long will they be there?'

'They left this morning.'

'What?'

'Well, you know their ultimate destination is Malta. I told you that.'

'Yes, you did. When will they get there?'

'It's the most dangerous part of the trip, entirely through waters that are at least partly controlled by the enemy. So I understand that they will be going flat out In which case they should be there in twenty-four hours.'

'If they get there.'

'Well, of course there is an element of risk. But Duncan has always come through.'

'That is the sort of statement I detest. You'll let me know when they arrive.'

'Yes, I can do that. But Kristin, you must understand . . . while they are still technically under my command, once they report for duty in Malta, I no longer have anything to do with them. So I will not be able to give you continuous bulletins on what's happening to them.'

'I'm sure you have friends in high places in Malta, Jimmy. I'll see you tomorrow night.' She blew a kiss into the phone before replacing it. 'Red tape,' she growled. 'We are drowning in a sea of red tape. Like that blithering idiot of a shipping agent who tells me that as I am a non-essential traveller there is no prospect of my getting a berth on a ship to Gibraltar, much less Malta.'

Which had been a life-saving ruling, as far as Alison was concerned. But she decided against saying it. 'But the boys are all right?' she commented.

'So far.' Kristin rang the bell.

'You do realize that you are continually putting the admiral in an impossible position.'

'I'm dealing with that. I gave him a copy of the *Kama Sutra* to read. As long as his back holds up he shouldn't have a problem.'

'Really,' Alison said severely. 'You are deliberately misunderstanding me.'

'One should always misunderstand people deliberately. To do so inadvertently can be embarrassing. Harry! Open a couple of bottles of Bollinger. Bring one up here and you and Lucia share the other. Mr Duncan has reached Gibraltar safely.'

'That is good news, milady.' Harry hurried back down the stairs.

'Kristin!' Alison said. 'I'm serious. Talking about embarrassment! You are continually asking the admiral to reveal classified information. He could be cashiered.'

'Rubbish! We're engaged to be married.'

'He's not supposed to reveal ship movements to anyone, even in the marriage bed.'

'Well,' Kristin growled. 'He had better not reveal them in anyone else's marriage bed.' Alison gazed at her with her mouth open, and she hurried on. 'That is behind me. Thank you, Harry.'

Harry poured, and placed the ice bucket with the bottle on the sideboard, then withdrew.

Kristin raised her glass. 'To the flotilla.'

'And Duncan.' Alison drank.

'Of course. Now tell me, when is this nanny of ours turning up?'

'Actually, tomorrow. That reminds me: I must make sure Harry keeps Lucifer locked up until she's settled in.'

'You cannot be serious. That could take weeks.'

'No, no. As soon as she's moved in I'll introduce them in

controllable circumstances. I just don't want the poor girl reduced to a nervous wreck on her first day.'

Kristin drained her glass, got up, and refilled it, then moved restlessly around the room. They would be at sea now, racing across the sparkling blue waters of the Mediterranean . . . with German and Italian bombers raining destruction upon them, not to mention the Italian fleet. How she wished she could be with them. With Jamie!

She had been very foolish. Very impulsive. But she had never denied that she was impulsive. And of course, even if they had parted on the best of terms, they would still have had to part, as he was so hell-bent on his duty. But life without Jamie was not conceivable. And now, even if he came back, she was committed to the admiral. He was a man she greatly admired, and a true friend. And he was by no means bad in bed, even if, as she had suggested to Alison, he could not by any stretch of the imagination match Jamie's virility . . . and his approach to sex was in any event entirely lacking in imagination.

That she could accept, at least for the time being, and could possibly be improved by giving him the right material to study... supposing he was not too embarrassed to read it. But there was also the fact that, although she knew he was trying hard to suppress it, or at least not be obvious about it, he could not help being authoritarian. She recognized that this was an essential part of being, first of all, commander of a ship, and even more, an admiral. Even Duncan was authoritarian when at sea. She had always been quite prepared to accept this. But it had always ended the moment they stepped ashore, and even more definitely, the moment they had entered the front door of her house.

Jimmy had not yet come to terms with that essential rule, even if she had warned him from the start that interference in her lifestyle was not something she was prepared to tolerate. And once he was her husband . . .

Douglas Morant had attempted to dominate her life, and he had had some reason, as when she had found herself, with great enthusiasm, in his bunk – she had volunteered to accompany him as cook on his summer's cruise, and her parents, under the erroneous impression that the heir to a

title would have to be beyond reproach, had not objected –
he had been exactly twice her age. Another reason, no doubt
for Don Diego Ojeda de Santos Lopez to feel absolutely
confident in his integrity as such things as statutory rape
were rare in Spain, certainly amongst the nobility.

And she had been happy to be a subservient wife and
pupil, bound up in the euphoria of being able to leave the
convent, which she had always hated – she had previously
run away twice and been hauled back in disgrace – and a
huge wedding and the excitement of being pregnant. But that
was not something, for all her teasing of Jamie, that she
really wanted to repeat. It was not that she was afraid of it,
or that she did not like children; it was the enormous chunk
it took out of one's life that irked. And Jimmy was already
dropping hints of how much he wished to be a father, while
there was still time.

'Kristin,' Alison said, 'you are making me nervous. You're
not worried about them, are you?'

Kristin poured herself a third glass of champagne, and
then sat down again, legs crossed. 'Of course I am worried
about them. Aren't you?'

'Well, yes. But no more so than when they were on patrol
in the Channel. I mean, they're all very experienced. They're
not going to do anything foolish.'

'Well . . .' Kristin raised her head. 'Lucifer is barking.'

Alison went to the window and looked down. 'It's a taxi.
And . . . my God! It's Rebecca Strong.'

Kristin joined her. 'What in the name of God is she doing
here?'

'Lucifer's in the hall. I'd better go down.'

'Don't hurry.'

'Oh, really, Kristin.'

Alison slid down the stairs as she might have done a ladder
on a ship, but even so she was too late. Harry had opened
the door to the sound of the bell, and Rebecca Strong was
staggering round the porch with two enormous white paws
wrapped round her neck. As her arms were wrapped round
the dog in an effort to maintain her balance, they suggested
that they were indulging in a somewhat intimate two-step.

Rebecca Strong was not a big woman, but her figure, always, Alison remembered, somewhat voluptuous, was also clearly muscular, as her crisply handsome features remained calm, even when being licked by a huge tongue, but then, she had encountered Lucifer before. Only her shoulder-length yellow hair looked slightly dishevelled; fortunately, her mink coat was open.

Alison reached the foot of the stairs and took over, as Harry was looking helpless. 'Lucifer,' she snapped, 'do get down.'

Lucifer subsided down Rebecca's front, taking a good deal of her blouse and several buttons with him. Harry averted his eyes.

'He remembers you,' Alison explained, reassuringly.

'And I remember him,' Rebecca agreed, tucking the blouse back into the waistband of her skirt, refastening the one remaining button, and making sure her coat was undamaged. She ruffled Lucifer's head. 'It's nice to know some things never change.' Her accent was New England.

Alison extended her hand. 'Welcome back. I really didn't expect to see you again. I mean, so soon.'

Rebecca pulled off her gloves and squeezed the fingers. 'I had a less eventful passage this time. Do you think my chauffeur could come in out of the cold?'

'Of course.' Alison opened the door again. 'Tell me his name.'

'I have no idea. It's a taxi.'

'You have come by taxi from . . .?'

'Southampton.'

'Ah.' A mere matter of sixty-odd miles! She pulled the door wide. 'Do come in,' she invited. 'Mind the dog.'

The driver got out and approached, giving a startled exclamation as Lucifer approached him with an enthusiastic gurgle.

'Lucifer!' Alison commanded, and grabbed his collar. This did not do a great deal of good, as she was dragged forward with him, but she managed to break the full force of the assault, and the driver skipped round him and ran for the shelter of the house. 'Harry!' Alison shouted. 'Take this gentleman into the kitchen and make him a cup of tea. Or he may prefer something to drink.'

'He's quite harmless, really,' Rebecca Strong explained,

as the visibly shaken man was escorted past her. 'Just a little boisterous.'

'Mrs Strong!' Kristin announced from the top of the stairs. 'Creating mayhem, as always.'

'Kristin!' Rebecca started up. 'As young as ever!'

Kristin did not look amused. As far as she was concerned, Rebecca Strong had endless faults. She claimed a girlhood friendship – they both had Swedish mothers who *had* been friends – she was nine years younger; and she had clearly had a profound effect upon Jamie when he had pulled her out of the English Channel and then put her to bed. Worse, she was married to a billionaire, and was thus potentially wealthier than herself. And worst of all, she was the only woman, or man, for that matter, who Kristin had ever met who was impervious to conversational put-downs: as she was never embarrassed, never appeared to notice sarcasm, or even to be aware of it, she was quite impossible to snub.

Rebecca was already mounting the stairs and insisting upon an embrace. 'It's so good to see you again.'

'How did you get here?'

'Well, obviously, I came by taxi.' Having hugged her reluctant hostess, she stepped past her and continued up the stairs. 'I just love this room.' She took off her coat and draped it over a chair, surveyed herself in the mirror behind the sideboard. 'Hm. No scratches. But I will have to change my blouse.'

'I meant, how did you get to England?'

'Equally, obviously, I came by boat.'

'And this time you weren't torpedoed,' Kristin observed, regretfully. There would have been no Jamie available to rescue her.

'Well, you know what they say: lightning never strikes twice in the same place. I consider that I am now immune from torpedoes.'

Alison had followed her. 'Well, have a glass of champagne. And, ah . . .' She looked at her watch. It was just past six.

Rebecca accepted the glass. 'Oh, I mustn't stay. Just long enough to make myself decent.' She sipped. 'That tastes good.'

'I can probably lend you a blouse.'

Rebecca surveyed her; even as a nursing mother there was no contest. 'It'd be a tight fit. Not to worry. My bags are in the car. I'll get something out in a minute. When I've had a drink and a chat.'

'Well, do sit down,' Alison invited, as Kristin seemed determined to leave the hostess role to her. 'And you have come here from Southampton.'

Rebecca sat on the settee and crossed her knees. 'That's where we docked, a couple of hours ago.'

'And you came straight here?'

'Well, you see, I'm sort of here on official business, and once I get up to London I'm going to be taken over by brass hats. And I so wanted to see you all again. So I thought I'd drop in here first. Is Duncan coming in tonight?'

'No,' Kristin said.

'He's all right, isn't he?'

'As far as we know, he's fine.'

'That's great. I'd so like to see him again, and thank him again, for all he did for me and Dad. If Duncan isn't around, I suppose there's no chance of seeing that lovely kid, Jamie whatever-his-name-was.'

'Who did even more for you, as I recall,' Kristin said.

Rebecca giggled. 'He was so embarrassed.'

Alison decided it would be a good idea to change the subject, and raised her glass. 'Well, your very good health. You say you're here on official business. Your Dad's all right, is he?'

'Oh, sure. He's beavering away, developing his bombs for the British Government. Actually, now we're all in it together, there's a strong possibility he'll be coming over to the States to work with our people at some secret site down in New Mexico or somewhere. I'll be seeing him when I go up to town tomorrow.'

'So this business—'

'Oh, it's all very hush-hush.' She smiled at them both, brightly.

'And your husband . . . George, wasn't it, doesn't object to your flitting to and fro across the Atlantic?' Kristin inquired.

'George is dead.'

'Oh, I'm so terribly sorry,' Alison cried.

'He wasn't very young.'

'What did he die of?' Kristin inquired, her tone suggesting did you use arsenic or a gun?

'He had a stroke. It was all rather sad. I was really quite fond of him. But it was mercifully quick. No hanging about in a comatose state.'

'Yes,' Alison agreed. 'That must have been a great relief.'

'And I assume he left you all his money,' Kristin remarked.

'Well, there were a few minor bequests. But on the whole, yes.'

'Inherited wealth,' Kristin said, drawing on her own experiences, 'helps a lot in cushioning grief.'

'Oh, it does. Now tell me about that delightful old admiral. What's he up to, nowadays?'

Kristin and Alison exchanged glances, and Alison refilled their glasses. 'The same old thing,' Kristin said.

'He was, is, I suppose, such a sweetie. He saved my life as well, you know.'

'Did he?' Now Kristin's tone suggested, what a foolish thing to do.

'You mean, in Norway?' Alison asked.

'Well, yes. It was rather a hoot, really. There I was, sitting on my cot in this cell, absolutely starkers, with this German's arms round me, and the door burst open and there were both the admiral and that sweet kid Jamie. Well, it was tricky, because this German bastard had his pistol out and was pressing it against my head. Both the boy and the admiral were armed with rifles, but Jamie didn't seem to know what to do. Not the admiral. Cool as a cucumber, he levelled his gun and shot the German's head off. I was covered in blood.'

'Oh, brilliant,' Alison cried. 'He never told me he did that. I never even knew he could shoot.'

'Apparently, when he was a young man, he won a shooting prize at some place called Bismuth or something.'

'I have an idea you mean Bisley.'

'Is that a fact?'

'Are we allowed to ask –' Kristin had clearly been keeping quiet with an effort – 'what you and this German were doing, or intending to do, sitting together naked on your bed, before he got his pistol out?'

'Oh, he wasn't naked,' Rebecca corrected. 'I was. When they arrested us, you see, they took away my clothes.' She looked from one to the other of the faces in front of her, and drank some champagne. 'Apparently it's standard procedure. Although . . .' She frowned. 'They didn't take away Daddy's clothes. I never thought of that before. Isn't that odd.'

'They were probably,' Kristin suggested, 'looking for a witch's mark. You know, a third tit, or something.'

'What a hoot.'

'But they didn't find anything?' Alison was genuinely interested.

'Well, of course they didn't. I'd know if I had a spare tit. Actually, they never laid a finger on me. They were waiting for some Gestapo people to come and pick me up.'

'That was before this fellow decided to share your cot,' Kristin suggested.

'No, no, it wasn't like that at all. It was the next morning, when Duncan and his people attacked the post. It was all pandemonium, and this captain burst into my cell. I think he intended to use me as a shield or a hostage or something.'

'But he spared the time to take off your clothes.'

'No, no. They had taken away my clothes the previous night. But then Jamie and the admiral turned up. I was terrified, but as I said, the admiral was magnificent. Do you see him often?'

'Well, of course,' Kristin said. 'We're getting married.'

'Are you? Of course, you're wearing an engagement ring. I didn't notice before. Oh, it's lovely.'

'Even if it's not as big a diamond as yours,' Kristin remarked, acidly. 'But then, Jimmy is only an admiral. Tell me, why are you still wearing yours, and your wedding band, if you're a widow?'

'Because I like them. Besides, it keeps away mashers.'

'Say again?'

'A masher,' Alison interpreted, 'is unwanted male attention.'

'But to think of you and Jimmy,' Rebecca said. 'Oh, how absolutely marvellous. I'm so glad he took my advice.'

Oh, shit! Alison thought. She had actually felt that the evening might end without a punch-up.

'I beg your pardon.' Kristin's voice was sinisterly quiet. 'Did you say, your advice? To marry me? You and Jimmy Lonsdale discussed me?'

'Well, you know what men are like, particularly when they have just rescued a damsel in distress who happened to be nude at the time. They couldn't find my clothes you see, and they were in a hurry to leave before any German reinforcements arrived. So, do you know, I had to wear Jamie's shirt and socks all the way home. And his duffel coat.'

Alison got up, hurried to the door, and pulled it open. 'Harry!' she shouted. 'Bring up another bottle of champagne, will you, please?'

'So,' Rebecca went on, apparently oblivious to the rumbling explosion about to occur in front of her, 'the admiral and I spent a lot of time together on the voyage home. Because of the fuel problems it took about three days.'

'All of which you spent in Jamie's shirt.' Kristin was a woman who liked to get her facts exactly right.

'Well, yes. But Jamie was working in his engine room, trying to keep the boat going. So the admiral started to come on a little heavy. I didn't take offence. I knew exactly what was going on in his mind, and he had saved my life. But, I mean, I was a married woman. I had no idea that George was about to drop dead, and I did know that he was about the most jealous man I had ever met.'

'And you couldn't risk a divorce and all those millions,' Kristin pointed out.

'Absolutely.'

'So you suggested that he take up with me.'

'Well, it seemed the obvious thing. I mean, you're a good-looking woman, and you have some money, and you're a widow, and . . .' She gazed at Kristin, eyebrows arched. 'Did I do the wrong thing? But I can't have, if you're going to get married. You know, I never really expected him to go as far as that. Isn't it amazing how things so often turn out for the best.'

'Yes, it is,' Kristin agreed. 'Didn't you say you had a train to catch?'

'Did I? Anyway, it's too late for that now. I'll find a hotel in Southampton for the night.' She looked at the clock on the mantelpiece. 'Seven. I should be going, though, or I'll miss dinner. You know what these provincial hotels are like. If you'll just allow me to get a bag and change this wreck.' She stood up, put her glass on the sideboard. 'It's been great, seeing you again and having a chat. I'm only sorry I missed Duncan. I mean, he actually saved me twice. Once from a watery grave and once from the Gestapo. When you see him tomorrow do give him my best regards.'

Kristin also stood up. 'We won't be seeing him tomorrow, or any time in the next few months. He's gone away.'

'Gone away?' Rebecca looked at Alison, as if supposing the marriage had broken down. 'Gone away where?'

'He's in Malta.'

'Kristin!' Alison protested. That was supposed to be top secret.

'Malta?' Rebecca cried. 'You're kidding! What a hoot. Tell you what, when I see him, I'll give him your love. Both your loves.'

'I beg your pardon,' Kristin said. 'You mean you're going to Malta?'

'Well, amongst other places. I shouldn't be telling you this, it's terribly hush-hush. But that's why I'm here. Well . . .'

'Alison,' Kristin said. 'I think we should invite Rebecca to stay for dinner.'

All at Sea

'Oh, I couldn't,' Rebecca protested. 'I'd be putting you out.'

'Not in the slightest,' Kristin assured her. 'In fact, I think you should stay the night.'

'But—'

'My dear Rebecca.' Kristin carefully avoided looking at Alison. 'You have just got off the boat after a no doubt tiring and traumatic crossing of the ocean. You are not due in London until tomorrow, and you have nowhere to stay. You say you have your luggage in the taxi?'

'Well, of course.'

'Then Alison, I suggest you get Harry and the driver to unload Rebecca's gear, pay the driver off, and send him home. Tell Lucia there will be a guest for dinner, and in the meantime, prepare one of the spare rooms. Then we can all have a jolly evening together.'

Alison looked at Rebecca. 'Would you like to do that?'

'Well . . . it would be tremendous. But I wouldn't want to put you out.'

'You won't. And we'd love to have you. I won't be long.' She shot Kristin a glance, and went down the stairs.

Kristin got up and refilled their glasses, then sat beside Rebecca on the settee. 'Now tell me why you are going to Malta.'

'Oh, I can't. It's a secret.'

'But you're going on government business. How are you getting there? By boat?'

'Well, they tell me it's the only way. Flying is reserved for emergencies.'

'So I believe. I never knew you worked for the government. Which government?'

'Washington, of course.'

'But you were working for our government when you were here last year.'

'I suppose I was, in a manner of speaking. But it was with the blessing of the State Department. They wanted to get Dad out of Sweden before the Nazis nabbed him as much as anyone. But the success of that business meant that I had a certain cachet with your secret service, and while George was against my ever getting involved again, especially when he heard I had been torpedoed and then captured by the Nazis, after he died, and we got involved in the War, they came back to me again. You know how it is, with two governments, both with the same aim in life but with different ideas on how to get there. You guys are having a pretty tough time in North Africa, so you're hollering for help, mainly in the field of materiel. Seems this guy Rommel has the superior tanks, and your people would dearly like to get their hands on our Grants, or better yet, a few Shermans. Well, we want to help if we can, but we sure don't want to pour valuable and sensitive materiel into a theatre which could collapse tomorrow, and leave our new gear in the hands of the Afrika Korps.'

'And they've sent you to find out if we can hold on? You're a woman.'

'Nice of you to notice.'

'What I mean is, do you suppose anyone in Cairo is going to tell you anything, or show you anything?'

'We have a secret weapon. You remember that guy Chadwick?'

'Chadwick,' Kristin said thoughtfully. 'Wasn't he the fellow who masterminded your trip to Sweden? And then masterminded your escape, via Duncan. And the admiral, of course.'

'You got it. He was quite big in MI6 even then. Now he's even bigger. He's apparently running their office in Cairo, and it seems he's willing to receive me and show me around.'

'You mean you seduced him just as you seduced the admiral and that boy Jamie.'

'Don't be a schmuck. I spent the whole of that goddamned trip trying not to *be* seduced.'

'I suppose I'll have to take your word for that. But how does Malta come into it?'

'It's on the way to Egypt, right? Part of what we want to know is how viable it is as a route for getting materiel to Alexandria.'

'Hm. You weren't supposed to tell me all that, you know. I could be a German spy.'

'Shit! I'd forgotten that. Are you a German spy?'

'Have another drink.' Kristin poured. 'So you have a place on a convoy for Malta.'

'For what it's worth.'

'And who are you travelling with?'

Rebecca frowned, 'I'm not travelling with anybody. I told you. No one is supposed to know that I'm even going.'

'But I know,' Kristin pointed out.

Rebecca's frown deepened.

'And I think,' Kristin went on, 'that it is ridiculous for a billionairess . . . you are a billionairess?'

'I have no idea. The accountants are still arguing about it.'

'Let's look on the bright side. It is absurd for a billionairess to take a long journey without a lady's maid.'

Rebecca stared at her with her mouth open.

'If anyone objects to this,' Kristin went on, 'you have to stick that little chin of yours out, and say, no maid, no trip.'

Rebecca closed her mouth, and then opened it again. 'You want to come with me, to Egypt, as my maid?'

'You can fire me, in Malta.'

'You are absolutely stark raving mad.'

'Is there any other way to be? I can be very stimulating company. Alison, my dear girl. Is everything fixed up?'

'Everything is under control. Your bags have been taken up, Rebecca. And dinner will be in half an hour.'

'And you're sure I'm not putting you out?'

'Not at all. It's such a pleasure to see you again.'

'And we have the most tremendous news,' Kristin announced.

Alison raised her eyebrows.

'Rebecca has invited me to accompany her to the Mediterranean, as her maidservant.'

'What?!'

'Although you know, Rebecca dear, I don't really think I'm cut out to play a servant.'

Relief rushed through Alison's nostrils.

'I think,' Kristin said, 'that I should be your secretary. A high-profile diplomat like you would never travel without a secretary.'

Alison poured herself a glass of champagne, and drained it in a single breath.

She sat on Kristin's bed while her mother-in-law drank her morning cup of coffee. 'You do realize that this whole idea is not only absurd. It is impossible.'

'What is absurd, and what is not,' Kristin pointed out, 'is entirely in the mind. As for being impossible, nothing is impossible if you set your mind to it. I wish to visit Malta, but there are no berths to be spared. Except for someone travelling on official business. Rebecca is travelling on official business.'

'And you seriously suppose that Jimmy will let you go?'

'Jimmy is not going to know I'm going, until I've gone.'

'He calls virtually every day.'

'And I will take his call, every day, until the day I am not here, when you will take his call.'

'Me?'

'Well, of course, my dear. Who else?'

'And what am I supposed to tell him?'

'That I have been called away to . . . I think Scotland would be best, to visit a sick aunt.'

'Do you have an aunt in Scotland?'

'I do not have an aunt anywhere, to my knowledge. But he doesn't know that. The only things he knows about me are what I have told him.'

'And you expect me to lie, to an admiral?'

'I don't think you want to let this admiral business clutter things up: you are no longer in the service. But you see, as he is an admiral, he has the power to mess me about. If he were to find out the truth, too soon, he could have me removed from the ship in Gibraltar. Ergo, he cannot find out the truth until I am actually on the boat to Malta, when it will be too late to stop me. No convoy is going to turn back, even for an irate admiral. Now be a dear sweet girl, and agree to act on my behalf.'

Alison scratched her head, and tried a different tack. 'And when you're torpedoed, blown up, killed?'

'I have thought of that.'

'Have you?' Alison was astonished.

'I am seeing Hamilton this morning.'

'Who is Hamilton?'

'My English lawyer. I am making out a new will, which will state that should anything happen to me, the entire estate is to go, jointly, to you and Duncan.'

'Oh, my God! Do you think Duncan will like that?'

'Of course he will. He adores you. And the estate will go through you to Baby Duncan. In any event, as you are joint heirs, neither of you can do anything stupid without the consent of the other. However, I am also going to make out an affidavit or whatever they call it, stating that until either Duncan or I come home, you will be in sole control of the estate and everything in it.'

'You really are sticking your neck out. Suppose I withdraw all of your available cash and abscond with the milkman?'

Kristin gave a shriek of laughter. 'You'd never do that.'

'How can you be sure?'

'Because the milkman is such an unattractive man.' She squeezed her hand. 'Darling, not even my worst enemy has ever accused me of being a fool. I am giving you complete control of my current account. It is fed from my investment accounts, in the amount of ten thousand a month.'

'What did you say?'

'It's actually more than it sounds, and you'll find it'll cover everything. The surplus every month is reinvested, but Hamilton will look after that. Of course, if you wish to spend it all, supposing you can in this ration-ridden country, you're welcome.'

'Ten thousand pounds . . . a month?' Alison checked, faintly.

'The point is that it will require the signatures of both Duncan and yourself to increase the transfers or to sell any of the investments. Of course, if both Duncan and I were to get killed in this stupid war, then it will all be yours, in trust for Baby Duncan.'

'Kristin!' Alison took the coffee cup from her mother-in-law's hands and placed it on the bedside table, then held the hands. 'Just to lie there, and talk so calmly about dying . . .'

Kristin squeezed her fingers. 'It has to happen one day, you know.'

'I know that. But why rush it?'

'I'm not rushing anything. I am not a good enough person to die young. And in any event, the odds against it happening are huge. But I would be stupid not to consider every eventuality, and to put everything in order.'

Alison sighed. 'Will nothing change your mind?'

'No. It's been too long since I last really adventured. This will be the greatest adventure of my life.'

'What about Lucifer?' She was almost wailing.

'He's yours until I get back. He adores you.'

'Kristin . . .'

Kristin leaned forward to kiss her. 'Darling, I am coming back. Now I must get dressed, and we'll rouse my new employer.'

'Lieutenant-Commander!' Captain Jardine was not a tall man, and his very broad shoulders made him appear shorter than he actually was; his handshake was very firm. Combined with his lantern jaw he made Duncan think of a slab of the Guernsey granite he remembered from his boyhood. But right now he was smiling. 'Welcome to Valetta.' He gestured at a chair before his desk, then sat himself and indicated a sheet of paper lying on the blotting pad. 'Your coming is announced. That is some record.'

'Thank you, sir.'

'Happy with your berths?'

'They're a bit far into the harbour.'

'Deliberately so. We get raided at least once a day. You missed this morning's visit, but they'll be back tomorrow. The idea of tucking you away in that little backwater is that maybe they won't notice you. You had no trouble getting here?'

'Not really, sir. We were spotted by some aircraft, which came down for a closer look, then flew off again. I think they mistook us for Italians.'

'Exactly so. That is something we must capitalize on. Of course we have limited time to do this. The first time you go into action, both Jerry and the Eyeties will realize that you are not theirs. That makes me want to use you to maximum effect, the first time. But at the same time, we can't delay using you for too long, because there are undoubtedly Italian agents here in Malta who are in constant touch with the mainland. Obviously, as you will have noticed, we have armed guards on constant patrol around the perimeter fence to keep prying eyes away, but the buggers do manage to get through, and of course, a large number of our domestic staff are Maltese. These are in the main loyal and trustworthy, but there are always bad hats to be found. Now, while as soon as I was informed that you were joining us, I got hold of some material, I must confess that I have never actually been on an MTB.'

'You're welcome to carry out a tour of inspection, sir.'

Jardine nodded. 'I will avail myself of that invitation. However, how exactly do you live?'

'Sir?'

'Your domestic arrangements. Do you have cabins?'

'My executive officer and I both have a small cabin, as do the other officers on their boats; the crew sleep together forward.'

'And, ah . . .'

'There are heads, sir. Although at sea, of course, fresh water is at a premium.' It was his turn to pause.

'Oh, there is no problem with that. Well, there is a problem, of course. These are small islands, and our only source of supply is rain. But we'll not stint you a shower or two. There are shore establishments for both officers and men, and you and yours are welcome to make use of them. Liberty?'

'They do need some time off.'

'Of course. But you will have to operate a shore watch system. I quite understand that you cannot all be on standby all of the time, and like you, I am sure, I would estimate that when you go into action you would be most effective *en masse*, as it were. However, as this may not always be possible, I must ask that two boats are always available, fully manned and fuelled, at all times.'

'Understood, sir.'

'Well, then . . . I'll see you in the club.'

* * *

'Someone has certainly blown the hell out of this place,' Lowndes remarked, standing with his hands on his hips to survey what would once have been an entire block but was now a pile of rubbled white stone, a matching colour, Jamie thought, to their spanking new white trousers and jumpers.

'Makes you think of London,' Jackman argued.

'Naw. This is worse,' Morrison said. 'More concentrated.'

'What do you think, Jamie?' Lowndes asked. Since Gibraltar, and his attempt to defend their actions, the four men had become fast friends.

'I've never been to London,' Jamie confessed.

'Never been to London?' Jackman was scandalized. 'Never been to the Windmill?'

'What's the Windmill?'

'It's a cabaret. It ain't cheap, mind. But when you get inside . . . nothing but naked girls.'

'You mean that's allowed?!'

'Well . . . they can't move, see. And they all have their pussies shaved. But they're there to be looked at.'

'You ever seen a naked woman, Jamie?' Lowndes asked.

'Of course he has,' Morrison declared. 'He put that Yankee woman to bed, last year. Had to strip her to do it. Of course, you weren't with us then, Bert.'

'Wish I had been. Tell us about it, Jamie. Did she have big tits?'

'Oh, bugger off,' Jamie suggested. More than ever he didn't want to be reminded of Rebecca Strong, because that started him thinking of Kristin. Someone had once written, out of sight out of mind, but that poor sod had clearly never met anyone remotely like Kristin. Every day, and even more, every night, she haunted his thoughts. The idea that he might never see her again . . . but why should he see her again? He did not suppose he haunted *her* thoughts. She was probably married by now, and so, perhaps, after the war and he returned to his father's garage . . . but he was resolved not to do that. The sight of the Bentley, or worse, the Sunbeam, pulling in for fuel, would be more than he could bear.

'Sailor, you wanna girl?' the boy asked.

'Eh?' Jamie blinked at the urchin.

'You got a girl?' Jackman asked.

The boy looked over their faces. 'You want four girls?'

'Now that might be an idea,' Lowndes agreed, obviously activated by the talk of the Windmill.

'Just so long as there's no risk of a punch-up,' Morrison warned. 'The skipper would definitely have my stripes if it happens again.'

'Good girls,' the boy promised. 'No trouble.'

'You game, Jamie?'

Jamie hesitated. He was so complimented to be taken up by the older men, so anxious to be considered one of them, but the thought of undergoing another experience like the one with Pamela . . .

'Listen,' Lowndes said.

The sound of a siren wailed across the island.

'Air raid!' Morrison snapped.

'No planes,' said the knowledgeable youth. 'Assembly for crews.'

'That's us,' Morrison said 'On the double.'

Jamie gave a sigh of relief.

All the crews had been fairly close to the harbour, and were assembled in half an hour. Duncan surveyed his officers. 'The RAF reports that a convoy has just left the south end of the Straits of Messina making south, almost certainly for Benghazi. They are sending out a squadron of bombers. We will intercept the convoy after the bombing raid, when it may well have become scattered. Now as you know, we stand a fair chance of being mistaken for Bagliettos, certainly at a distance. To enhance our chances of getting up close and personal, we will furl our ensigns once in sight of the enemy and not fly them again until about to open fire. Please remember that we six are all they have down here, so I don't want any heroics that may be costly. We go in together, line up our targets, and fire our torpedoes. Then we get out at full speed. While going in, by all means use your six-pounders, but you are not to hang about to engage anyone in a gun battle. The RAF sighting was a brief one, and they were not certain about escorts, but there will certainly be an escort. Remember that while they may be shooting at us, and as I have said, you may reply if your gun has nothing better to aim at, our prime objective is to use our torpedoes on the freighters, who are carrying materiel for the use of the Africa Korps; that materiel is essential for their survival. Now, there will be radio silence once we leave the harbour. The enemy will certainly be listening. Let me repeat: speed is the essential when we attack. We go in, and we get out. No boat can stop and give assistance to another. That must be clearly understood, no matter how much it may go against the grain to abandon a comrade in distress. Any questions?'

There were none, but a look around their grim faces left him in no doubt that they were up for it.

'Then good luck, and good hunting.'

They saluted, and boarded their vessels.

'All well down there, Jamie?' Duncan asked into the intercom.

'Aye-aye, sir.'

'Very good. The drill is the same as usual. When we engage, you'll assist Wilson.'

'Understood, sir.'

'Switching on now.' He turned the key and the engine came to life. Immediately the other boats also started up. The lines were taken in, and the six boats slipped down the long, narrow harbour, the bulk of the castle rising on their right. It had clearly been bombed several times, but yet looked as solidly impregnable as he knew it had proved in the past. Built by the Knights of St John after their expulsion from the island of Rhodes by the Turks, it, and its gallant defenders, had had, in the middle of the sixteenth century, to survive the full might of the empire of Suleiman the Magnificent, an army, it was said, of more than a hundred thousand men, supported by a fleet of several hundred galleys. Yet a force of a few thousand knights and their retainers had held out, and eventually the Turks had gone away, never to return.

By a surprise attack, Napoleon Bonaparte in 1798 had actually captured the island, but he had known he could never hold it in a sea dominated by the Royal Navy, and besides, his destination had been Egypt, and so he had sailed away after a few days. Now, after more than a hundred and forty years, it was again under siege, but only from the air. Even with German support, Benito Mussolini was not going to risk a physical assault, certainly while the Navy was still around. He wanted, and needed, complete mastery of the Mediterranean first.

The flag, fluttering in the breeze, was dipped to the six little boats as they glided out of the harbour mouth. The flotilla responded, and then the helms were put down to round the islands on the south side. They had received no further information, but Duncan did not suppose that finding the convoy was going to be difficult; with the speed at their disposal they could overhaul it no matter where it might be.

The islands fell away behind them, and they streaked across a calm sea. Although they had only been here for a couple of weeks, and it was still February, they had come to consider this weather as the norm, however dire the warnings of the locals and old hands that it could change suddenly and violently should a mistral, the cold, dry but often very strong north-westerlies arising in the south of France, come storming out of the Gulf of Lyons.

But those winds seldom got as far as Malta, and today conditions were perfect. As they had about a hundred miles to go, Duncan had Wilson serve an early lunch, along with the now de rigueur salt tablets. It was 1400 when Rawlings, as usual in these circumstances on lookout, said, 'Aircraft, green fifteen, about ten thousand feet.'

Duncan levelled his glasses. 'Out of the south-east. She should be one of ours.'

'She's spotted us.'

The plane was definitely descending.

'Shall we furl the flag, sir?'

Duncan considered, briefly. If the aircraft was hostile, and she identified the flags, their presence would undoubtedly be relayed to the convoy. On the other hand, if she was British . . . and that seemed indicated by the direction from which she was approaching . . . the decision had to be his. 'No. If we do that, she may well assume we're Italian, just as we're hoping the convoy will do. And she will almost certainly be armed. Maintain course and speed.'

The aircraft dropped lower yet, and now they could make out the red, white and blue roundels. The White Ensign was streaming out behind each boat, and had to be visible at some distance. But she continued to approach, and now began to circle above them.

Cooper appeared. 'Should we man action stations, sir? Just in case?'

'It is not in our remit to shoot down an RAF plane, Mr Cooper, even if he makes a mistake. We must just hope he doesn't. But he could be trying to tell us something. Check it out. Remember, we do not reply on the air.'

'Aye-aye, sir.' Cooper disappeared, while Duncan surveyed the rest of the flotilla, willing them not to overreact. But as always they were prepared to take their lead from him.

Cooper was back in the hatch. 'Yes, sir. He says: You are too far south. Convoy disarrayed by air attack. Now seventy-five miles north-east of you.'

'Mr Rawlings, use our lamp and signal: Many thanks. Then make to flotilla: Course zero-seven-five, fifteen hundred revolutions.'

'Aye-aye, sir.'

'It'll be past five before we get there,' Cooper remarked. 'There isn't much twilight in these latitudes.'

'Which is what I have in mind,' Duncan said. 'We'll come at him out of the setting sun, and then hopefully disappear again into darkness.'

'Aye-aye, sir!' Cooper said enthusiastically.

As always in these circumstances, time began to drag. Jamie came up for a breath of fresh air, and gave his usual confident report on the engine, and it was he who, at 1630, said, 'Smoke, bearing green five.'

Cooper was on the helm, and both Rawlings and Duncan levelled their glasses.

'Spot on, sir,' Rawlings said.

'I would say one of those ships is on fire.'

Rawlings looked again. 'It would appear so, sir.'

'Action stations, Mr Rawlings. And signal the flotilla: Furl ensigns; time to split. Then take the tubes.'

'Aye-aye, sir.' Rawlings rang the bell and then got busy with his lamp.

'You'll take the gun, Mr Cooper. You may fire as and when you find a target. I will be concentrating on the torpedoes.'

'Aye-aye, sir.' Cooper exchanged his cap for his steel helmet and left the bridge.

Duncan also changed hats, then wrapped his hands round the spokes of the wheel. It was time for one hundred per cent concentration. Behind him, Rawlings completed his transmission and received the necessary acknowledgements. Then he stowed the lamp and furled the ensign. By now the crew had taken up their stations on deck, and Jamie had left the hatch to join Wilson in the mess.

Duncan looked left and right and saw the flotilla diverging. As he was in the centre, he continued straight ahead, maintaining his cruising speed; time enough to increase his revolutions if and when he was identified as an enemy; at twenty knots it was that much easier to line up a target.

Again there was an agonizing wait, although it was actually only a few minutes. The convoy was now fully visible to the naked eye. There were several obvious freighters, two of which had fires on board, although neither seemed to be out of control. There were also four destroyers, two on either side. They were flying the Italian flag, and from one of them, presumably the flotilla leader, there was a flashing light. As Duncan did not understand Italian, he could only guess what she was saying: she wanted identification.

She was the most tempting target, but had to be ignored in favour of the freighters and their precious cargoes. This was a new experience for him; he was now in the position of those Schnell-boat skippers he had spent so many hours trying to destroy.

'Jamie,' he said down the hatch. 'Get up here and unfurl the ensign.'

'Aye-aye, sir.'

Duncan glanced at the rangefinder: four miles. That was maximum range for his torpedoes, and he had not yet been challenged, so he kept going; having selected his target, what appeared to be the largest of the freighters; he was sure he could see tanks on her deck.

There was a flash of light from in front of him. It was a warning shot, as it was aimed over his head and plunged harmlessly into the sea behind him. But the next one would be in earnest; they were close enough for the ensign to be identified. His target was now clearly visible, in the gap between the two starboard destroyers; it was simply a matter of allowing the slight angle of deflection to offset the forward movement of the ship. 'Stand by!' he said into the tannoy. The men on deck braced themselves, and he lined it up, and then thrust the throttle forward.

412 leapt ahead, leaving a huge wake behind her. The other boats were doing the same, their engines screaming at the evening sky, their ensigns also now streaming in the breeze. Three thousand yards! 'Fire one!' he shouted. 'Fire two!'

The torpedoes splashed into the water and raced away from even the speeding motor boat, behind Duncan huge plumes of water leapt skywards as the destroyers opened fire. And now the six-pounder barked, and again. Cooper was firing at the nearest warship, and although most of his shots were wide, there was a larger than usual flash of red from the destroyer's deck.

'Good shooting, Mr Cooper!' Duncan shouted, even as he twisted the helm to bring the boat about and make for the shelter of the growing darkness behind him. As he did so he heard the sound of an explosion, and then another, and looked over his shoulder to see flames shooting skywards, from two separate locations. He had no idea if they had been caused by his torpedoes, but the flotilla had scored two hits. And all without—

'Shit!' Rawlings said. He had retuned to the bridge. 'Begging your pardon, sir.'

Duncan looked to starboard, and saw the pall of flame, in the wrong position. 'Damn!' he agreed.

'Do we . . . can we . . .?'

'No, Mr Rawlings. That would cost us another boat. The Italians will pick up any survivors: they're seamen like ourselves.'

He wondered who it had been.

'Here we are, ladies.' The purser himself had escorted the two glamorous, and apparently important, mink-clad women down to their cabin. Now he opened the door for them.

Kristin stepped past him. 'It's terribly small.'

'Well, madam, this is not a passenger vessel.' He signalled the sailor behind him to bring in the two suitcases.

Kristin surveyed the bunks, one above the other. 'You mean we're members of the crew, or something?'

'Madam, every cabin on this ship except for the captain's, has an upper and lower berth.'

'Hm,' Kristin commented, contemplatively.

'It's only for a few days,' Rebecca said, soothingly, but she also looked around herself. 'I don't see the bathroom.'

'Madam?'

'The bathroom. A place where people do, well, whatever they need to do in bathrooms.'

'There is a washbasin,' he pointed out.

'Excuse me?!'

He was now starting to look slightly desperate, his feelings not helped by the continued presence of the sailor, who had returned to the corridor, but remained there, grinning. 'There is a bathroom at the end of the corridor.'

'Used by . . .?'

'All the other passengers.'

'Holy shit!'

'There are only twelve, all told. I am instructed to invite you to sit at the captain's table for dinner,' the purser hurried on, placatingly.

'Just how many tables are there, in a boat this size?' Kristin asked.

'There is just the one table, madam.'

"I see. In that case, you may tell him we accept.'

'Thank you.' He turned to the door, and turned back. 'This door must never be shut.'

'What?'

'In the event of an emergency, you see, it could jam. You secure it on this brass hook here, which keeps it slightly open.'

'And leaves us at the mercy of every curious passer-by.'

'It is apparently regarded as necessary,' Rebecca said. 'That sweet kid Jamie whatever-his-name-was, explained it to me when I was on that MTB. And I had nothing on.'

'That seems to be your only enduring memory of the whole episode,' Kristin remarked, scathingly. 'She had just been torpedoed, you see,' she explained to the purser, whose mouth was open.

'You mean you have been torpedoed before, madam?'

'I don't much like that 'before' bit,' Rebecca said. 'Are you saying that it is likely to happen again?'

'Oh, no, no. Well, of course, there is a risk. But it is a very small one. Now ladies, two more things. You should both equip yourselves with a sizeable waterproof bag. If you do not already have such a bag, I have them for sale in my office. In this bag you will carry your passport, any other important documents, your valuables and money, and any other . . . ah . . . items you may regard as essential should you have to leave the cabin or the ship in a hurry. This bag you will carry with you at all times, and you will sleep with it beside you at night. You also must have your life jacket with you at all times. There will be a lifeboat drill before we leave the Solent.'

'You mean we wear this bag to dinner with the captain?'

'He will expect you to, madam.'

He left the cabin, and Kristin and Rebecca looked at each other. As Rebecca had been delayed in London, this was the first time they had been alone together in a week. In fact, as they were both realizing, it was the first time they had ever been alone together.

'How the other half live,' Kristin commented, taking off her coat and hanging it on the hook behind the door.

'How tragic for them.' Rebecca hung hers on top of Kristin's.

'But you've had to do this before. Like last week.' Kristin placed her suitcase on the lower bunk, opened it. 'I mean, rough it on a boat.'

'I,' Rebecca informed her, 'crossed the Atlantic on the *Queen Mary*. With an en suite cabin. You may use the two lower drawers in that bureau.'

'Locker.'

'What?'

'At sea, a bureau is known as a locker.' Kristin took out the two dresses she had brought with her and hung them in the wardrobe. 'What about the time before? When you were blown up?'

Rebecca leaned against the bulkhead with her arms folded, watching her at work. 'Then I travelled by a neutral American ship. She was not blown up. That happened after I had transferred to a small Portuguese ship for the last leg, Lisbon to Southampton. That was supposed to be an overnight trip.'

Kristin was transferring her underclothes to the locker. 'Well, the only time I have been at sea in a cabin this small was in a yacht, and as I owned the yacht it didn't matter. I have never slept in an upper bunk in my life. I suppose we'll have to toss for it.' She arranged her toiletries around the basin.

'Excuse me,' Rebecca said, hefting her suitcase on to the bunk in turn. 'You seem to forget that at this moment I am your employer.'

'Oh, yes?'

'I am also doing you a favour in allowing you to be here at all.'

'I see. Well, if I'm climbing up there, there is something you should know.'

'You snore. Don't worry about it. Sound rises. Although . . .' She looked up at the deck above them. 'It doesn't have very far to go.' She closed the empty suitcase, and began arranging her toiletries in turn, carefully moving Kristin's to one side.

'I do not snore,' Kristin announced. 'But I do not wear clothes in bed, either.'

'Don't you? Oh! Well, snap. And we can't shut the door!'

'It should be an interesting trip. Are you a lesbian?'

'What?' It was almost a shriek.

'Just checking.' Kristin was delighted; it was the first time she had seen Rebecca disconcerted.

'You mean, just because I sleep in the nude . . . but you do, too. Are you saying . . . but you're a married woman. Were. And now you're engaged again.'

'If you intend to go through life without sampling everything it has to offer, you are wasting an awful lot of breath that could probably be better used by other people. Next thing you'll be telling me that you've never slept with anyone save George.'

'Of course I have not.'

'Good God! Despite this weakness you have for always

being naked when there's a crisis? Wasn't he more than twice your age?'

'Well . . . yes. Wasn't Lord Eversham more than twice yours?'

'Do you know, that's absolutely true. When we got married.'

'But you got around to adultery just as soon as you could. Sampling life.'

'Exactly. And I intend to go on doing so. And it strikes me that as we are here, shut up together in a tiny prison cell, well . . . you really are a very attractive woman, you know.'

'There's the siren,' Rebecca said. 'We're casting off. Let's go see what's happening. And then, I think we should visit the purser's office and get those little bags.'

'I thought,' Rebecca said, 'that we were going to visit your old home. Not stay in a hotel.'

'This is not an hotel,' Kristin pointed out. 'It is the house where I was born and bred.'

The two women stood on the Madrid pavement looking up at the immense, palatial house, while the traffic rumbled to and fro behind them, and passers-by stared at them.

'And what is it now?' Rebecca asked.

'The house where I was born and bred.'

'Come on.'

'I haven't been here since 1936,' Kristin said, dreamily. 'My God! Six years! I came down to sort out the estate, after Daddy died. Do you know, I almost stayed. I wanted to. The divorce had been so messy. But I was advised to shut it up and go back to England. The Civil War was just starting, and Madrid was controlled by the Communists. Already there were stories of atrocities. Do you know what they did to the wives and daughters of anyone suspected of being a Nationalist?'

'Do I want to know something like that? But I suspect you are going to tell me, anyway.'

'Well, they were gang-raped, of course.'

'Of course.'

'That needn't have been so bad. But then they shaved them. Everywhere!' She put one hand on her head and the other on her crotch, as if performing a yoga exercise. 'Can you imagine?'

'I'd rather not, if you don't mind. So you skedaddled back to the UK and left it sitting here. I'm surprised it's still standing.'

'Oh, it got knocked about a bit during the various bombardments. But Carlos was here, looking after it. And he's had it repaired. Well, mostly.'

'Who's Carlos?'

'My lawyer.'

'And he managed to survive, even though he was your lawyer?'

'Lawyers,' Kristin pointed out, 'always survive. Here he is, now.'

The car had just parked at the curb. And now the dapper little man, bald but with a pencil moustache, and impeccably dressed in a three-piece suit, hurried towards them. 'Donna Kristin!' he cried in Spanish. 'When I got your telephone call I could not believe my ears.' He seized her hand to kiss the glove. 'You have come back to live?'

'Sadly, not right now. I am on a boat.'

'You have brought your yacht to Spain? But that is very dangerous, at this time. I mean to be at sea.'

'I am not on my yacht, Carlos. I am on a freighter, which is presently berthed in Gibraltar. But as it is going to be there for a couple of days, I thought I'd come up and see for myself how things are going. Will you open up?'

'Of course, Donna. Of course.' He looked at a spellbound Rebecca. She did not speak Spanish, but had been able to gather that Kristin was a somebody in this neck of the woods.

'This is my close friend, Señora Rebecca Strong.'

'Señora!' He kissed her hand, in turn. 'Now, if you will come with me.' He led them up the wide front steps to the door to the porch.

'I congratulate you,' Kristin said. 'It looks in surprisingly good shape.'

'Well, the cleaners come in every day. And the workmen are just about finished the renovation. Another couple of weeks should do it.' He unlocked the door and ushered them in.

'Wow!' Rebecca stood in the centre of the parquet floor of the huge entry hall, gazed at the suits of armour against the walls, at the grand staircase leading up to the first floor gallery, above which there rose three more galleries, and then the huge dome of the roof.

'Does it remind you of home?' Kristin inquired with malicious innocence.

'You have got to be joking. How old is this place, anyway?'

'It was built in 1552.'

'What?'

'Of course, in 1552 not even the Pilgrims had yet landed. Did you know that one of my ancestors sailed with Cortez? It was the loot he brought back from Mexico that built this house. Now, Carlos,' she reverted to Spanish, 'Señora Strong and I intend to have a long, hot bath. I assume my room is ready?'

'The girls will be here in half an hour. I telephoned them as soon as I heard from you.'

'That was very thoughtful of you. And there is hot water?'

'Oh, yes, Donna.'

'Excellent. Then we wish paella for dinner. I have not had a paella for six years.'

'Of course, Donna. And the wine?'

'Marquis de Caceres white. Put six bottles on ice.'

'Of course.'

Kristin held Rebecca's hand. 'Let's go look at the rest of the house.'

'Do I get a room too?'

'Do you wish for a room too? My bed is big enough for four.'

'I thought we had done with that stuff. It just isn't me.'

'Do you know,' Kristin said, 'it isn't me, either, really. But the challenge . . .'

'Of having an affair, with either sex?'

Kristin gave one of her roguish smiles. 'Of pulling your leg.'

'This is tremendous,' Rebecca said, taking a sip of wine in between digging her fork into the piled plate of paella in front of her, 'I mean, the work, the skill, that went into it. The detail.' She had, earlier, watched in wonder as the two Spanish maids laid on by Carlos had carefully prepared the huge pan on top of the gas ring in the kitchen, explaining in broken English that the temperature had to be sufficiently high that the rice would just stick to the sides.

'It is nice,' Kristin agreed.

'They seemed so skilled.'

'Every competent Spanish woman can cook a paella. Lucia does a marvellous one. But getting the ingredients in England . . . it requires special rice, for a start.'

Rebecca drank some more wine. 'I can't thank you enough for bringing me here, Kristin. For showing me how . . . well, I suppose you would have to say, how the other half lives.'

'It's always worth knowing, that. When this stupid war is over, I will visit you in the States, and you can show me how that half lives. This is, if you're still there.'

'Eh? Why shouldn't I still be there?'

'Well, I've been thinking about your problem.'

'I have a problem?'

'Of course you do. You have the most serious problem any woman can have: lack of sex.'

Rebecca put down her fork.

'Don't get your knickers in a twist. I accept that you don't want to have sex with me. I can't imagine why, but I suppose it takes all sorts. I can understand, having only ever known sex with a man old enough to be your father, you are severely inhibited. But if you don't do something about it, now, it is going to get worse, and you are going to wind up a lonely old woman. That being so, we have to find you a man.'

'Chance would be a fine thing.'

'Don't tell me you're against that as well?'

'Of course not. But you see, in my position . . . I have to suppose every man who wants to get close to me is after my money.'

'I think you could be selling yourself short. But in any event, the man I have in mind for you would not be after your money. I mean he doesn't have any of his own, just his service pay, but he is absolutely as straight as a ruler. And we know he fancies you.'

'May I ask of whom we are speaking?'

'Why, Jimmy Lonsdale, of course. I'm sure that he is going to be knighted, one of these days. If you were to marry him, you'd become a lady. I mean in the titular sense. Rebecca, Lady Lonsdale. Doesn't that sound nice?'

Rebecca drank some wine. 'It sounds entrancing. But isn't there a tiny matter that you have overlooked?'

'Have I?' Kristin was genuinely surprised.

'Admiral Lonsdale is your fiancé.'

'Ah. I've been thinking about that too, and I have come to the conclusion that it would not be a good idea for us to marry.'

'But —'

'It was rather a hasty decision. On my part. Things were a little . . . fraught at the time. I have now realized that it would be a disaster, for both of us. I suppose he just can't get this admiral thing out of his system. I mean, I'm sure he's a great leader of men, and probably women as well: Alison has a high regard for him. But I don't want to be led, anywhere, or commanded. Don't get me wrong. He really is a sweetie, and he's not too bad in bed, either. He's just not me.'

'Kristin,' Rebecca said. 'You are a hoot.'

They stood together at the rail as the freighter slowly pulled away from her berth, to the accompaniment of a cacophony of noise, sirens wailing, men shouting, engines grinding: the entire convoy of twenty ships together with its six escorts was getting under way at the same time.

'I don't think I thanked you properly for that experience,' Rebecca said.

'Actually, you did.'

'Well . . . have you taken Jimmy there? To that house?'

'Good God, no. We only got engaged at Christmas.'

'Well, I think it would be the ideal place to honeymoon.'

'You have got to be joking. He's an admiral. Do you think he'd ever get permission to honeymoon in a place like Spain? Anyway . . . I told you. It's not going to happen.'

'Kristin . . .'

'Excuse me, ladies.' The purser was there, inviting them to dine at the captain's table, as always.

Captain Albury had become a friend, over the voyage; he clearly enjoyed entertaining two such attractive, and enigmatic, women – he had no idea why they were going to Malta, save that as they *were going,* it had to be both important and secret.

His officers equally would have liked to get closer to them, but had to yield priority to their superior, although they endeavoured to keep their end up. 'I hope you like your new lifeboat, Mrs Strong,' First Officer Laidlaw remarked. Like everyone else on board, he assumed that Rebecca was the senior of the women, as they were on the passenger list as Mrs Strong and secretary. This misapprehension suited Kristin well enough as she wanted to take no risks of it getting back to Jimmy where she was and what she was doing, certainly until it was too late for him to do something about it.

'I'm sure it's very nice,' Rebecca agreed. 'I haven't actually been in it, yet. Am I going to have to?'

'That is extremely unlikely. We are the centre ship of the convoy. Any Italian sub would have to work his way through all the outside ships to get to us.'

'You are very reassuring,' Kristin remarked.

'I don't understand why we have had to change boats anyway,' Rebecca said. They were seated one on each side of the captain, with Laidlaw on her left, and her comment was made at large.

'Ah, well, you see,' Albury explained. 'When you came on board at Southampton, no one knew who you were. The purser assigned all our passengers to a boat station, virtually by rote. But now that we have got to know you . . . 'A' boat is commanded by me, personally.'

'That's not so good,' Kristin pointed out. 'Much as we would enjoy your company while drifting about. Aren't you supposed to go down with the ship?'

'I am supposed to remain with the ship until everyone else is off,' he corrected. 'But my boat would continue to stand by until I am picked up. But as Mr Laidlaw has said, it is extremely unlikely to happen.'

'Do you think,' Kristin remarked, returning to the cabin from her visit to the bathroom, 'that they are as confident as they sound? Or are they just stringing us a line?'

'The latter.' Rebecca was already in bed. Now she watched

Kristin's long, splendidly muscled legs climbing the ladder past her nose. 'You're not seriously going to break it off with Jimmy?'

Kristin swung her legs on to the bunk and lay back with a thump. 'As a matter of fact, I am very serious.'

'I hope it has nothing to do with what I said, about us on the boat . . .'

'Discussing me,' Kristin said, and switched off the light.

'It was something hypothetical. Just a conversation. But the fact that he did something about it must show that he had it in mind all the time. And you've just admitted that you'll never find a nicer guy.'

'Go to sleep,' Kristin recommended.

She did so, very rapidly, to be awakened, it seemed only minutes later, by the clanging of a bell and the wail of a siren.

PART THREE

The Storm

Blow wind, swell billow, and swim bark.
The storm is up, and all is on the hazard
William Shakespeare

Ladies in Distress

L ucifer's barking alerted Alison to a visitor. She went to
the window, looked down at the chauffeur-driven command
car, and muttered, 'Shit!' then ran for the stairs. 'Harry!' she
shouted. 'Take Lucifer out the back.'

Harry hurried into the hall. 'Come on, old chap. Food,
food.'

Lucifer galloped behind him, and Alison opened the door.
'Jimmy!' she cried. 'What a pleasant surprise! Or has something happened?'

The admiral embraced her. 'Indeed. Tremendous news!'

'Come in. Come upstairs. I'm in Kristin's sitting room.
Tell me,' she invited over her shoulder as she led him up the
stairs.

Lonsdale had entered the house somewhat cautiously,
braced for a physical assault, but as there was none, he hurried
behind her. 'Duncan has had one of his successes.' He puffed
as he reached the top of the stairs.

Alison was already at the sideboard. 'Is it a sherry success,
or a champagne one?'

'I think sherry will do.'

'Then sit down.' She handed him a glass, then sat beside
him on the settee.

'He and his flotilla attacked a convoy east of Malta, and
sank two ships.'

'Brilliant! And they're all right?'

'Well, actually, they suffered a casualty.'

'Oh, my God! Who?'

'Partridge. *416*. Did you know him?'

'Doesn't ring a bell. And his crew?'

'I'm afraid so. They may not all be dead. But the boat blew
up, and as you know the flotilla is under strict instructions

not to risk their boats trying to rescue survivors when in a battle situation. I'm sure the Italians would have picked up any.'

Alison shivered and drank some sherry. 'It's good of you to come all the way out here to tell me.'

'Actually, I came out here to find out what Kristin is doing?'

'Oh! Ah! I told you on the phone . . .'

'That she had to go to Scotland to be with a sick aunt. That was over a week ago. When is she coming back? I mean, by now the aunt must either have recovered or be dead.'

'Ah!' Alison said again. Kristin had actually been gone nine days. She would have to have been in and out of Gibraltar by now, and be on her way to Malta 'To tell you the truth, Jimmy, she's not in Scotland.'

'What? You told me—'

'I told you what Kristin told me to tell you. She didn't want to upset you.'

'What? Then where is she?'

'On a ship, I think.'

'What?'

'You know how she wanted to visit the houses in Spain . . .'

'Oh, my God! She didn't! She must have absolutely flipped her lid. Well . . .' He put down his glass and stood up. 'I'd better—'

'I don't think she's still there,' Alison ventured.

'You mean she's on her way back? Already? Well, I'll—'

'I don't think she's on her way back, either.'

'Just what do you mean?'

'I know she was stopping off at Gibraltar. But then she was going on to Malta.'

Slowly Lonsdale sank back into his seat, and as an afterthought picked up his glass and drained it. 'That's not possible.'

'Not possible are not words with which Kristin is familiar.'

'It is not possible because there is no ordinary passenger traffic between Gibraltar and Malta, at this time. Every ship out of Gib is filled to capacity with supplies, weapon, troops, and VIPs on official business. There is no room for tourists.'

'I know. She went with Rebecca Strong. Do you remember the American woman? You went with Duncan to get her and her father out of Norway.'

'I do indeed remember Rebecca,' Lonsdale admitted. She was not a woman he would ever forget. 'How the hell did she get involved with Kristin, again? If I remember rightly, Kristin did not exactly take to her.'

'I suppose because they are so alike. Rebecca was on her way to Malta on official business.'

'What official business?'

'It's something to do with possible American aid to our people in Egypt.'

'How the hell did Rebecca Strong get involved in something like that? She's not in the diplomatic service, is she?'

'Apparently she has hidden depths.'

'I thought she was married to some rich, and very possessive, American?'

'Yes, she was. But he died, and left her footloose and fancy free. And very rich herself.'

'Good heavens,' the admiral commented, thoughtfully.

'So, when Kristin discovered that she was going to Malta, she talked her into taking her along. As her secretary.'

'Good heavens!'

'So there you are. I'm sorry about the deceit. Kristin really didn't want to agitate you. Anyway, I don't know how long they had to spend in Gibraltar, but they must be on their way again by now.'

'I see. And do you have any idea when they are coming back?'

'Well, it could be a little while. Rebecca was actually on her way to Egypt. As I said.'

'You mean Kristin is going to Egypt?'

'Ah . . . I don't think she had that in mind. As she seems to have been and done everything else, I'm quite sure she's seen the Pyramids.'

'Are you saying that she may be thinking of staying on in Malta? That woman is stark, raving mad. I've a good mind to have her arrested.'

'I don't think that would be a very good idea,' Alison ventured. 'She'd be absolutely furious.'

'*I'm* furious!'

'Well, it's up to you.'

Lonsdale regarded his empty sherry glass. 'Don't you have anything stronger than this?'

'Holy shit!' Rebecca tumbled out of her bunk and landed on her hands and knees. 'God Almighty!' she shrieked, as Kristin came out of her bunk in turn and landed on her back. She collapsed on to her face.

'Oops!' Kristin acknowledged, and switched on the light. 'Let's rush!'

Rebecca rolled over and sat up, feeling herself for possible broken bones. 'That hurt. You must be as heavy as your beastly dog.'

'When we get back to England, I'll remind Lucifer you said that.' Kristin handed her her mink. 'Put this on.'

'Why?'

'Don't you remember what the purser said: when the alarm goes we must get on deck as quickly as possible.'

'I can't possibly go on deck in a mink coat.'

'I know. You prefer to be in the nud when being torpedoed. If I'd known you were going to make a habit of it I wouldn't have come. But we don't want to distract the captain; we're in his boat, remember. Come along now.'

'You have to give me time to put something on.'

'I have given you your mink. You don't have the time for anything else.' She inserted Rebecca into the coat, then into her life jacket, pulled the strings tight. 'In this straitjacket, no one will look at you twice. Here's your ditty bag.'

The purser appeared in the doorway. 'Oh! Ah! Excuse me, ladies, but you should be on deck.'

Kristin had already put on her coat, now she added her own life jacket. 'We're on our way. How long have we got?'

'Oh, we're not sinking.'

Kristin glared at him. 'Then what the fuck is going on?'

'The convoy is under attack, and we must take proper precautions.'

'Shit!' she remarked, as they followed him up the stairs and out on to the deck. Here, with the ship blacked out, it was utterly dark, save for various flashing lights and the white wakes of the other ships. 'How on earth do they avoid running into each other?' she asked at large.

The only other women on board were four nurses, and the six women had been herded together beneath the bridge wing. Eating in a general mess they were all acquainted, even if the nurses were always down at the far end of the table. One of them now remarked, 'They don't, always.'

'Your profession,' Kristin reminded her, 'requires you to bring comfort and hope to people, not doom and gloom.'

'Gee!' Rebecca commented. 'Look there!'

As the convoy was still steaming at full speed, the incident was already some miles astern, but they could hear the sound of the explosion, and see the flames shooting skywards,

'One gone,' a nurse said.

'Why aren't we stopping to pick survivors up?' Kristin asked. 'There must be some survivors.'

'We don't stop for anything,' the nurse said. 'Our job is to get as many of us to Malta as we can.'

'You mean those people are just going to be left to drown?' Rebecca was aghast.

'A destroyer may see if it can help.'

'I think you are in the wrong profession,' Kristin announced. 'God damn, but my feet are freezing.' She went to the door, and encountered a large sailor. 'Open up,' she said. 'I'm just nipping down to get a pair of socks.'

'And for me.' Rebecca had followed her.

'I'm sorry, ladies,' the man said. 'No one is to go below until the emergency is over.'

'Oh, yes? And suppose I really need to go?'

'Well –' he peered at her, anxiously – 'you don't, do you?'

'Oh. pffft! I'll tell you this,' she told Rebecca, 'from here on I am sleeping fully dressed, down to my shoes.'

'Snap,' Rebecca agreed.

After an hour they were allowed back to their cabins, and despite their churned up nerves, went back to sleep for a couple of hours.

'Actually,' Rebecca said, as they got dressed. 'We were never in any danger. I told you, lightning never strikes twice in the same place. There is absolutely no risk of this ship being torpedoed.'

'I'm prepared to believe you,' Kristin said. 'Because I want to. But you'd better be right.'

It was a magnificent, warm day, with nothing but blue skies. The convoy had reformed and was steaming east at full speed, which actually was not very fast. Kristin had been counting. 'We left Gibraltar with twenty ships and six escorts. Now there are only eighteen ships and five escorts. Does that mean,' she asked the captain, who had joined them for breakfast, 'that we have lost an escort as well as two merchantman?'

'No. One of the escorts stayed behind to see what he could do about survivors.'

'Thank God for that.' Rebecca said.

'Did they get the sub?' Kristin asked.

'I don't know. They dropped a lot of depth charges but I don't think there was any conclusive evidence of its destruction.'

'Anyway,' Rebecca said brightly. 'We must be past halfway.'

'Well, not quite. We'll be halfway by this evening. Unfortunately, the nearer we get to Malta, the nearer we also get to Italy.'

'Another doom and gloom merchant,' Kristin growled, as they went up to the boat deck, where the steward had arranged deck chairs for them. They were both wearing shirts, slacks and sandals, with their hair tied up in bandannas, and stretched out comfortably in the increasingly warm sunshine, their life jackets and survival bags beside them. 'You should have told him your theory.'

'He'd probably have pooh-poohed it.'

'True.'

'Coffee, ladies?' The steward was back.

'That would be very nice,' Kristin agreed.

Rebecca was surveying the row of lifeboats. 'I know I should have asked this before, but somehow it didn't seem important until last night: are there lifeboat places for everyone on board?'

'Of course, madam. Board of Trade Regulations. Not like the old *Titanic*, eh? Ha ha.'

'Ha ha,' Kristin agreed. 'But I think it's unlikely that we are going to run into an iceberg down here. What about if we're hit, and some of the lifeboats are damaged and became unusable?'

'That's almost impossible, madam. If a torpedo hits, it's on or below the waterline, not on the boat deck. But if by some freak it were to happen, it's allowed for.'

'How?'

'Well, you see that row of orange boxes over there? Those are inflatable rubber life rafts. If we had to abandon ship, those are fired overboard. When they hit the water they automatically inflate. They can carry ten men. And women, of course. I'll just get the coffee.'

'Nice of him to include us at the end,' Kristin growled.

'You're not scared, are you?' Rebecca asked. 'Not you.'

'Do you know, I never thought I would be. I mean, I've been in enough blows at sea, and in boats a fraction the size of this. But then, everyone had a job to do. There's no time to be scared. And I was at Dunkirk, with people being blown up all around me. And I was in a fight with an S-boat. We even got hit. But I was with Duncan, and, well...'

'Jamie,' Rebecca suggested, helpfully.

Kristin shot her a glance. 'He was there too, yes. And I wasn't scared. There wasn't time, I suppose. But last night, seeing that ship just blow up without even seeing who was shooting at it, and knowing that even if you survived that you'd be drifting about in the darkness, wondering if you were going to be picked up . . . it's not so much fear as the sheer inconvenience of it. Not being in control. Do you know what I would like to see right this minute, more than anything else in the world?'

'Well . . . Malta, I suppose.'

'Duncan's flotilla, coming over the horizon at full speed to take care of us.'

'That would be a lovely sight, wouldn't it? It could still happen.'

'Your coffee, ladies.'

The tray was presented, and they took the cups and saucers and plates with the little biscuits.

'Will there be anything further?'

'A couple of glasses of sherry, at eleven o'clock.'

'Eleven o'clock, madam.'

'Just make sure it's Harvey's Bristol Cream. Not Bristol Milk, mind. That's too dry. Bristol Cream.'

'I'm not sure we have any Harvey's sherry on board, madam.'

'Oh, for God' sake!'

'This isn't the *Queen Mary*,' Rebecca reminded her.

'Oh, pffft. Look, just make sure it's sweet sherry.'

'Yes, madam. I will see what can be done.'

'What do you think those are?' Rebecca asked, pointing. Kristin and the steward both looked.

'I would say . . .' Kristin said.

'Aircraft!' the steward interrupted.

Kristin turned her head to glare at him, and discovered that he had gone quite pale. And at that moment the alarm bell started ringing.

'This is the captain speaking,' the voice said over the tannoy. 'We are informed that the approaching aircraft are Italian, and therefore hostile. We shall be dispersing and taking avoiding action. All passengers will leave the deck and assemble in the saloon, wearing life jackets.'

'For God's sake,' Kristin complained again.

Rebecca was on her feet. 'We'd better do as he says.'

'If you would, madam.' The steward was replacing the crockery on his tray with some clattering; his hands were shaking.

Kristin and Rebecca went down the ladder into the saloon, where the rest of the passengers were gathering, chattering to each other. Of the other ten, four were the nurses and six were army officers. These were wearing uniform, and endeavouring to appear calm. The purser appeared. 'Life jackets, please, ladies and gentlemen. Life jackets, please.'

Kristin and Rebecca pulled on their jackets, and tied the strings. 'He seems to be taking this more seriously than the submarine,' Rebecca muttered.

'He could have a point,' Kristin suggested, remembering her conversation with Duncan; if an armoured battleship appeared to have no hope of surviving an air attack, what were the chances of an unarmoured freighter? On the other hand, Duncan had said that speed was the key to avoiding air attack, and the ship certainly seemed to be going faster than at any time since the voyage had begun. 'Excuse me,' she said to the still fussing purser. 'Do you know how fast we're going?'

'I would say all of twelve knots, madam.'

'Twelve knots. And what is our maximum speed?'

'That's it.'

Kristin sat on a settee. Duncan had said forty knots was what would be needed.

Rebecca sat beside her. 'Isn't that good?'

'No.'

'Ooh!' cried one of the nurses. 'Look at that!'

They gathered at the windows to watch great plumes of water rising around another ship as the first bombs were dropped. These all seemed to have missed, but ... 'Excuse us ladies,' said the boatswain, entering the saloon at the head of four of his men, who immediately started closing the steel shutters over the ports.

'If you do that,' Rebecca pointed out. 'We won't be able to see what's happening.'

'If we don't do that, madam,' he replied, 'that glass is liable to shatter and you'd have shards flying everywhere. That could be dangerous.'

A few minutes later they were enclosed, and at that moment the ship heeled violently as she altered course. There was a chorus of screams from the nurses and exclamations of alarm from the men as they lost their footing and staggered about.

'Just be calm, ladies and gentlemen,' called a man wearing the insignia of a colonel, who had also dined at the top of the captain's table and seemed to be the senior officer present. 'I think it would be a good idea if we all sat down.'

'Absolutely,' Kristin agreed, and regained the settee, which she and Rebecca shared with two of the nurses.

As there weren't quite enough seats for everyone, the officers sat on the floor. No one said anything any more, as the ship heeled this way and then that, and occasionally gave a violent shudder.

'I think he's getting the hang of it,' Rebecca commented.

But almost as she spoke there was a violent explosion

from close at hand. The lights in the saloon went out, and them came on again, flickering, and from outside they could hear shouts of alarm and the bell started again, urgently.

Kristin found that she was clutching Rebecca's hand. 'I hope they're going to tell us what to do next.'

The door opened and the purser reappeared. 'Ladies and gentlemen,' he shouted. 'The ship has been hit, and—'

His voice was drowned by another explosion, louder than before, and he pitched forward to lie on the deck.

'He's bleeding,' Kristin snapped, and nudged the nurse beside her. 'Do something.'

The nurse gulped, but fell to her knees beside the unconscious man, while Kristin realized that the lights had again gone out but that she could still see – there was a huge rent in the outer bulkhead. At the same time she also realized that the engine had stopped beneath her, but the ship was still heeling.

'Holy shit!' Rebecca gasped.

There were shouts all around them, drowned in a blast on the tannoy. 'This ship is sinking. Abandon ship. Every man for himself.'

'He could've mentioned us,' Kristin growled. She grabbed Rebecca's arm, dragged her to her feet, and towards the now opened door. This was jammed with people trying to get out, all encumbered by their life jackets. But they half-pushed, half-fell through: the door was on the downwards side of the list.

They staggered into the open air, and across the deck to the rail, where Kristin saw that the water was only a few feet below them. Now she smelt smoke, and looking round saw it rising above the forward section of the ship. A glance above her head revealed the lifeboats on this side, hanging in their davits in shattered strips of wood.

'Fuck it!' she muttered. 'Listen, we have to get off.'

'She's going over,' Rebecca protested. 'She'll crush us!'

'Just jump, and swim like hell.' Kristin climbed over the rail and dropped into the water; it was so close she hardly made a splash. She looked back up. The ship was certainly listing above them, but for the moment was not actually rolling any further. 'Come on!' she shrieked.

Rebecca hesitated a last moment, then climbed over the rail and dropped beside her.

'Now swim,' Kristin told her.

They struck out vigorously, Kristin using an overarm stroke, and Rebecca a breast stroke. They were aware of people all around them, shouting and gasping, even bumped into one or two, but were concentrating only on getting away from the stricken ship. Then there was a huge whoosh that sounded like a giant sighing in distress, and a wave picked them up and hurled them forwards, before the suction pulled them beneath the surface.

Their life jackets brought them back up in seconds, gasping, spitting, vomiting salt water, and then vomiting some more as they swallowed oil.

'Jesus!' Rebecca gasped. 'I'm dying.'

'I thought you were used to this sort of thing,' Kristin panted. 'Come on, we have to find a boat.'

They were surrounded by pandemonium. Above their heads the planes were still wheeling and bombing. Their own ship had disappeared beneath a huge area of turbulent water which still surrounded them. Looking around Kristin saw that two other ships were on fire . . . and the survivors were steaming away as fast as they could. Bastards, she thought. But they were lucky bastards, merely obeying orders.

And there were no boats to be seen, only bits of shattered wood floating around, and, she saw to her horror, dead bodies. There was still a lot of shouting, but it was diminishing. She wondered how long they could survive, in the water. Their life jackets were supporting them, and the sun-heated sea was quite warm at the moment, but she remembered how cold the air had been in the middle of the night. And her fur had gone down with the ship!

'Are we going to die?' Rebecca gasped.

'Could be. What a fucking waste. I mean, you and I could probably buy the Bank of England between us, especially now that it seems to be about bust. And here we are, floating about the ocean waiting to disappear.'

'Ooh!' Rebecca shouted. 'Oh, my God! Something touched my leg. Oh . . .'

'It was my toe, silly. Fuck it! My shoes have come off.'

'Ooh!' She seemed to sag in her life jacket. 'I thought . . .
Do they have sharks in the Mediterranean?'

'As a matter of fact, they do,' Kristin said. 'I once saw a
whopper, outside St Tropez. It was just after lunch, and we
left the harbour behind this huge two-hundred-foot job.
They'd obviously just finished lunch as well, and their chef
came on deck with a bucket full of scraps and leftovers which
he proceeded to empty over the side. Next thing this monster
emerged, a great white thing. Very impressive.'

'You have no idea how much that cheers me up,' Rebecca
said.

'Lady Eversham! Lady Eversham! Over here!'

Kristin turned her head. Viewing the world from the
perspective of water level in a still disturbed sea had limited
her understanding of what might be happening around them.
But now she saw, only a few feet away, one of the orange
life rafts, fully inflated, hanging over the side of which with
outstretched hand was one of the nurses. She was in an
extremely bedraggled state, but Kristin had never seen a more
beautiful sight.

'Come on!' she told Rebecca, and swam towards the hand.

There were actually two nurses in the raft, and a few moments
later both Kristin and Rebecca were on board, lying in the
bottom and panting, while water drained out of their hair
and their clothes.

'Are we glad to see you,' Rebecca panted.

'Where did you find this thing, anyway?' Kristin asked.

'It found us. It bumped into us.'

'How nice of it.' Kristin sat up and turned on her knees.
'Jesus!'

The noise had diminished, and was now principally
composed of the cries of the sea birds circling overhead. The
dinghy was surrounded by debris . . . and dead bodies. It was
obvious that not a single lifeboat had been launched; presumably they had all been destroyed in their davits. There were
another couple of the life rafts to be seen, and there seemed
to be people in them, but they were some distance away.
Apart from that the sea was empty.

'Do you know what time it is?' Rebecca asked.

Kristin squinted at the sun, which, if still overhead, was slightly off the perpendicular. 'I would say about one o'clock.'

'I have a watch,' volunteered one of the nurses. She wore it on her lapel.

Kristin peered at it. 'It's stopped. Water must have got into it.'

'Oh! Oh, gosh! It was a gift from my mother.'

'Well, I should think someone will be able to fix it, when we're picked up.'

'When do you think we'll be picked up?' asked the other girl.

'Just be patient. Tell me your name.'

'Elizabeth Shortly, milady.'

'And you?'

'Audrey Stone, Lady Eversham.'

'And how do you know my name?'

'The purser told us. He told everybody.'

'I wonder if he survived,' Kristin said thoughtfully, her tone suggesting that if he had, he might not, much longer. 'And do you also know who this lady is?'

'Well, no, milady. Is she a lady too?'

'I think you need to rephrase that,' Kristin suggested. 'This is Mrs Rebecca Strong, and she is the richest woman in America.'

'Eh?' Rebecca awoke from a brood.

'Well, one of them,' Kristin said, magnanimously.

'We never had lunch,' Elizabeth grumbled. 'I am so hungry.'

'And we never had our sherry.'

'Oh for a drink. Anything,' Audrey said.

'Our things,' Rebecca said. 'Our bags with our things. We haven't got them.'

'There's a fact,' Kristin agreed. 'But you must be used to that.'

'I need to go,' Audrey said.

'For God's sake. You haven't had lunch, and you say you're thirsty, how can you need to go?'

'Well . . . I just do.'

'Oh, well, drop your knickers and put your bottom over

the side. You'd better hold her hands, Elizabeth, so we don't
have to fish her back out.'

'Look, there are two paddles strapped to the side, there,'
Rebecca said. 'Shouldn't we use them?'

'Where were you planning to go?' Kristin inquired. She
lay back, resting her head on the rubber gunwale, looking
up at the sky, and realized that she had lost her sun glasses
as well as everything else. She closed her eyes, and felt
Rebecca lying beside her.

'Do you think the captain survived?'

'If he did,' Kristin said, 'he should be drifting around with
us. But somehow I think he did the proper thing, and went
down with his ship. Not that he could have had a lot of time
to brood on it. That thing sank like a lead bucket with a hole
in it.'

'He seemed such a nice guy.' Rebecca brooded for a few
minutes. 'How long can we survive without food or water?'

'Without food, quite a long time, I believe. Several days.
Maybe as long as a fortnight.'

'Gee!'

'But without water . . . two days, maybe.'

'Oh! Can't we drink our own urine?'

'Supposing we had any, and could stomach it. And had
anything to catch it in.'

'Shit.' Rebecca rested her head on Kristin's shoulder.
'Kristin, I'd like you to know that if I ever did have an affair
with a woman, it would be you I'd choose.'

'Now she tells me,' Kristin remarked. But she gave her a
hug.

'Ah, Eversham, my dear fellow. Come in, come in.' Captain
Jardine beamed. 'Great news, eh? Great news.'

'Partridge has been picked up, sir? And his people?'

'Eh? Partridge? Ah, no. Nothing yet.'

'Oh.' Duncan's face fell.

'That doesn't mean he's lost. No, no. The Italians are always
dilatory at reporting prisoners of war. And of course, when
they report it, they will also have to report the action, which
will involve admitting the loss of two of their ships. A brilliant action. Oh, indeed. Their lordships are very pleased.

Although of course they expected nothing less of you and your people. Absolutely. But this news about your mother! I must say, you must have been terribly worried when what was left of the convoy arrived two days ago. And you gave no sign of it. If I may say so, Lieutenant-Commander, you are a remarkable fellow.'

Duncan sank into the chair before the desk, uninvited. 'I'm afraid, sir, that I have no idea what you are talking about.'

'What?' Jardine sat down himself, behind the desk. 'You knew your mother was on her way?'

'My mother, sir? On her way where?'

'Why, here, of course. She was with convoy MJ 18. The one that docked two days ago. You mean you did not know this?'

'I did not know this, sir,' Duncan said, with difficulty preventing himself from shouting. 'You are saying that my mother is here in Malta?'

'She is now, yes. Or . . . ah. Hm. You did not know she was coming?'

'You say she came in on that convoy two days ago?' And has made no effort to contact me, he thought. What the devil is she playing at now?

'No, no,' Jardine said, clearly now as confused as himself. 'That convoy lost four ships to enemy action. Your mother's was one of them.'

'Oh, my God!'

'Quite. Absolutely. But she was picked up, by a destroyer, and came in this morning. There were four women on a life raft. And, one of the survivors is a lady who we are told is the Dowager Lady Eversham. She would be your mother, wouldn't she?'

Duncan stared at him.

'Isn't that a great relief?'

'It is a great relief, sir.' Or it would be, he thought, if I had known she was missing in the first place. And . . . he looked at his watch. 'May I ask what time she arrived?'

'About eight this morning.'

'And it is now 1600.'

'I know, my dear fellow. You should have been informed immediately. But you see, she had no identification.'

'Sir?'

'She, and her companion, had only the clothes in which they were found, and—'

'Did you say, companion, sir? Oh, my God! Not my wife?' But that was impossible. Alison would never have abandoned Duncan junior for such a crazy, irresponsible adventure. And surely to God she would not have brought the baby with her!

'Oh, no, no. A woman called Strong.'

'Strong,' Duncan muttered. 'Oh, no.'

'You know this woman?'

'Yes, sir, I do.'

'Thank God for that.'

'And you are saying that Mrs Strong and my mother were in this life raft together?' But they hate each other, he thought.

'Indeed. With a couple of nurses. Now, the point is, this Strong person claims to be a US government official. And it so happens that the brass here were, are, expecting someone of that name.'

Duncan scratched his head.

'Absolutely,' Jardine agreed. 'She claims to be the woman they are expecting, but she cannot prove it.'

'Just as the other woman is claiming to be Lady Eversham.'

'No, no. She is not claiming to be anyone, at this time. It was the nurses she was with who identified her as Lady Eversham, but when asked how they knew this, all they could say was that they had been told by the purser of the ship in which they were sailing, and he, poor chap, seems to have drowned, along with all of the officers. So the people here are both confused and worried. If these people are not who they claim, well . . .'

'Yes, sir,' Duncan said wearily. 'Am I allowed to see my mother?'

'Of course you must see her. That is what we want, why I sent for you. You see, while the police were puzzling what to do about the situation, I mean, two women both with possibly very high profiles but without a shred of identification to back up their claims, someone suddenly remembered that there was, right here in Valetta, a naval officer named Lord Eversham, so they contacted me. And I sent for you.'

And you could have told me that in one sentence instead of wasting half an hour, Duncan thought. 'Of course, sir. I hope you are not telling me that my mother is in a police cell?' That is, he thought, presuming it is still standing.

'Oh, no, no. Nothing like that. She's in hospital.'

'You said she's all right.'

'I believe she's all right. But twenty-four hours in a life raft, with no food and no water, and no shelter, well . . .'

'Yes, sir. If you'll excuse me.'

The Mission

'Lieutenant-Commander Lord Eversham,' the nurse said, looking up appreciatively from her notes. 'This gentleman is waiting for you.'

Duncan turned to survey the crowded hospital waiting room, and the man who had just got up and was coming towards him. He was definitely not Maltese, but he was wearing a lounge suit rather than a uniform, which was surprising. 'Lord Eversham? John Edwards. My card.'

Duncan looked at the piece of cardboard, frowned, and the man touched his lips. 'Not here, please, milord. Shall we go up? There is an elevator.'

He escorted Duncan to the lift, but before the doors closed they were joined by three other people, and could do no more than gaze at each other. They reached the third floor, and followed another corridor, past busy wards and bustling nurses, to gain a lobby, occupied by a sister, seated at a desk . . . and another man wearing a lounge suit, who rose at their appearance.

Duncan could keep quiet no longer. 'Am I allowed to ask what is going on?' he inquired. 'Is this chap MI6 as well?'

'Yes, he is,' Edwards said. 'As to what is going on, we would like you to help us ascertain that.'

'I came here to see my mother.'

'Quite. Lady Eversham is in this private ward, just beyond that door. She is sharing it with the lady who was in the life raft with her. All we require from you is confirmation that it is Lady Eversham, but more importantly, we are told that you can identify the other lady.'

'Well, I can't do that until I see them, can I?'

'Of course,' Edwards said, smoothly. 'Sister.'

She got up and went to the inner door.

'But before I see them,' Duncan said, 'I would like you to tell me why they are under arrest.'

'They are not under arrest, milord. We are merely protecting them until their identity is established.'

'Protecting them from whom? Or what?'

'Like you, sir, I only obey my orders.'

'I see. Just tell me, what happens if I am unable to identify them?'

'Well, sir, that would be a different matter. But . . . you *are* going to identify them, aren't you?' He was anxious.

'Sister.'

She had been waiting patiently. Now she rapped gently, and then opened the door. 'Lady Eversham? You son is here.'

'I should think so too,' Kristin remarked.

The nurse looked at Duncan and waggled her eyebrows, questioningly.

'Par for the course,' Duncan assured her, and entered the ward.

This was a bright and airy room, with an open window allowing fresh air to ruffle the flowers in the vase on the table. There were two beds, and both women were sitting up. They wore bed gowns and their hair had been neatly brushed, but . . .

'Mother?' Duncan kissed her cheek, and wiped cream from his lips. 'What happened to you?'

'Don't you know what happened to me?'

'I know your ship was sunk. But this stuff on your face . . .?'

'That is a cream which they hope will counter the worst effects of my sunburn. I spent twenty-four hours in a rubber dinghy with no protection from the elements. So did Rebecca.'

Duncan moved towards the other bed, hesitated. 'Mrs Strong?'

'My name is Rebecca.' Rebecca pointed out. 'And aren't you going to kiss me as well?'

Duncan obeyed, and she gave him a tissue to wipe away some more cream. Standing between the two beds, he looked from one to the other. 'But you're both all right?'

'Of course we're not both all right,' Kristin said. 'In addition to being roasted for twenty-four hours . . .'

'Actually,' Rebecca said, 'It was only twelve hours. The other twelve were in darkness, or before the sun got hot.'

'As I was saying,' Kristin went on, 'in addition to being roasted alive for twenty-four hours, we had nothing to eat and nothing to drink in that time, either. And these beastly people won't allow us anything solid to eat yet, or anything except milk and mush and water to drink. I wish you to sort that out, Duncan. Explain to them that I am a carnivore who will become very angry if I do not get a fillet steak in the near future, and that I am also used to a glass of sherry every morning, a glass of whisky every evening, and a glass of champagne with my dinner. I only drink Bollinger.'

'I'll see what I can do.'

'What you can also do,' Kristin pointed out, 'is get us out of here, and to a boutique or something: we have no clothes save what we were wearing when the ship went down. And they're not in good shape either.'

'My shirt is torn,' Rebecca explained.

'We have also lost all our identification, and all our money,' Kristin continued. 'And please find out if those two girls are all right.'

'What two girls?'

'Elizabeth and Audrey. I cannot remember their surnames. They were in the raft with us, but were taken off somewhere when we arrived.'

'Were they service personnel?'

'They were nurses.'

'I imagine they've gone to a military hospital. I'll check it out. Now you must just relax, Mother. Everything will be taken care of,' Duncan said, 'after you tell me, and the gentlemen waiting outside . . .' he glanced over his shoulder; the door was ajar, so Edwards was undoubtedly hearing every word.

As Kristin had realized. 'Are they gentlemen?' she asked. 'I think we need proof.'

Duncan sighed. 'They are the ones who require proof, Mother. This I can provide. But they also want to know what you are doing here. So do I.'

'I suspect that they already know what I am doing here,' Rebecca said. 'All they want is to be sure is that it is me.'

Duncan looked at his mother.

'I'm with her,' Kristin explained. 'Well, I couldn't let her make such a dangerous journey on her own.'

'She also wanted to check out her Spanish property,' Rebecca put in. 'Which we have done, and to make sure you were all right.'

'So you just packed a few things and put to sea. And Jimmy let you? Don't either of you realize there is a war on? And from our point of view, this is the centre of it?'

'Jimmy Lonsdale is history,' Kristin announced.

'What? You're engaged.'

'Not any more. He is now engaged to Rebecca.'

'What?'

'That's just an idea of your mother's,' Rebecca said. 'I doubt he even remembers what I look like, much less who I am.'

He remembers what you look like, Duncan thought, if only from the neck down. He took refuge in what he considered to be the pertinent issue. 'He still should never have let you come on a jaunt like this.'

'Ah,' Kristin said. 'He doesn't know. Actually, he probably does know by now. I told Alison not to tell him until there was no question of him stopping me. She may have done so by now.'

'You have involved Alison in this?'

'Well, she had to know.'

He glared at her, then decided not to say what first came into his mind. 'Well, I have to work on getting you out of here. Although I'm not sure where you are going to go. Those hotels which are still standing are pretty full. I'll be in touch in a little while.' He bent over his mother for a kiss and the door opened wide.

'May I come in?' Edwards asked.

'You are in,' Kristin pointed out.

'Well, you see, I need to speak with Mrs Strong, urgently.'

'So speak.'

'In private.'

'That is obviously impossible. But you can speak, anyway. We have no secrets from each other. Not now.'

*   *   *

'Are all your people stuffed shirts?' Rebecca asked, closing the bedroom door behind herself.

'To be official, in this day and age, you have to be a stuffed shirt.' Kristin stood in the middle of the floor surrounded by boxes and clothes; it was not a large room, but it was the best Duncan had been able to find, and it was in the best hotel Valetta still had to offer. 'You know, I understand that these people are having a rough time, but this selection is appalling. And there is not a mink to be had for love or money.'

Rebecca, who was still wearing the shirt and slacks in which she had been shipwrecked, although freshly laundered, and darned – she was also carrying an armful of parcels which she now deposited beside Kristin's – surveyed the chaos. 'I don't suppose there's a lot of call for furs in this climate.'

'It's the principle of the thing. How did your meeting go?'

'It was somewhat chilly. I had to tell them that as far as shipping our tanks through the Med to get here en route to Alexandria was concerned, my verdict would have to be negative.'

'That must have gone down like a lead balloon. So how do the tanks get to Alexandria?'

'It'll have to be round the Cape of Good Hope and up the Red Sea and the Suez Canal.'

'Won't that take a very long time?'

'A week or two longer. But at least most of them will get there.'

'And they were happy with that?'

'No. But it's my decision.'

'So what happens now?'

'They're arranging for me to go on to Cairo just as quickly as possible.'

'You mean you're going to risk another sea voyage?'

'No way. I'm flying.'

'Is that safer?'

'It has to be better than being sunk again. The third time might not be so lucky.'

'I thought you said that lightning—'

'Forget it. I may not be torpedoed or bombed again, but

I'm sure those bastards will think up some way of getting at me. So, it may be goodbye in the near future. Anyway, the good news is that I saw the girls.'

'And?'

'They're recovering well. They send you their love.'

'How sweet.' Kristin sat on the bed. 'Well, we knew we were going to be separated.'

'Yes. I'm sorry. Rubbing shoulders with you has been great fun.'

'And for me, too. Despite your inhibitions.'

'But you're staying with Duncan. For how long? He could be here for months. Maybe years.'

'Yes. Well, I have one or two things to do.'

'In Malta?'

'Why not?'

Rebecca sat beside her. 'Duncan really isn't in the frame, is he?'

'I have no idea what you are talking about.'

'Kristin, darling, you have come more than two thousand miles, at the risk of your life, to be with your son. We have now been in Malta for two days, and we have dined with him once. You haven't even been to look at his boat.'

'Well, I've been shopping, haven't I?'

Rebecca regarded her for several moments. 'I really thought we had become friends. Confidantes.'

'Oh, we are. Definitely. You are going to marry my fiancé, remember?'

'Just tell me what's going on. Your real reason for being here.'

'Ah –' there was a rap on the door – 'I'll get it.' She got up and hurried across the room, opened the door.

'I wish you to know that I have done as you wished, milady,' the bellboy said.

'Thank you. Was there a reply?'

'The gentleman said to thank you, milady.'

'And?'

'That was all he said.'

'Shit!'

'Milady?'

'Just an expression. Forget it.'

'The gentleman was in company when I saw him,' the bellboy explained.

'Ah. Yes. I understand. Just a moment.' She went to the table, carefully avoiding looking at Rebecca, opened her new handbag, and gave him a handful of notes, recently supplied by Duncan, as he had paid for her new clothes, and for those of Rebecca, when she had been able to spare the time to go shopping. As she did so . . . 'What in the name of God is that racket?'

'It is the air raid siren, milady. You, and the other lady, should go to the shelter. It is in the basement.'

'At least,' Rebecca remarked, as they sat together in the midst of a cluster of hotel guests and staff, listening to the bangs and crashes and explosions from above them, 'we can't be sunk.'

'The next time I get close to an aeroplane,' Kristin said, 'I am going to throw a rock at it.'

'Just make sure it's not the one I'm travelling to Cairo on. What's that?'

'The all-clear, madam,' said the man seated close by. 'Let's hope the hotel is still standing.'

'Shit!' Kristin said. 'All of those clothes, lying on the bed!'

There was dust and smoke everywhere, but the hotel had not been hit on this occasion, and they found the bedroom exactly as they had left it.

'There's a relief,' Rébecca said. 'Now, we simply have to get ready for tonight. Let's see what you bought.'

'Tonight? I haven't bought anything for tonight. Specifically.'

'Oh, don't tell me you've forgotten we're invited to dinner at Government House? I found this rather attractive green thing. It's nice and slinky.' She opened a large paper bag she had left lying on the bed, took out the deep green silk gown. 'Voila! And the accessories.' She waved the gloves, handbag and shoes. 'Must keep the natives happy.'

'I'm sure they'll be very happy.'

'Well, show me yours.'

'I told you, I didn't buy one.'

'What?'

'I'm not going. You'll have to offer my apologies.'

'You mean you are declining an invitation to dinner at Government House? He's a sir.'

'So? I'm a lady. That is my title,' she added, modestly.

'He's the king's representative.'

'There is some doubt as to whether I actually have a king, at this moment,' Kristin pointed out. 'Only a dictator.'

'But . . . don't you have an English passport?'

'I do. I also have a Spanish passport and a Swedish passport. Actually, the word is had; they are all at the bottom of the sea.'

'If you don't come,' Rebecca said, 'you won't be invited again.'

'That will be a great relief.'

'And you'll be socially ostracized.'

'My darling Rebecca, I have been socially ostracized all of my adult life. For that to change now would probably give me a heart attack.'

'Oh, you are impossible –' Rebecca pointed – 'it's to do with that message you got, isn't it? Which was a reply to one you sent.'

'As a matter of fact, yes. And it's all worked out rather well, don't you see, with you going to spend the evening wassailing with the local aristocracy. Just don't hurry back. Go for a midnight swim or something.'

Rebecca stared at her. 'You . . . have invited someone to come here this evening?'

'I don't know if he'll come, mind. There was no actual reply.'

'A man?'

'Well, of course he's a man. I told you, I only go for women when there are no men around.'

'You have a lover! Here in Malta?'

'There wouldn't be much point in coming all this way if he wasn't.'

'I think you could at least tell me who it is? As I'm in on the secret anyway. Is it someone I know?'

Kristin considered. Then shrugged. 'In view of what you have told me about your chaste views on life, I would say that he is someone you know better than anyone else in England.'

Rebecca's mouth slowly opened as the penny dropped. 'I don't believe it.'

'That's up to you.'

She contradicted herself. 'But . . . I mean . . . how long has this been going on?'

'Jamie has been my lover for more than two years.'

'But . . . the admiral . . .?'

'I told you, that was a spur of the moment thing, that I rapidly realized was a mistake.'

'And you came all this way, and at such a risk . . .?'

'To be with Jamie? Wouldn't you? No, I don't suppose you would.'

Rebecca sat on the bed. 'I just don't know what to say.'

Kristin sat beside her and kissed her on the cheek. 'Then don't say anything. Just remember not to say anything to anyone else, either.'

Duncan stood on the dock and gazed at the smoking wreck. 'Who was on board?'

'Cawthray and Smart,' Matthews said, miserably.

'Well, I suppose that was better than if you'd all been there.'

'It's bloody fortunate that the rest of us didn't go up with her,' Beattie commented.

Duncan nodded. 'They are just going to have to give us permission to leave the harbour and disperse every time there's a warning.'

'With respect, sir, that would involve putting to sea at least once in every day, just about,' Wilcox commented.

'We'd at least be alive. And probably more importantly, our boats would still be afloat,' Duncan pointed out. 'Mr Matthews, see what you can do about replenishing your people's gear. I'll see Captain Jardine about accommodation pending repatriation.'

'Can't we remain with the flotilla, sir?'

'There aren't going to be any replacement boats.'

'I realize that, sir. But you may need replacement crews. And we can back up the shore maintenance.'

Duncan considered, and Beattie muttered. 'Here's the captain, now.'

Jardine hurried along the dock, stood with his hands on his hips, surveying the scene. 'There's bloody bad luck. Any casualties?'

'Two ratings, sir,' Duncan said.

'Damnation! Any other damage.' He looked pointedly at *412*, which had been nearest to the sunken vessel.

'We're checking now.' And at that moment Cooper, Rawlings and Jamie emerged on deck. 'Report.'

'Tight as a drum, sir,' Cooper said. 'The blast seems to have gone mainly upwards.'

'There's a relief,' Jardine said, 'And the others are all right?'

'Yes, sir,' Beattie said.

'So we still have a flotilla, even if it's only four boats,' Jardine commented. 'We may have a big job coming up in the near future.' The officers looked expectant. 'All in good time. It's top secret. There's a bigwig on his way from England to discuss it, see if it's practical. You'll be put in the picture then.' He turned to Matthews. 'I imagine you'll be glad to get home.'

'With respect, sir...' Matthews looked at Duncan for support.

'Sub-Lieutenant Matthews would like to remain with the flotilla, sir.'

'He no longer has a boat.'

'We may suffer casualties, which he and his crew could replace. Trained men, sir.'

Jardine looked at the assembled sailors. 'His people would be happy with this?'

'They want to stay, sir,' Matthews said.

'Very good. I'll have to square it with the admiral, but for the time being, you remain members of the flotilla. I think your people deserve liberty tonight, Lieutenant-Commander.'

'Thank you, sir. May I have a word?'

Jardine jerked his head, and Duncan followed him out of earshot. 'Well?'

'About tonight, sir. Do I have to attend?'

'Of course you do. An invitation to dine at Government House is a command. Besides, your mother will be there.'

'I'm afraid I won't be very good company.'

'Oh, come now. You've surely suffered casualties before. What about Lieutenant Partridge and his entire crew?'

'We don't actually know, as yet, if they are dead. But in any event, we certainly did not go out to dinner that night, and drink champagne and engage in puerile small talk.'

'Having an elaborate dinner, drinking champagne, and indulging in puerile chat is as good a panacea for grief as there is. Besides, it is our duty, always to present to the public an unflappable, totally confident exterior, no matter what the circumstances. Didn't they teach you that at Dartmouth?'

'I never went to Dartmouth.' Duncan confessed.

'Ah.' Jardine glanced at his sleeve. 'Of course. I had forgotten. Well, you come along tonight and drown your sorrows. You'll feel better for it.'

'What we're going to do,' Morrison said, 'is see if we can find that nipper who had girls available.'

'Aye-aye,' Lowndes agreed enthusiastically. 'Getting damn near blown up always has me raring to go.'

'Count me in,' Jackman agreed. 'Even if we do get the clap.'

'Jamie?'

'I think I'll skip this one, Mr Morrison.'

'Now, Jamie, you can't let something like this afternoon get you down. It's a fact of life, when you're in a war. The skipper's off to GH tonight, and you can bet he's not going to be weeping into his beer.'

'Champagne,' Lowndes corrected.

'Eh?'

'That's what they drink at Government House. Champagne.'

'Well, there you go. Jamie?'

'I'm sorry, Mr Morrison. I'm just not in the mood. I'd be a wet blanket.'

Morrison studied him for several moments, then nodded. 'All right, laddie. No one's forcing you. There'll be a next time, when you're feeling better.'

The three men went off together, muttering to each other. Undoubtedly discussing him, Jamie thought, wondering at his sudden lack of spunk.

If they only knew! But did he know himself, what he was

doing. She was here! All the waiter had given him was the name of the hotel, and the room number. And the words, After eight. But she was here. He couldn't imagine what might have happened to bring her all this way, and at such a risk. Kristin, drifting around the Mediterranean in a rubber dinghy! It was impossible to visualize.

After eight. In a posh hotel. Did he dare take the risk? But if he did not, he was indeed a coward . . . and he would regret it for the rest of his life.

He was really scared when he entered the hotel lobby at five to eight. He had spent the previous ten minutes standing across the street, making up his mind to take the vital step. He could not imagine what he would do, if someone took exception to the sight of a common sailor entering such obviously expensive portals . . . cut and run, or face it out?

He would be carrying a message. That was it. A message from his skipper to his mother. No one could object to that. But . . . the skipper was going to dinner at Government House! Surely Kristin would be going too? Was she just teasing him, making a fool of him? Would even Kristin come all this way to play such a cruel trick?

In any event, there was only one way to find out. And having come so far . . . he crossed the street. A few heads turned, but no one attempted to stop him as he parted the blackout curtains and walked confidently through the lobby to the elevator. This was empty, and he rode up alone to the fourth floor. This corridor also was empty, and a few minutes later he was rapping on the door of the designated bedroom, and was in Kristin's arms.

She kicked the door shut while kissing him, but when he managed to get his mouth free he had to say, 'Milady . . .'

'Looking over one's shoulder is always a mistake,' she said. 'Except for the purpose of avoiding future mistakes. I wish you to forgive me for that moment of madness. Can you?'

'I can forgive you anything, milady. But . . . which mistake?'

Kristin released him, took off her dressing gown – she wore nothing underneath – and got into bed. 'They were both aspects of the same mistake.'

He sat on the bed beside her, caressed her shoulders and breasts.

'Your face is peeling.'

'It is awful, isn't it? Are you going to stop wanting me?'

'Oh, milady –' he hugged her – 'when I think of you being torpedoed—'

'I was bombed. Actually, I think that was worse.'

He hugged her. 'If you had died . . .'

'I didn't. And it was an experience. That is what life is all about, experiences.'

'So what happens now?'

She pulled her head back. 'I beg your pardon.'

'I meant, about the admiral.'

'The admiral is history. As I said, the whole thing was a mistake. Jamie . . . do you remember me saying that I wanted to have you in a bed?'

'For a whole night,' he said dreamily.

'Well, I'm not sure we can quite manage that, tonight. But I have travelled two thousand miles, and been sunk, to reach this position. I don't think we want to waste it.'

'Mother is all right, is she?' Duncan asked, steering Rebecca to one side of the crowded drawing room.

'Ah. Well. She's feeling a little off colour. The sunburn, you know. Perhaps I should have said, she's feeling too much colour.'

'She's put up a monumental black.'

'I have an idea that blacks, whether monumental or not, do not interest your mother.'

He raised his eyes to the ceiling. 'But you, Mrs Strong, if I may say so, look absolutely stupendous, enhanced by your sunburn.'

'It's very nice of you to say so. And it's thanks to your generosity. I will pay you back, I promise. But I thought we were on first name terms.' She looked past him. 'Oh, my God!'

'I'm sorry. Did I . . .' He became aware that people were standing at his elbow.

'Lord Eversham,' the Governor's ADC said, 'I believe you know Admiral Lonsdale.'

Duncan turned, mouth open. 'Admiral . . . . what . . .?'

'Got in this afternoon,' Lonsdale explained.

'By—?'

'I flew. This is a flying visit, eh? Mrs Strong. Rebecca! How good it is to see you again, and looking more beautiful than ever.'

'And you, Admiral,' Rebecca said, faintly. 'You're here—?'

'Military matters,' Lonsdale explained. 'Hush-hush. But then, you also are here on secret matters, I understand. With Lady Eversham.' He glanced left and right.

'Mother isn't here tonight,' Duncan explained.

'But she is in Malta?'

'Oh, yes. But . . . ah . . .' He looked at Rebecca for assistance.

'Sunburn.'

'What?'

'And heat exhaustion.'

'What?'

'If you'll excuse me,' the ADC said, not wishing to become involved in what he could see was a looming crisis. 'I know you old friends have a lot to talk about.'

The admiral ignored him. 'Sunburn? Heat exhaustion? What the devil . . .'

'Well, you see, she had to spend twenty-four hours in a life raft, and was rather overexposed.'

'But she was travelling with you. Wasn't she?'

'Yes. And I was with her. In the raft.'

'Doing what?'

'Well . . . floating about. Getting sunburned.'

Lonsdale looked at Duncan in bewilderment.

'Their ship was bombed, and sunk, you see,' Duncan explained.

'Good God! Why wasn't I informed about this?'

'It only happened a few days ago.'

'And now you say she's ill. I must go to her.'

'Ah,' Rebecca said. 'She's not actually ill. Just not in the mood for dinner parties.'

'But she's all right.'

'Oh, yes. It would take more than a few bombs to ruffle Kristin.'

'I must go to her.'

'You can't possibly leave the party before dinner,' Rebecca pointed out. 'Think of the seating arrangements. And I should think she's in bed by now.' Almost certainly, she reflected.

Lonsdale looked as if he would have protested further, but at that moment the dinner gong went.

Both Rebecca and the admiral were seated near the head of the table, and the governor. Duncan, to his great relief, was well down the other end. Perhaps Lonsdale was here on official business, but that he had also come for Kristin was almost certain. Did she need warning? He doubted it. But neither could he doubt that there was going to be a bust up that would make an Italian air raid seem like a children's tea party.

He tried to catch Rebecca's eye, but she was busy swanning the governor with her charm and her charisma, ignoring not only him but the admiral, seated obliquely opposite her. She was carrying out some agenda of her own. And when the meal finally ended, and the ladies had returned from upstairs while the men finished their port, the admiral grabbed a seat beside her for coffee.

'I really would like to know what happened,' he said.

'We were bombed, and the boat sank. Kristin and I were lucky. There weren't all that many survivors.'

'You know that she wasn't supposed to be there at all.'

'I think that's something you need to discuss with Kristin.'

'You're staying at the same hotel?'

'We're sleeping in the same room. Accommodation is a little limited in this old town. Where are you staying?'

'They're putting me up at the officers' mess. This is a flying visit.'

'So you said. And you figure on taking Kristin back with you?'

'Of course I do.'

'Well, I guess that is also something you'll have to discuss with her, tomorrow.'

'I'm going to be very busy tomorrow. And I'm flying back tomorrow night. I'd like to take you to your hotel and talk with her tonight.'

'She'll be asleep.'

'Then we'll wake her up. This is important. Hello, people are leaving.'

He held her hand to help her to her feet, while her brain was spinning. It was not yet midnight – obviously, with everyone under such stress and so busy, long nights were not on – and Kristin had warned her not to return before then. That meant . . . the risk of total disaster: Kristin might be able to weather any storm, but that poor kid, if the admiral should find him in bed with his fiancée!

'I have a car available,' the admiral said.

Rebecca looked left and right, but there was no sign of Duncan. He had obviously remembered how pally she and the admiral had been on that trip back from Norway and decided to let them get on with it. Shit, shit shit! On the other hand . . . and Kristin would be so pleased.

Lonsdale ushered her into the back seat of the command car, sat beside her, while the driver awaited instructions. 'Which hotel is it?'

Rebecca took a deep breath. 'Jimmy! Do you remember that voyage back from Norway?'

'Well, of course, my dear. It's not something I ever intend to forget.'

'I shall never forget it, either. And now, seeing you again, so unexpectedly . . . I had never expected to see you again, you know.'

'I was always sure we would meet again, some day.'

'And you were right. But it may never happen again. Jimmy, let's spend a little time together.'

'Eh?'

'Tell your driver to take us to the north side of the island, so that we can look at the sea, as we did on that trip.'

'Ah . . . you heard the lady, driver.'

'Aye-aye, sir.' He engaged gear and they drove out of the city.

Rebecca rested her head on the admiral's shoulder. 'Do you think I am being foolishly romantic?'

'Of course not. But— .'

'Do you like romantic women?'

'Well, I . . . ah . . . I don't really know any. I mean . . .'

'Oh, I know. Kristin isn't romantic. She is the ultimate realist.'

'Yes. But you do realize, well . . .'

'That you are engaged. I told you that was what you should do, remember?'

'Well, you said it might be a good idea.'

'Oh,' she said, sitting up. 'Isn't that beautiful!'

The car had stopped on a bluff in between two clearly manned watchtowers, overlooking the sea, and the moonlight was streaming across the water.

'What's out there?'

'Well, I suppose, Sicily. But it's sixty miles away.'

'Only sixty miles?'

'This is called the Sicilian Channel. It's about the narrowest part of the Mediterranean. After the Straits of Gibraltar, of course.'

'Can we take a walk?'

'Well . . .'

'The driver can wait a few minutes, can't he?'

'Certainly, madam,' the driver said. 'If the admiral wishes it. But I should point out that this is a restricted area, and we are likely to be run in.'

'Pooh. This is an admiral. Please wish it, Jimmy. I'm beginning to feel like Cinderella.'

'It's quite chilly out. And you haven't a wrap.'

'You can put your arm round me.'

He hesitated, but she was already out of the car. 'Blow your horn if there's any trouble.'

'Aye-aye, sir.'

The admiral followed Rebecca, tentatively put his arm round her shoulders; again she rested her head against him. 'You're shivering,' he said.

'It's colder than I thought. Maybe I'm still suffering from exposure.'

'Then we'd better go back.'

'No, please. You could let me use your jacket. Until we go back.'

'Ah . . . yes, of course.'

He took off his shell jacket and wrapped it round her shoulders.

'Gee, that feels good. I'd love to go to Sicily,' she said. 'Will you take me there, after we've won the war?'

'Eh?'

'We are going to win the war, aren't we?'

'Well, of course we are. But there's a good way to go yet. And, well...'

'You're worried about Kristin.'

'Well . . .'

'When one is floating around in a rubber dinghy, expecting to die, one is inclined to share confidences. Even Kristin.'

'I'm not sure I know what you mean,' he said uneasily.

'Kristin feels that she inveigled you into proposing. That for you to marry her would be a mistake. She is, well, I suppose we should say, a wild child. Or a wild woman, now, I suppose. She's not going to change, because she doesn't want to change. Is that very upsetting, you having come all this way to get her back?'

'I didn't actually come all this way to get her back.'

Rebecca raised her head. 'You didn't?'

'I told you, I'm here on a professional matter. But as I knew she might be in Malta, I did intend to take her back, yes. And frankly, I wasn't looking forward to it.'

Rebecca stopped walking. 'I seem to have lost something.'

'Well, you see, I have an unpleasant duty to perform. Or actually, an unpleasant decision to make.'

'And you feel it will upset Kristin. Therefore it is something to do with Duncan.'

'I really would not like to pursue this. It's top secret.'

'I get you. Do you have the time?'

He looked at his wristwatch. 'Just coming up to one.'

'Then I suppose we could be getting back. My tits are frozen. But you mustn't disturb Kristin. And no matter what happens, if you're around when this business is over, I mean, the whole thing, I really would like to explore Sicily with you.'

'I think we want to leave that until the war is over.'

'You're so practical,' she agreed. 'Now tell me, when are you going to be knighted?' She cocked her head. 'What's that noise?'

'That,' the admiral said, 'Is my driver, blowing his horn. Urgently.'

The knock on the door woke Jamie. 'What—'

'You were sleeping,' Kristin explained.

'Oh, milady . . .'

'I didn't wake you, because that is what I wanted, to lie beside you in a bed, and listen to you snore.'

'Do I snore?'

'Very gently. Very sweetly.'

There was another knock, more peremptorily.

'Jesus!' he said. 'What time is it?'

Kristin stretched out her arm and lifted the clock on the bedside table. 'Three.'

'*What!*'

'I'd better see who that is.' She threw back the sheet and got out of bed.

'But—'

'Don't worry. I'm not going to admit anyone who could possibly be hostile.' She went to the door.

'But aren't you going to put something on?'

'Being greeted by a naked woman always throws the opposition,' she explained. 'Especially if he happens to be an admiral.'

'Oh, my God!' Jamie sank beneath the sheet.

Kristin opened the door.

'Kristin! Well, really . . .' Rebecca said.

'Are you alone?'

'Of course I'm alone.'

'Then you may come in. That must have been one hell of a party.'

Rebecca entered the room, pushing hair from her eyes. 'I,' she announced, 'have just come from the police station.'

Kristin closed and locked the door. 'I've never been associated with a criminal before,' she said. 'I'm not sure it's good for my image.'

'Oh . . .' Rebecca gazed at the bed. Only Jamie's head was visible. 'Oh, good Lord!'

'You do know each other,' Kristin reminded her. 'As I understand it, very well.'

Jamie sat up. 'Good evening, Mrs Strong.'

Rebecca sat in the one chair.

'Now tell us,' Kristin invited, 'of what crime have you been convicted?'

'Of course I have not been convicted. I was with the admiral.'

'At three o'clock in the morning, being arrested. I think that is probably grounds for a divorce. It is certainly grounds for breaking an engagement.'

'It was not like that at all.'

'That's what they all say,' Kristin pointed out.

'We were walking, on the cliffs, and it was apparently a restricted area. And these MPs suddenly popped up and arrested us. They were terribly officious. They wouldn't believe that Jimmy was an admiral, even after he was identified by his driver. So they took us all off to the police station. Jimmy was absolutely furious.'

'And frustrated,' Kristin suggested. 'But why wouldn't they believe that he was an admiral? Wasn't he in uniform?'

'Well . . . yes. But he'd taken his dinner jacket thing off.'

'For you to lie on?'

'To put round my shoulders,' Rebecca said, primly. 'I was cold.'

'What an exciting life you lead. Well . . .'

'I think I had better be off, milady,' Jamie suggested.

'Don't tell me you're going to be arrested, too?'

'Well, no. I was given the night off. But . . . well . . .' He looked at Rebecca.

'Of course,' Kristin agreed. 'If she gets in with us, you could be distracted. Ah, well . . . tomorrow night?'

'Well . . .' He looked at Rebecca.

'Oh, don't mind me,' Rebecca said. 'I won't be here. I'm flying out at six. My God! That's only fifteen hours away. I have got to get some sleep.'

Jamie got out of bed, and Kristin took him in her arms for a long kiss. 'Now the entire trip is worthwhile,' she said. 'Tomorrow night.'

'If I can, milady.'

'You can and you will. I'll be here. All night.'

'Well . . .' He reached for his pants.

'Hey,' Rebecca said. 'Don't I get a kiss as well? Seeing as how we're all in this together?'

Jamie looked at Kristin.

'Oh, give her a treat. I suspect she's had a frustrating evening. But I would put your pants on first.'

'No way,' Rebecca said. 'I believe in payment in kind.'

'Come in, Lieutenant-Commander,' Captain Jardine invited. 'I'd like you to meet Admiral Berkeley. Admiral Lonsdale I believe you already know.'

Duncan shook hands with the two men, somewhat apprehensively; he had never been in the same room with two admirals before: he could not imagine what had brought about this honour . . . or was he about to be court-martialled? Even Jimmy Lonsdale was looking exceedingly grim. What could Mother have got up to now?

'Sit down, Commander,' Berkeley invited, and Duncan took the straight chair in the centre of the room, placing his cap on his knees. 'We have invited you here this morning,' Berkeley said, 'because we are faced with a critical and potentially disastrous situation.'

Duncan could only wait.

'Tell us what you know of the *Napoli*?'

'She is Italy's latest battleship. Or she will be, when she is completed.'

'She is completed, Commander.'

Duncan gulped.

'At present she is in Brindisi, and we are informed by our agents that she is about to begin her sea trials, in the Adriatic. Now, her specifications are obviously top secret, and we have been unable to access them, but we do know that the Italians were given copies of the plans for *Bismarck* and *Tirpitz*. How much of this know-how they have used is uncertain, but shore observations by our agents indicate that she is bigger than any other unit in the Italian fleet, and therefore bigger by some distance than any capital ship we presently have in this area. Now, we may remember *Bismarck* and feel that we will get the bugger eventually. However, conditions are completely different here to what they were in the North Atlantic last year. *Bismarck* was hundreds of miles from any port of refuge, and completely lacked either a destroyer screen or air cover, and as I am sure you remember, it was air attack that crippled her rudder and left her helpless. *Napoli* will never be operating more than a couple of hundred miles from a base, and she will have all the support that she requires, once she begins operations. If Mussolini can add her to his Littorios, we would be faced with an overwhelming force.

'Now, obviously, we have to stop her completing her trials. And again, obviously, air attack would seem the answer. After all, two years ago we sank two battleships in Taranto. But frankly, that was a stroke of luck. It was a surprise attack, there was limited anti-aircraft protection, and the Luftwaffe were not involved. And because of the shallowness of the harbour, no one at that time considered that an attack with torpedoes was feasible. Well, we proved that it was feasible, and as you know, the Japanese developed the idea with devastating effect at Pearl Harbor. As a result, every navy in the world is aware of the risks of air attack in harbour, whether from bombs or torpedoes, and is prepared for it. A week ago, as soon as we discovered where she was, we launched an air strike. The enemy was waiting for us and of eighteen planes only six returned; they did not score a single hit. We can see no reason why any further strikes will be more successful.

'Well, then, surface craft. Unfortunately, owing to various mishaps, we have no surface craft capable at this moment of taking on *Napoli* in a gun battle, and in addition, we know that the Strait of Otranto is mined from one side to the other. This rules out the use of submarines, as well. One tried to get through a fortnight ago, and has not been heard of since. Surface craft would have even less chance of making it, supposing they weren't blown out of the water by enemy aircraft before they got within range. However, the mines are mainly contact, and are moored ten feet beneath the surface.' He paused to stare at Duncan.

'I understand, sir. You consider that a motor boat drawing only four feet and made of wood, could get over the obstructions.'

'Do you think it can be done?'

'We could certainly have a go.'

'Ahem,' Lonsdale remarked.

The other men turned their heads to look at him.

'It's not on.'

'Sir?' Duncan asked.

'Perhaps you can get through the minefield. But do you seriously suppose that you will be allowed to get within torpedo range of the battleship? You'd be sunk before you got within ten miles of her, either by her own guns, or by the Brindisi defences, or by aircraft.'

Berkeley looked at Duncan.

'If you will excuse me, sir.' Duncan got up, went to the huge chart of the Mediterranean pinned to the wall, and took the dividers from the table beneath it. 'It is about four hundred miles from Valetta to the bottom of the Adriatic. That is to say, ten hours at full speed. And then another hour or so to Brindisi. If we left here at 1800, we could do the entire journey in darkness, and carry out the attack at dawn.'

'Brilliant!' Berkeley cried, and looked at Lonsdale.

'And you seriously think that you can sink a ship like *Napoli* with two eighteen-inch torpedoes?'

'We'd use the whole flotilla,' Berkeley said.

'Which I understand is now down to four boats.'

'That should be sufficient to do the trick. *Napoli* doesn't actually have to be sunk. If she could just be put out of action for a few months, that would give us the time, perhaps to get a KGV battleship down here to sort things out.'

'All very pat,' Lonsdale said. 'So tell me this: it may well be possible for the flotilla to get into the Adriatic under cover of darkness. It may even be possible for them to score a couple of hits. But it will then be broad daylight with another ten hours of broad daylight to come. How are the boats supposed to get back here under attack from an enemy who will by then be fully activated?'

'Well, of course, there is a risk involved. There is a risk in any military operation.'

'That isn't a risk. It's a cast iron certainty. None of them will get back. Four boats, sixty-eight men.'

'A single destroyer,' Berkeley said quietly, 'would be over two hundred men.'

The two admirals glared at each other.

'I was sent here,' Lonsdale said, 'because since the beginning of this war the MTBs have been my particular responsibility. I am therefore required by their lordships to determine the feasibility of this scheme, and report my opinion. I am bound to tell you, Admiral Berkeley, that I do not regard the plan as in any way feasible. You are sending these men and their boats to almost certain death.'

'Have you the power to forbid the exercise?'

Lonsdale sighed. 'You are in command, here on the ground. I can do no more than give you my professional opinion, and copy that opinion to the Admiralty.'

'I accept your criticism and your reservations. However, the matter is too urgent for us to wait on a final judgement from their lordships. I have discussed the situation with Admiral Cunningham, who as you know is our supreme commander here in the Mediterranean, and he agrees with me that our situation would become very nearly untenable were the *Napoli* to be allowed to complete her trials and combine with the three Littorio class battleships Mussolini already has in commission. To prevent that happening, with the very likely consequence of Italy being able to dominate this area, which would almost certainly entail the loss of Malta, any risk must be run, and every sacrifice considered necessary should be made.'

Lonsdale swallowed.

'However,' Berkeley went on, 'I am willing to leave the last word to Commander Eversham. Just now, Commander, you expressed the opinion that the venture was feasible. You have now heard the professional opinion of Admiral Lonsdale that it is not. Would you care to reconsider your opinion?'

Duncan looked from face to face. He knew Jimmy was right, that he would be leading his men, or most of them, to almost certain death. But if they could cripple or even seriously damage the super-battleship, it would be a great victory. And if even one boat got back, it would be a triumph.

Both admirals had been studying his face. Now Berkeley added, 'It goes without saying that your crews must all be volunteers.'

Duncan took a deep breath. 'They will volunteer, sir.'

The Hazard

'Thank you, Commander,' Admiral Berkeley said. 'As of this moment, that is your rank. Now, obviously speed and secrecy are paramount. When can you sail?'

'My boats are fully fuelled, sir. We can sail tonight.' He grinned. 'And be back tomorrow night.'

'Brilliant. What will you tell your men?'

'That we are required to undertake a vital but most hazardous mission for which they are required to volunteer.'

'And you are quite sure they will do so?'

'I am, sir. But in case anyone does not feel up to it, I have an entire spare crew, from *415*, to draw on.'

'Excellent. Captain Jardine, will you see that Commander Eversham has everything he may require in the way of charts and known enemy dispositions.'

'Aye-aye, sir.'

'Well, then, Commander –' Berkeley held out his hand – 'good luck and good hunting. I look forward to hearing all about it, tomorrow night.'

Lonsdale walked back to the flotilla's moorings with Duncan and Jardine. 'I noticed,' the admiral remarked, 'that you did not exactly endorse Admiral Berkeley's opinion as to the feasibility of this operation.'

'I'm not sure *he* actually claimed it was feasible, sir,' Duncan pointed out. 'Only that it has to be done.'

'Yes,' Lonsdale commented, drily. 'What am I supposed to tell your mother? I'm an old friend of the family,' he explained to Jardine.

Duncan observed that he had not mentioned the fact that he and Kristin were engaged. 'I don't think you should mention it at all until I return. I assume—'

'I am returning to England this evening. Actually we fly to Gibraltar and then on from there.'

'And you're taking Mother with you?'

'I hope to do so, certainly.'

'Sir?'

'I don't think it's something we should discuss at this moment. We'll be in touch as soon as you're back.' He paused on the dock to look down at the four moored boats, and the still evident wreckage of *415*.

'Will you come down, sir?' Duncan asked.

'No. I don't think that would be a good idea. I will wish you, and all your people, the very best fortune in the world. If anyone can pull this off, you're the man.'

Duncan shook hands. 'Captain?'

'I'll come down,' Jardine said. 'We need to go over your charts and see if you need anything extra.' He also shook hands with the admiral. 'It's been an honour to meet you, sir. It's only a pity the circumstances couldn't have been more felicitous.'

'I thank you.' Duncan surveyed the assembled crews. 'I thank you all. The operation starts now. That is, all liberty, or contact with anyone beyond the perimeter fence is off limits. I suggest you all turn in and have as much sleep a you can, because the next twenty-four hours are going to be strenuous. We cast of at 1800. Stand down.'

The ratings wandered off, muttering at each other. Duncan did not suppose there was a man amongst them who was not at least apprehensive, although he had done his best to be upbeat about the exercise, stressing their advantages of speed, darkness and surprise, but they all had to understand the risks.

And himself? In these circumstances it was a blessing to be in command, with too much to think about to be scared. It was tantalizing to think that Mother was only a mile away, and he could not say goodbye to her, perhaps for the last time. But then, distance did not matter in these circumstances; it would not have mattered if Alison and Baby Duncan had been in the Valetta hotel with her, he still would not have been able to say goodbye. He simply had to be positive, and assume he was going to come back. However . . .

He clapped Matthews on the shoulder. 'Don't look so glum, Bob. As of 1800 you're in command of this base, at least until we come back. You'll have another boat of your own in the near future.'

'Yes, sir,' Matthews acknowledged. But he still looked desperately unhappy.

As always before an op, the skippers assembled in the mess of *412*. 'You all know the drill,' Duncan told them. 'Absolute radio silence until we're back here tomorrow afternoon, and no boat will show lights. You have your charts, and you know the course. We should be off Taranto at first light; hopefully everyone will be too surprised to react immediately to our appearance, that is, supposing we're observed at all and not mistaken for Bagliettos. Then it should only be another hour or so to Brindisi. There we go in, loose our torpedoes, get the hell out of there again, and return here at full speed. The return trip will have to be made in daylight, and we can expect to be under continuous attack, so we will split up as far apart as we can. One small, fast, motor boat is more difficult to find, and attack, than a flotilla of four. Any questions?' He waited a moment, then said. 'Good luck and Godspeed. We'll have a champagne supper tomorrow night.'

They returned to their boats, and Duncan went down to the engine room. 'We'll be operating at full speed for roughly twenty-four hours, Jamie.'

'She'll cope, sir.'

'I never doubted that. Now you go off and get some rest.' He turned to the door, checked, and turned back. 'You and I have known each other a hell of a long time, Jamie.'

'Yes, sir.'

'And we've had a few experiences together.'

'That we have, sir.'

'So I feel I know you well enough to say . . . this is a tricky one.'

'I kind of suspected that, sir.'

Duncan hesitated, then held out his hand. 'Godspeed, Jamie.'

Jamie squeezed the offered fingers. 'And to you, sir.'

*   *   *

The door closed, but Jamie remained looking at it for several seconds. He doesn't think we're going to make it, he thought. And he has so much more to lose than I. All of that money, the car and the yacht, a beautiful and loving wife, and now a baby as well. Even that adorable dog. But all that matters to him is his duty.

So, that is all that can matter to me, too. Because I am losing something of no less value, as Kristin had told him: the love and desire of a beautiful woman. She had been utterly contrite last night, and both loving and demanding. She had confessed that the idea of marrying Admiral Lonsdale had been an aberration, that she intended to end it before he returned to England, and to remain in Malta for as long as he was stationed here. And she had been looking forward, as had he, to another night together, at the very least. Now that was not going to happen, and she would not know why for at least twenty-four hours. No doubt she would be furious. But if he was not there to explain personally, she would then make preparations for her return to England.

He wondered how she would take the news, of the deaths of the only two men he felt that she had ever loved?

'Excuse me, Lady Eversham,' said the voice on the phone, 'But an Admiral Lonsdale is here to see you.'

'Ah,' Rebecca said. 'Actually, I am not Lady Eversham. But she's right here. Just hold on a moment.' She put her hand over the mouthpiece; Kristin was just emerging from the bathroom, towelling herself. 'Jimmy's here. You have to see him some time.'

'Of course. Now would be best.'

'I hope you're going to put something on.'

Kristin put down the towel and picked up her dressing gown.

'You can't go downstairs in just that.'

'I am not going downstairs at all. He is coming up. Confrontations are always best in private.'

Rebecca sighed and moved her hand. 'Will you ask the admiral to come up?'

'Of course, madam.'

She hung up. 'I'll make myself scarce, shall I?'

'Of course not. You're involved. Aren't you? You never did tell me exactly what happened last night, apart from the fact that he took off his jacket . . . . and the pair of you got yourself arrested for performing an indecent act in public.'

'You know that's not true,' Rebecca said, defensively, 'And you didn't tell me, either.'

'But you could see what *we* had been doing. All I need to know now is whether or not Jimmy is still my fiancé.'

'Well . . . yes.'

'What? You mean, nothing happened at all?'

'Quite a lot happened. But . . . well . . . oh, here he is.' She hurried to the door in response to the knock. 'Jimmy! How nice to see you.'

'She means, again,' Kristin pointed out.

The admiral looked both surprised and apprehensive. 'Rebecca?'

'We share a room, remember?'

'And everything else,' Kristin put in. 'Do come in, Jimmy.'

Lonsdale entered the room, even more apprehensively, and Kristin gestured him to the one chair. She herself sat on the bed, while Rebecca closed the door and used the dressing stool.

'Rebecca tells me you're going back today,' Kristin remarked.

'I take off at six.'

'Quite literally a flying visit. Did you accomplish everything you wanted?'

'Frankly, no.'

'Well, you can't win them all.'

'There's a seat on the plane for you.'

'Now, Jimmy, unlike you, I hate flying visits. As I am sure you know, I had quite a job getting here. So I think I'll hang around a while longer.'

'There's no point in your doing that.'

'I don't know what you mean.'

'I mean it's quite likely that Duncan may not be here much longer.'

'You mean they, he's, being recalled to England? Oh, that's splendid. In which case, I will come with you. If Rebecca has no objections.'

'Rebecca?' He looked at her, flushing.

'Well,' Kristin said. 'I've never been one to muscle in.'

'My God! You mean, you think . . .'

'She's always jumping to conclusions,' Rebecca explained.

'Oh, I . . .' He pulled himself together, clearly reminding himself that he was an admiral, a commander of men. And women. 'Duncan is not being returned to England at this time. He is leaving Malta, very shortly, for a new assignment, and he may not be coming back. I can't tell you anything more than that. It's top secret. So . . .'

'You mean the flotilla is being moved to Alexandria. Why didn't you say so? I'll come with you tonight, Rebecca.'

'I'm not sure there'll be room.'

'Nonsense. They can't stop you travelling with your secretary.'

'I'm supposed to have fired you, remember?'

'But you've realized that you can't do without me. I would get on the phone to them right away and explain the situation.'

Rebecca looked at the admiral.

Lonsdale took a deep breath. 'Kristin, I wish you to come with me.'

'And I have explained that I am not yet ready to return.'

'But I do not wish you to remain in Malta by yourself.'

'Oh, for God's sake! Don't you think I can take care of myself? Anyway, I'm going to Alexandria, with Rebecca.'

'I am sorry. My mind is made up.'

Kristin gave him her most imperious stare. 'It is my mind that matters.'

'Kristin, if you force me, I will go to Government House this afternoon and have an order signed for your deportation.'

Kristin stared at him with her mouth open.

'Jimmy . . .' Rebecca began, uneasily.

'I'm sorry, Rebecca. I'm being forced to it.' He got up. 'A car will call for you at four. Kindly be dressed and waiting. And Kristin, I wouldn't do anything stupid like running off and trying to hide somewhere. Malta is not a very large island, and the police know it far better than you do. You'd simply wind up in a prison cell.'

Kristin pulled off her engagement ring and threw it at him.

*   *   *

'Excuse me, sir –' Cooper hovered in the doorway of Duncan's cabin – 'Captain Jardine is here.'

Duncan had been studying the chart of the Adriatic Sea in conjunction with the *Mediterranean Pilot*. This was obviously the pre-war edition, but he didn't suppose anything much had changed, as regards wind, weather, water depths or wave formations. Brindisi, now, was a different matter. It had been the principal Roman Adriatic port – then known as Brundisium – since before the empire, had seen the ships of Pompey, Caesar, Mark Anthony and Augustus, alongside its piers and wharves. It had greatly expanded since those days, and the *Pilot*, as an English publication, could not be expected to be up to date as regards its more recent fortifications. More than ever their principal weapon would have to be surprise.

But the reappearance of the captain was disconcerting. He stood up. 'Sir?'

'Will you excuse us, Mr Cooper,' Jardine said.

'Sir.'

Cooper left the cabin, and Jardine closed the door.

'There's not too much room, sir,' Duncan commented, and offered him the chair. He sat on the bunk. 'Nothing wrong, I hope.'

'There's nothing particularly right. We've had a message from our agent in Brindisi, in which he states that *Napoli* is preparing to sail. The message is timed six hours ago.'

'But that's excellent news, sir. It means that we may not have to penetrate Brindisi Harbour to get at her.'

'Agreed. But she is supposed to be capable of more than thirty knots. If she sailed six hours ago, she could be up the north end of the Adriatic by now. For you to catch her will involve an extra ten hours at sea, there and back, all in broad daylight, before you even start your return journey.'

'That could be tricky, yes. But if I heard you correctly, sir, your agent estimated that she was *preparing* to leave, six hours ago. It is very unlikely she cast of the moment the message was sent. In fact, if my experience us anything to go by, it takes several hours, except in cases of extreme emergency, for the average battleship to clear port, much less one embarking on a maiden voyage. Nor is it likely that she would begin such a voyage at dusk. My guess would be that she is planning to leave tomorrow morning. This could be to our best advantage, if she has just cleared the harbour when we arrive.'

'Your optimism does you credit, Commander. So tell me what you make of the weather report we have just received, that there are severe storms over Venice and Trieste?'

'Ah. I have just been reading about Adriatic weather. Coming out of Central Europe it can spawn a fierce northerly wind, called the bora, something like the mistral. But because the Adriatic is confined by the Apennines to the west and the Balkan Mountains to the east, and is thus restricted in scope, it gets funnelled and can be quite strong. Of course there isn't sufficient fetch for a big swell, but it can throw up some sharp and quite steep waves. Maybe fifteen or twenty feet.'

'Is that serious for your boats?'

'It should not be, per se. But I suppose it could interfere with our aim, and therefore the effectiveness of our torpedoes.'

'But you're prepared to go ahead, despite these two pieces of rather negative news?'

'Do we have a choice, sir? And as regards getting in and out, a bit of bad weather, which will probably be accompanied by low cloud and rain, could be very helpful to us. I've used the weather before, in Biscay, to get out of a tricky situation.'

'Hm. However, there is one aspect of the situation you haven't mentioned.'

'Sir?'

'A fifteen-foot wave necessarily creates a fifteen-foot trough. The minefield is only ten feet below the surface.'

'Ah. Good point.'

'I think you need to mention that to your commanders.'

'I will do that, sir. But I don't think there is much we can do about it, save hope that the weather doesn't reach the Straits of Otranto until after we pass through it tomorrow morning.'

'And on the way back?'

Duncan grinned. 'We'll have to keep our fingers crossed.'

Jardine regarded him for several seconds, then held out his hand.

Duncan called his skippers together for a last time to put them in the latest picture. 'We will of course have to investigate Brindisi first,' he told them. 'I, as the lead boat, will do that. If I signal Go, follow me in because our target will be there. If I do not signal, or signal Negative, continue your course to the north, spreading out. Our target will be somewhere up there. Again, the operative signal will be Go. Whoever makes that signal will be assumed to be commencing his attack and all other boats will steer to that point.'

Then it was time to prepare for sea. It was just on six and growing dark when he gave the order to cast off, at the same time looking over his shoulder towards the airport from which a plane had just taken off. He wondered if the admiral was on board . . . and if he had Mother with him? And if he had told her what was happening? And what had been her response?

But right now, Mother had to be history. As did Alison and Baby Duncan. 'Cast off, Mr Rawlings,' he said, quietly.

It was a beautiful night, moonless, but also cloudless; the sky was filled with stars. Whatever might be happening over Venice, several hundred miles away, it had not yet reached here.

'Normal watches,' Mr Cooper,' he said, but stayed on the helm until the end of the Second Dog Watch at 2000, when he went below for supper and bed.

He was up again at four, having slept soundly, although at full speed the engine noise was considerable. But the sea remained calm and the movement regular.

'No wind yet, sir,' Rawlings commented, as he took over the Morning Watch from Cooper.

'I don't think we should complain about that, Mr Rawlings.' Duncan swept the northern horizon with his binoculars. They had to be within sixty miles of the Italian coast, but there was no sign of any activity, anywhere. But that thought had to be inspired by apprehension; why should there be any activity? No one knew they were coming, yet.

The darkness was beginning to fade. He looked over his shoulder, saw the other three boats in line astern of him, as ordered; it was his plan to draw any enemy activity in the strait to allow the others to get through.

At forty knots there was always a considerable breeze on the bridge, but now it had definitely freshened, both from the feel of it on his face and the increase in the motion of the boat. While as the darkness faded, he could make out the white horses to either side. But the sea was still no more than slight, perhaps two to three feet, and in another couple of hours they would be through the minefield.

'Sun-up,' Cooper remarked, as a glow spread across the eastern horizon.

Both he and Rawlings were on the bridge, and Rawlings now said, 'Land. Wide to port.'

'Spot on,' Duncan agreed.

The course was north-east by east; he had no intention of closing the shore until it was time to turn up. But that time was nearly on them.

'Land to starboard,' Cooper said.

'Corfu,' Duncan remarked. 'Another fifteen minutes.'

The Strait of Otranto was about forty miles wide.

He thumbed the intercom, 'Report, Jamie.'

'All going well, sir.'

'I am about to alter course, when we shall be just over an hour away from Brindisi. We shall be in the minefield in fifteen minutes. You'll come up then.'

'Aye-aye, sir.'

'All hands, prepare for action stations.'

At this speed, he couldn't risk them on deck, but he wanted everyone in the mess, just in case they touched a mine. Which was a meaningless precaution, he knew: if they touched a mine they would go up like a firecracker.

'Altering course, now,' he said, and carefully eased the helm to port. 'Check astern, Mr Cooper.'

'All following, sir.'

The sun had now cleared the eastern horizon, and there was every promise of an absolutely beautiful day, except . . . it was cloudless overhead, and to the south and west, with excellent visibility; the headland to port was clear and even green. But to the north there was a patch of cloud, dark, and growing almost visibly, while the wind had freshened some more; from the sea state he estimated it as Force Four to Five, fifteen to twenty knots. But the waves remained no more than moderate, perhaps four feet. And they had to be in the minefield by now. His hands involuntarily tightened on the wheel as he looked down at the surging blue water to either side.

'I have smoke, green fifteen,' Cooper remarked. 'Estimated distance fifteen miles. Would that be the end of the field?'

'Or she's using a swept channel,' Duncan said, never taking his eyes from the sea in front of him. 'Can you identify?'

'Too small for a battleship. In fact . . . I would say she's a freighter.'

'Is she approaching?'

'At this moment, no, sir.'

'Just keep an eye on her. Astern, Mr Rawlings?'

'All looks correct astern, sir. But I have a flashing light, red ten.'

'A beacon, you mean?' He found that hard to believe, in time of war.

Rawlings studied the horizon for some moments through his glasses. 'It's not a beacon. I would say it's Morse. But in Italian.'

'Then we'll have to ignore it.' He cast a hasty glance at his watch. 'We should be through. Course is three five oh for the next hour. Take the helm, Mr Cooper.'

The tension had left him feeling quite exhausted, for the moment. He thumbed the intercom. 'You may like to know that we are through the minefield,' he announced, and listened to the spontaneous burst of applause coming up through the hatch.

He looked to port, made out the flashing light. It was definitely signalling.

'What do you reckon he'll do, as we haven't responded?' Rawlings asked.

'What he should do is have us investigated. I imagine he is on the phone now, rustling up an aircraft or two. However, as we are dealing with Italians, and it is very early in the morning, I think there's a good chance of it being an hour or so before he gets much response.' He levelled his glasses ahead. 'Brindisi! Signal flotilla, Mr Rawlings. Good luck. I'll take her, Mr Cooper. Check that smoke to starboard.'

'It's not approaching, sir. So far so good, eh?'

'Almost too good to be true. Now, keep your eyes glued on those breakwaters. *Napoli* is a big ship; she should stand up like a skyscraper.'

Cooper turned his glasses to the north-west. The flotilla was now parallel with the coast, distance about fifteen miles, but gradually closing. 'Nothing, there, sir. You don't suppose . . .'

'She's around. She's put to sea. The question is, how long ago. Mr Rawlings, make to flotilla: Negative. Target at sea. Spread out until located.'

'Aye-aye, sir.'

Duncan adjusted his course to due north as they passed the port. Now the clouds in front of him were clustering very close, dark and black, and the wind was howling, while the seas were big, with deep troughs and breaking crests, into which *412* smashed with bone-shaking force.

'Mr Rawlings,' Duncan said, 'Signal: Reduce speed as necessary,' and himself brought the revolutions down to fifteen hundred to avoid the risk of hull damage. The movement immediately became easier, but remained severe.

'Signal from *413*, sir,' Rawlings said. 'Large vessel bearing green ten.'

Beattie was about half a mile away to starboard. Cooper levelled his binoculars in the required direction. 'Well, glory be,' he said. 'that's a battleship.'

As he spoke, Rawlings said, 'Aircraft approaching from the west, sir.'

'They'll have a job finding us in all this spray,' Duncan said. 'Make to flotilla, Mr Rawlings: Go.'

He decided against resuming full speed until he had to. The battleship was about ten miles away, steaming north at about fifteen knots, he estimated. So the MTBs would close her over the next hour.

'Keep an eye on those aircraft, Mr Cooper,' he said. 'Mr Rawlings, sound action stations. And unfurl the flag.'

'Aye-aye, sir.' Rawlings rang the bell, and the crew came on deck.

'Prepare for sudden alterations in speed,' Duncan warned into the tannoy. 'Topsides, Jamie.'

He looked right and left. *413* was on his right, *417* beyond her, another half mile further on. Linton had brought *414* up on his left. All the boats now had their ensigns streaming in the wind, and all were bucking and plunging in the big seas. But they were all practised torpedo-boat skippers and would know that firing had to be timed to the wave formation, as the torpedoes would travel in a straight line from the angle of release, just as in the old days of sailing ships the guns had to be fired on the upward roll.

'They've spotted us,' Cooper remarked.

He was talking about the planes.

'Do we signal the flotilla to take evasive action?'

'No we do not, Mr Cooper. Not until the attack has been carried out.'

Cooper gulped.

'Ships astern, sir,' Rawlings commented.

'Such as?'

'Destroyers, I would say.'

'Range?'

'Ten miles, maybe.'

'Then they won't catch us before we attack.'

Four miles.

'Man the tubes, Mr Rawlings. Mr Cooper, I don't think our popgun will make even a dent in that armour, but you may fire at the deck.'

'Aye-aye, sir,' they answered together, and left the bridge to go forward.

Duncan watched pillars of water rising out of the sea in front of them; the bombers had miscalculated their speed and overshot. Three miles. By the time the planes came round again the flotilla would be within range.

But now the warship itself was alerted, and along the sides there came a ripple of red. She was using her secondary armament, but with the boats bucking and dipping, and the seas now breaking in every direction, accuracy was difficult.

He glanced right and left. The other boats were still in line and clearly still operational. Two nautical miles, four thousand yards. Maximum range, but the sea around him was being peppered with shot. One moment more, he thought. One moment, as he lined the boat up on the battleship's midship section. She was making no attempt to take evasive action; her captain was obviously confident that the torpedo boats could not get close enough to deliver without being sunk.

'Fire one,' he shouted 'Fire two!'

The words had hardly left his mouth when there was a violent explosion.

The blast seemed to check the boat in mid-plunge; Jamie was thrown across the mess cabin and landed on the starboard bulkhead, momentarily dazed. He looked around him, not sure whether to expect water pouring in or hear a final explosion as he was hurled into oblivion.

But the MTB was still afloat and plunging ahead, although from the motion clearly out of control. The reinforced glass of the cabin window was cracked but not shattered. 'Mr Wilson?' he asked. 'Mr Wilson!' he shouted.

There was no response. He staggered to his feet, half fell against the ladder, clawed his way up to the bridge, and looked around himself in consternation. Duncan lay where he had been thrown, against the mast, and was clearly unconscious, if not dead. While the boat was careering in circles, being thrown left and right by the waves, water flew everywhere.

He fell against the console, grasped the wheel. The boat had turned away from the battleship, and the wind was now behind them, and blowing the flames from the burning foredeck over the bow rather than aft to consume the rest of the ship. But it also meant that they were now heading back towards the chasing destroyers . . . save that the destroyers had disappeared, obliterated by the heavy rain that had suddenly started, crashing on to his bare head – his hat had come off at some time.

Behind him he heard two huge explosions. Somebody's torpedoes must have struck. But there was no time to consider celebrating. The rain was even tending to dowse the flames, but this was to leave the foredeck exposed for the shambles it was, with the planking torn up, and bodies scattered everywhere. It really was a miracle that they hadn't gone down like a stone, and indeed, if they were still afloat, the bow was already lower in the water that it should be. Hastily he reduced speed to a thousand revs.

It was time for an instant decision. He doubted the rain was going to last more than fifteen minutes, at which time, if he continued on this course they could be a sitting duck for the destroyers. But if there was a hole in the bow, to turn up to the sea would bring foundering that much closer. On the other hand, he reckoned land was only about twenty miles away. Albania? Or Yugoslavia? Albania was occupied by the Italians, Yugoslavia by the Germans. Or was it? They had certainly invaded the country, but he had read somewhere that the Yugoslavs were resisting. It was their best bet. Their only bet, he reckoned.

The new course brought the seas on to his beam, but he had steered his father's boat in similar circumstances in the English Channel, and as he had expected, at twelve knots the MTB skated up and down the sides of the waves more comfortably than when she had been smashing into them.

This was satisfactory, but there was so much to be done, and he couldn't leave the helm. 'Mr Wilson!' he shouted down the hatch. 'Mr Wilson!'

It seemed an eternity, then Wilson emerged, blood rolling down his cheek from where he had been thrown against he bulkhead. 'Jesus!' he muttered. 'What happened?'

'We stopped one. Listen, we're making water forward. Can you get into the engine room and start the pump?'

Wilson stared at Duncan still slumped against the mast. 'The skipper's hurt!'

'So are a lot of others. But we can't do a lot for them if we sink. The pump, Mr Wilson. The pump!'

Wilson disappeared, and a few moments later there came the reassuring clack of the pump accompanied by the swish of water streaming over the side. Wilson retuned. 'There's a bloody big hole in the bow. It's above the waterline, but there's a hell of a lot of water down there. We shouldn't be steering so close to the seas.'

'There's a clutch of destroyers back there. I reckon our best bet is to beach her.'

'Beach her?' Wilson peered forward into the suddenly murky morning. 'Beach her where?'

'There's land just over there.'

'Oh, yes? And we spend the rest of the war in an Eyetie prison camp?'

'That has to be better than drowning. Anyway, it needn't happen. Can you take the helm?'

'Not me. I don't know anything about steering. I'm a bleeding cook.'

'True,' Jamie agreed, glancing at his face. 'Well then, do something about the skipper.'

Wilson dropped to his knees beside Duncan. 'God, he's out cold. You sure he's not dead?'

'Why don't you find out? I think he hit his head when he was knocked off his feet.'

'He's breathing. But he's hurt bad. Look at the way he's lying. He's broken something.'

'Is there any blood?'

'Some.'

'But he's not actually bleeding?'

'I don't think so.'

'And he's unconscious. Leave him for the time being, and see what you can do about the chaps on deck. They can't all be dead.'

Almost he thought the cook was going to say, 'Aye-aye, sir.' Instead he slid down the short ladder to the deck.

Jamie concentrated. The rain was still teeming, which effectively concealed them from the Italians. But it also meant that he could not see more than a hundred yards in front of himself, and the howling of the wind meant that he couldn't hear anything, either. Helming the boat in the cross seas, which, if quietened by the rain, were still big and breaking, was an exhausting business, and every so often one came on deck, moving the bodies to and fro and no doubt bringing curses from Wilson, although he couldn't hear them either.

He had no watch. The actual time wasn't important, but

he would have liked to know how much time had elapsed since he had taken control. Of course even that would be meaningless, as his starting point had been pure assumption. He had estimated that they had to be no more than twenty miles from the Yugoslav coast. He had slowed right down to hardly more than ten knots; even so they had to be pretty close. But the bow was sinking ever lower.

Wilson climbed back on to the bridge, dripping water from the waves flooding the deck. 'You know there are only eight down there?'

'I didn't count.'

'There were fourteen,' the cook said, morosely. 'That means six went overboard when we were hit.' He looked astern.

'Well, there's damn all we can do about them now,' Jamie said. 'How about the others?'

'They're all dead.'

'*All* of them?' Jamie couldn't believe his ears.

'I reckon that shell fragmented when it hit. Lucky for us, I guess. If it had kept on going as solid shot it'd have torn the guts out of us.'

'Mr Cooper?'

'He's not there. Must've gone overboard.'

'Shit! Mr Rawlings?'

'He has a big sliver of shrapnel sticking out of his chest. You think I should push them over?'

'No.'

'It'd be as good a burial as they're going to get.'

'When this weather clears a stream of dead bodies floating about will tell the Eyeties we came this way.'

Wilson blew through his teeth. 'You have a cold head on those young shoulders.'

One of us has to have, Jamie thought. But he said, 'I thought I heard the skipper groan just now. See what you can do.'

Wilson dropped to his knees beside Duncan, while Jamie realized that the rain was easing, and visibility was lifting. But it still wasn't more than a mile. A totally grey mile, of heaving, white-capped waves. And the bow was now nearly awash; he didn't reckon they had more than half an hour.

And remembered that these waters had seen two famous naval battles, Actium, in 31 BC, when the fleet of Augustus and Agrippa had shattered those of Antony and Cleopatra, and Lepanto in 1571, when the Christian fleet of Don Juan of Austria had beaten the Ottomans of Uluch Ali. The seabed beneath him must be littered with rotting ships and rusting armour. And maybe even a grinning skeleton or two. Soon to be joined by a few more.

'I think his knee is broken,' Wilson said. 'And maybe a couple of ribs.' As he felt about he was rewarded by a shout of pain. 'And he's woken up.'

'Get below and find something to splint him with,' Jamie snapped. 'And there are painkillers in the first aid locker.'

'I'm a bloody cook, not a doctor,' Wilson grumbled, but he went down the hatch; Jamie knew, because he had watched him, that he was actually a very capable medical orderly.

'Jamie,' Duncan gasped.

'I'm here, sir.'

'What happened?'

'We were hit, sir. I'm afraid we're taking water.'

'Let me speak with Mr Cooper.'

'Mr Cooper is no longer on board, sir.'

'What? Then find Mr Rawlings.'

'Mr Rawlings is dead, sir.'

'Oh, my God! Who have we got?'

'Mr Wilson, sir. And me.'

Duncan gasped, whether from pain or mental distress Jamie couldn't be sure. But at that moment Wilson returned with a couple of legs he had apparently torn off the collapsed mess table, as well as the First Aid box. 'Here we are, sir,' He knelt beside his captain.

'What? My God, I'm in pain. Wilson, you say? Wilson? Are you in command?'

'Ah . . . no, sir. Young Jamie's taken command. Well, he knows more about it than I do. Now, sir, open your mouth . . . here we go. Now take a swig of this.'

There was a gasp. 'What the—'

'Whisky, sir. Best thing.'

'Jamie,' Duncan muttered. 'Jamie! Where are we? What's happening? Where are we going?'

'We're closing the shore, sir. Soon be there.'

There was no reply, so he looked over his shoulder.

Duncan's head had sagged against Wilson's knee. 'Crikey! What did you give him?'

'A double dose of morphine.'

'In whisky? Shit!'

'Well, I have to straighten this leg and set it, eh? I wouldn't like him to be awake when I'm doing that. Can't you hold this fucking thing steady?'

'No, I can't.'

As he spoke, there was another violent check to the boat's forward motion.

The Aftermath

It was midnight when Lonsdale and Kristin landed at Gibraltar. They had not spoken throughout the flight, Kristin staring resolutely in front of her, but when they disembarked the admiral said, tentatively, 'These people will find you somewhere to sleep; we'll be on our way again tomorrow.'

Kristin regarded him for some seconds. 'Do I know you?' she asked, and followed the waiting Wren into the terminal building.

'I'm told I'm supposed to stay with you all night,' the young woman said, apprehensively, as she led her towards a waiting command car.

'Of course you must,' Kristin agreed. 'I'm an extremely dangerous criminal, being returned to England for trial. Didn't they tell you?'

'What?' She looked left and right, as if seeking an MP.

Kristin got into the back of the car. 'I am probably going to be hanged. Are you taking me to prison?'

'I was told to take you to The Rock for the night.'

'I suppose your prisons are all full.'

The Wren considered this while the car moved off. 'My name is Jennie.'

'How sweet.'

'And you are Lady Eversham. How should I address you?'

'Did you say that you are spending the night with me?'

'It's a twin-bedded room.'

'How inconvenient. But in circumstances of such rampant intimacy, I think you had better call me Kristin.'

'Oh, I like Christine. I think it is such a pretty name.'

'I'm sure it is. But it doesn't happen to be *my* name. I spell mine with a K, and there is no E on the end.'

'Oh! Ah . . .'

'So you see,' Kristin said, 'I am not only a dangerous criminal, I am also an enemy alien. I would sleep with your pistol drawn.'

'I don't have a pistol.'

'That could be unfortunate. Now I suggest we terminate this conversation. I need to have a brood.'

In fact, her sense of outrage was already diminishing; it was not an emotion she had ever allowed to interfere with her life before. Of course, this was the first time she had ever been deported from anywhere – although she supposed that she had been on the point of being deported from Guernsey by the Germans when Duncan and Jamie had so conveniently turned up. It was more the outrageous behaviour of Jimmy, acting as if he owned her; if she had not already ended their engagement, she would certainly do so now. And it might be necessary; from the way he had picked up and pocketed the engagement ring he had clearly not accepted her gesture as final.

What was really annoying was the thought that Duncan and Jamie had been sent off somewhere beyond her ken, or her ability to get to them. Rebecca had promised to see what she could find out, but she had no idea how long the American was going to be detained in Cairo, and if she would be coming back via England. It was all so frustrating, after she had gone to so much trouble, and taken such a considerable risk . . . to spend one night in Jamie's arms! And it had not even been a full night.

Even so, it was a night she would never forget, especially as it might be a few months before she could have another. She supposed, in cold, conventional, pedantic terms, she was totally irresponsible, in her pursuit of her desires. But was not desire the driving force behind every human action, whether it was the desire to be more powerful than anyone else, or more rich than anyone else, or more famous than anyone else? In her case, the desire was for experience, and as, because she was a woman, she could not go into action alongside Duncan – except illegally, she thought with some satisfaction – what was left to her, save love, and sex, and physical ecstasy?

'Is there anything else you would like, milady?' Jennie asked, anxiously, as she finished her midnight snack.

'I'm sure I could think of something,' Kristin agreed. 'But I don't think you're the one to provide it. Also, I'm very tired. Just let's go to sleep.'

'How long do you propose to keep up this schoolgirl sulk?' Lonsdale inquired, as they strapped themselves in for the flight home.

'Certainly until after you have apologized,' Kristin said.

'Then I apologize, unreservedly. I was acting in your own best interests.'

'I should remind you that the only person who is capable of knowing what my best interests are is me. However, I will accept your apology if you will tell me where Duncan and . . . his boat have gone, or are going.'

Lonsdale sighed, and looked at his watch. 'I imagine he's just about there now.'

'Where?'

'The Strait of Otranto.'

Kristin turned her head to look at him while the plane soared into the air. 'The Strait of Otranto? That's—'

'The mouth of the Adriatic Sea. He and the flotilla are on their way to Brindisi.'

'But the Adriatic is virtually an Italian lake.'

'I'm afraid it is. That's why I couldn't tell you before. The operation is top secret.'

Kristin stared at him. 'You have sent my son, and . . . and his crew, into the Adriatic? In their little wooden boats? Don't you realize—'

'That it is virtually a suicide mission. Yes, I do realize that.'

'You bas—'

'Kristin, *I* did not send them anywhere.'

'Then what are they doing? Why were you in Malta, anyway? It wasn't just to pick me up.'

'No, it was not. I was sent to Malta because the MTBs have been my babies since the War started. I was required to give my on the spot evaluation as to whether the proposed operation was viable.'

'And you went for it.'

'I told them it was a suicide mission. But I was overruled. I wasn't helped by Duncan's insistence that the operation was possible.'

'Well, he would, wouldn't he,' Kristin growled 'What was so important about this mission, anyway?'

'They were supposed to torpedo and if possible sink the new Italian super-battleship *Napoli*. There was no other means of getting at her.'

'And you think . . .'

'They left the same time we did, to make the crossing from Malta in darkness. They were due to enter the Strait at dawn, that is, just over an hour ago. They'll have reached Brindisi by now and completed the job, and be on their way back.'

'And you expect them to get back?'

'I think –' Lonsdale chose his words with care – 'that there is a good chance of at least one getting back.'

'You can sit there and say something like that to me?'

'What else am I supposed to say? It's happening, right this minute. And there is not a goddamned thing either you or I can do about it. I'm sorry, Kristin, but there are occasions in life we cannot control, no matter how much we might wish to.'

Again she stared at him, this time in wonderment, as she realized that he was genuinely upset; he had never revealed such passion before. 'When will you know?' she asked, her voice quiet.

'They have promised to inform me the moment they regain Valetta. Obviously they are maintaining radio silence.'

'And when should they get home?'

'Perhaps about six tonight.'

'Thank you, Jimmy. It is good of you to put me in the picture.'

'Kristin . . .'

'Right now, I don't think I want to do anything save wait.'

It was past noon when they touched down at an airfield in Kent, having fortunately encountered no German aircraft over Biscay, and after lunch it was a drive of three hours down to Lymington. Lonsdale accompanied her, but spoke little on the journey, only asking as they stopped before the house, 'Are you going to be all right?'

'Why should I not be all right?'

'Well—'

'Just let me know as soon as you hear something. There's Lucifer!' She got out as Harry opened the door, and a moment later was in the paws of the dog. 'There,' she said. 'I told you I'd only be gone a couple of hours. Dogs can't tell time,' she explained to an anxious admiral. 'I'm waiting to hear from you.'

Lucifer subsided and a few moments later she was in her sitting room with Alison, who had thoughtfully opened a bottle of champagne. 'I imagine you have a lot to tell me,' she suggested.

'A lot,' Kristin mused, sitting on the settee, and trying to select her words. 'Aren't you drinking?'

'Not right now. I think it gives Baby hiccups.' Alison sat beside her. 'Wasn't that the admiral in the car? Did he arrange for you to come back?'

'He collected me himself.'

'Good lord! I didn't realize he'd go that far! You mean he went to Malta just to get you back? Now there is true love.'

Kristin drained her glass and held it out. 'I'll have another. Jimmy did not go to Malta to collect me. He was required to go there on duty, and thought he might as well pick me up at the same time.'

Alison refilled her glass. 'It just goes to show how things always turn out for the best.'

'When I refused to come, he had me deported.'

'Oh! Well, if it was the only way, perhaps—'

'Jimmy Lonsdale is history.'

'Oh!' Alison tried to change the subject. 'Did you manage to see Duncan, and . . . ah . . .'

'I saw both Duncan and Jamie. Aren't you interested in why Jimmy had to go to Malta?'

'Well, I suppose it was something secret.'

'It was.' Kristin patted the settee. 'Come and sit down and I will tell you what it was.'

Alison obeyed, frowning. She listened in silence, then got up and refilled Kristin's glass, taking one for herself. 'It's half-past five.'

'Then they should just be getting back.'

Alison looked at the radio.

'I don't think there will be anything on the BBC for a while,' Kristin said. 'Jimmy promised to be in touch the moment he heard anything. I haven't told you how Rebecca and I were sunk.'

'*What*?'

'We spent a whole day drifting round the Mediterranean. Haven't you noticed anything about my complexion?'

'It's sunburned.'

'So you supposed I have spent the last week lying in the sun. Well, that is not entirely inaccurate. I will tell you exactly what happened.'

It was half past six when she finished, and Alison, who had just completed Baby Duncan's feed, was becoming increasingly restive. 'I've just remembered,' she said, 'that Malta is at least one if not two hours ahead of us. That means it's at least half-past seven there. If the flotilla was expected back at six . . .'

'Now you know there could have been any sort of delays . . .'

The telephone rang. Both women rose, but Alison got there first, Baby still on her arm. 'Eversham House.'

'Ah . . . Alison?'

'Yes, Admiral.'

'Is Kristin there?'

'She's here. And she has put me in the picture.'

'Ah. Um . . .'

'Please, Admiral. Tell me how the mission went.'

'The mission. Yes. It seems to have been a great success.'

Relief raced through Alison's body. 'Thank God!'

'Yes, indeed. Lieutenant Linton reports that at least three torpedoes hit.'

'You mean the battleship was sunk?'

'He couldn't confirm that. But she's certainly been badly damaged, and should be out of action for several months. That is actually the best we were hoping for.'

'Well, hallelujah! Did you hear that, Kristin? The op was a success.'

'I heard that,' Kristin said. 'And that the report was made by Lieutenant Linton. Would Jimmy care to explain that?'

'Admiral?' Alison asked.

She could hear him gulp. 'Yes. Well . . . only one boat got back. Linton's *414.*'

The receiver slipped from Alison's hand, and hung from its cord as she hugged the baby against her. Kristin put her arm round the younger woman's waist, and regained the receiver.

'Alison?' Lonsdale asked.

'It's me,' Kristin said. 'What happened to the other three boats?'

'We don't know. But . . .'

'What?'

'*Napoli* had left Brindisi when the flotilla got there, but they caught her up about an hour later, and went straight into the attack. Up to that moment they seem not to have been spotted, but then they were subject not only to fire from the warship but bombing from aircraft, and were being followed by a flotilla of destroyers. As I say, they seem to have scored three hits. Duncan's orders were to scatter the moment they had fired their torpedoes, and get home as best they could. This Linton did. He reckons he was saved by a sudden violent rain squall which cut visibility and was followed by mist. He also suspects that there was a good deal of confusion on the Italian side, with most of their attention being concentrated on getting *Napoli* back to port.'

'So, he doesn't actually know if the other boats were lost.'

'No, but . . . ah . . .'

'*Digame,*' Kristin shouted, reverting to Spanish as she was inclined to do when under stress.

'He saw *412* take a hit, moments before the rain arrived.'

'You mean he saw her explode?'

'He didn't see an explosion. But she was definitely on fire, then she disappeared into the rain and mist. And as I said, neither she nor either of the other boats made it back to Valetta. Kristin?'

Kristin hugged Alison.

'Listen,' Lonsdale said. 'They're all going to get gongs. And Duncan will get the Victoria Cross. I guarantee that.'

'Posthumously,' Kristin said.

'Well, yes. It will be a posthumous award. Alison will have to receive it.'

'What the fucking use is that to anybody?' Kristin inquired, and hung up.

'What in the name of God!' Wilson shouted, as he rolled across the bridge deck. He had been in the act of taking off Duncan's pants to discover exactly what had happened to him, and retained most of the material in his hands, the garment having been torn in half.

Jamie had been thrown forward, across the wheel, and now fell sideways as a wave broke against the hull and tried to drive it over. But they were stuck fast. He pulled himself up, gasping for breath, instinctively switched off the ignition, and stared into the gloom. Concentrating as he had been on coping with the beam seas he hadn't realized just how murky the day had become; the rain had slackened to a drizzle, but had been replaced by mist. But yet . . . he peered forward, and was sure he could make out something solid.

Wilson struggled to his knees. 'Are we sinking?'

'No. We're aground.'

The cook pulled himself up to stand beside the helm. 'Out here? Then we're done.'

'No we're not. Look!'

He pointed east, and another wave broke on the hull, forcing them to hold on to avoid being thrown over again. While now there was an ominous cracking sound from beneath them.

'Christ! She's breaking up,' Wilson shouted.

'So we have to hurry. Come on, we have to patch the skipper up first. Then we have to get out of here.'

'To go where, boy?'

'There!' Again he flung out his arm. 'Look, for Christ's sake!'

Wilson stared into the mist. 'I don't see anything. Or . . . wait a mo . . . there's something.'

'Land,' Jamie told him. 'The coast of Yugoslavia. Or at least one of the islands off the coast.'

'How do you know?'

'Because it can't be anywhere else. Come *on*.'

He knelt beside Duncan, peered at the exposed leg, bent back at a sickening angle. There was very little blood and no splintered bones to be seen, so he estimated the damage was confined to the knee. That was definitely at least dislocated. 'Give us a hand.'

Wilson knelt on the other side, and between them they carefully straightened the leg. Duncan moaned and moved restlessly.

'He's coming round,' the cook said.

'Not yet,' Jamie said, strapping the table legs into place. 'There you go. The best we can do, for the time being.'

'So what do we do with him now?'

'We get him ashore.'

'What? He'll drown. We'll drown. Oh, my God!'

From beneath them there came another loud crack.

'Of course we won't drown,' Jamie snapped. 'That water's only about four feet deep. We'll float him between us. Listen, get below, and pack a bag with some grub. Nothing that needs cooking. Biscuits and the like. All those chocolate bars you keep stashed away. Just leave room for the first aid kit.'

He went down the ladder himself, forward into the crew's quarters, to the locker where the firearms were kept. Here he was up to his ankles in water, while the stranded boat continued to shudder to the impact of each wave. But he felt sure the impacts were lessening in force; either the wind was dropping or the tide was falling – he didn't know if there was a tide, at least of any size, in the Adriatic.

He selected two rifles and two bandoliers, slung them, and went aft. Wilson was still packing a large canvas bag with food. 'Who are you aiming to shoot?'

'Anyone I don't like the look of, or who may not like the look of us.'

The water at the foot of the after companion was knee deep, and when he opened the engine room door he saw why; the hull was cracked wide open, and the precious Packard, on which he had lavished so many hours of devotion, was clearly never going to function again, unless it could be taken to a workshop and dried out within the next few hours, and that was not likely to happen.

He sighed, and went aft to Duncan's cabin. Here also there were a couple of feet of water. He pulled open the locker drawers and found another pair of pants, then in the desk located the skipper's service Smith and Wesson revolver; he had never fired a revolver himself, but there was always the chance that Duncan might recover sufficiently for it to be used in a scrap. The gun was loaded, but there was also a box of cartridges, and he took this as well. It would not fit into his pocket, but Wilson could add it to his collection.

Then he returned to the bridge, to find that Duncan had woken up, even if he was not fully functioning. 'Jamie!' he gasped. 'Thank God! I thought you'd abandoned me.'

'You know I'd never do that sir.'

'Where are we? What's happening? Why aren't we moving? That noise . . .?'

'I'm afraid we're stranded, sir. I did it deliberately, because we were sinking. We took a hit, forward.'

'Yes,' Duncan said. 'Yes. I remember. I thought we were done. Did the torpedoes get away?'

'They must have done, sir, just before we were hit. If they hadn't, we wouldn't be here now.'

Duncan gasped. 'God, my leg hurts.'

'I can imagine. I think the knee may be dislocated. Now, sir, we have to get ashore. The ship is breaking up.'

Duncan caught his arm. 'The flotilla!'

'I can't say, sir. It was a bit tricky. We had the battleship firing at us from in front, half a dozen destroyers coming up astern, and all these planes overhead.'

'A bit tricky,' Duncan muttered.

'What saved us,' Jamie went on, 'was a sudden heavy rain squall which lasted long enough for us to get out from under, as it were. But we had too much to do just keeping afloat to contact the others. And as we were making a lot of water, we decided our best bet was to beach her.'

'We, being?'

'Mr Wilson and me. We're the only survivors. With you,

of course. Everyone on deck bought it, or went overboard. There was no way we could turn back to look for them. Going by what happened to the other chaps, they were all probably dead anyway. I'm sorry about that, sir, but I had to make the decision, whether to try to save the ship or hazard her by turning back to look for those others.'

Wilson emerged from the hatch, his bulging haversack slung. 'It was Jamie did it all, sir. Took command, he did.'

'Well . . .'

'I know,' Duncan said. 'Someone had to do it. Thank God you were here, Jamie. You made the correct decision. Listen, did we score a hit?'

'I don't know if *we* did, sir. There were three big bangs.'

'Then maybe it was worth it.'

The rain was now no more than a light drizzle, and the mist had taken on a yellowish tinge to suggest that there could be a sun up there. The wind was also dropping all the time; if the boat was still swaying to every wave accompanied by dreadful grinding and cracking noises, the movement was becoming less violent.

Between them, Wilson and Jamie got Duncan down the ladder and on to the foredeck. There they paused for breath and to survey the eight dead men.

'Brave men,' Duncan said.

'Jamie said we should leave them, sir,' Wilson said. 'So as not to leave a trail.'

'Again, the correct decision. Well . . .'

Jamie looked at Morrison's upturned face. Lowndes lay close to him, but Jackman had disappeared, no doubt overboard. He wondered if they had found the boy who had offered them girls . . . was it only the night before last?

Duncan caught his expression. 'Morrison was a friend.'

'They were all my mates, sir.'

He dropped into the water beside the hull; as he had estimated, it was only just over three feet deep, had it been more than that, the MTB would not have stranded. The waves were still big enough to buffet him, but he had no doubt they could cope.

Wilson heaved Duncan over the side, and Jamie caught him.

'I can use my other leg,' he protested.

'And you'll need it, sir. But you'll need us as well. It's a fair distance.'

Wilson joined them, and they waded towards the shore, each holding one of Duncan's arms. It was slow going, over an uneven and uncertain bottom, patches of smooth and slippery rock being interspersed with sandy areas. Several times they all collapsed full length in the surge. But gradually they got down to knee and then ankle-deep water, and the going steadily got easier.

Jamie was by now more interested in the shore, which became steadily more visible as they approached and the mist thinned. It consisted of a rocky beach, behind which there was a pine forest. Whether it was an island he had no idea; he remembered reading that this entire coast was a mass of islands, so it seemed likely, but how far it might be from the mainland was also an unknown quantity. He realized that there were still one hell of a lot of decisions to be made, but their priority was to get to the shelter of the trees.

This they did as the setting sun finally broke through the clouds, and Duncan collapsed on the dry underbrush with a gasp, face contorted with pain.

'I have some morphine here, sir,' Wilson offered.

Duncan pushed himself up to sit with his back against a tree. 'I don't think that would be a good idea. We may need our wits. You wouldn't have any water?'

'I have a couple of canteens, yes, sir.'

They were all equally thirsty, which emptied one of the water bottles. They were still too churned up to feel like eating. Duncan looked at his watch, which was waterproof. 'Ten to five. What is your plan, Jamie?'

'Me, sir?'

'You're in command, remember?'

'That was while you were unconscious, sir.'

'I am still not fit enough to resume command. I'll be happy to go along with anything you have in mind. We obviously can't stay here for very long, and if a Jerry patrol comes along . . .'

Jamie considered. 'Very good, sir. I think the first thing we need to do is carry out a reconnaissance to establish just where we are. With your permission, I will have a look around.'

'It'll be dark in an hour.'

'This will be a preliminary recce, sir.'

'What about a fire?' Wilson asked. 'We're all sopping wet, and when that sun goes in it's going to get bloody cold.'

'No, fire, Mr Wilson,' Jamie said. 'There may be nasties about.'

Wilson looked at Duncan, who smiled through the pain. 'Mr Goring is in command, Mr Wilson.'

'I won't be long,' Jamie promised. He slung one of the rifles.

'Company!' Wilson muttered.

Jamie unslung the rifle again, turned to look at the four men coming through the trees. 'They're not German soldiers,' he said.

'But they've got guns,' Wilson pointed out.

'From what I was told in Malta,' Duncan said. 'The man you want to ask for is named Tito.'

'Hi,' Rebecca said. 'Remember me?'

'Good God!' Admiral Lonsdale said into the telephone. 'Mrs Strong!'

'Excuse me?'

'Well, Rebecca. This is a surprise.'

'I hope it's not an unpleasant one.'

'Good God, no. But . . . ah . . . where are you calling from?'

'I'm at the railway station here in Portsmouth. I thought I should make my number, right, before turning up at your office.'

'You mean you wish to come here?'

'I wish to see you. As I happen to be in England. I thought we might have dinner together. I'm happy to go Dutch.'

'Dutch? I don't think we have a Dutch restaurant here in Portsmouth. I'll have to ask around.'

'You know something, Jimmy? I am going to have to re-educate you. Just tell me where we can meet. That is, if you want to see me again.'

'Of course I'd like to see you again, Rebecca.'

'Then I'll be along as soon as I can find a cab. They seem to be a little thin on the ground around here.'

'No, no. Don't worry with a taxi. I'll send my car for you.'

'Gee. Now that's real sweet of you.'

'So,' she said, when, after a tentative embrace, she was seated before his desk. 'How are you keeping?'

'I'm very well. And better for seeing you.'

Which was no lie. In her smart new suit and matching hat she was more attractive than ever, certainly knowing, as he did, what lay beneath the material.

'Say, that's nice.'

He hesitated. 'About that night . . .'

'I won't say forget it, because I don't want to forget it. But I guess we'd both had a lot to drink.'

She waited, because she knew that he had very little to drink.

'I don't want to forget it either,' he admitted. 'But I behaved like the most utter cad.'

'For kissing me. And . . . well . . .'

'I am so terribly embarrassed about that.'

'Well, don't be. I like having a man's hands on my body. If he's the right man.'

'Yes, but at that time I was engaged to another woman. Kristin.'

'You mean you're not engaged to her now?'

'You saw her throw her ring at me.'

'Yeah. But Kristin, well . . . she's always been kind of impulsive. She'll come round.'

'Not this time.'

Rebecca raised her eyebrows. 'You didn't tell her about necking with me?'

'I'm not *that* much of a cad. But Kristin . . . I'm wondering if she ever did mean to go through with it.'

They gazed at each other for several seconds. Then he said, 'And you're in England . . .?'

'On my way home.'

'So, ah, was your mission successful?'

'I was shown everything I needed to see. I even had lunch with the great white chief, chap called Auchinlech. Now there's a mouthful. You know him?'

'Well, no. He's a field-marshal.'

'But you're an admiral.'

'A rear-admiral. That's the equivalent of a major-general in the army. Auchinlech probably has a dozen of those under his command.'

'Wow! Still, he seemed quite a decent guy, even if he didn't like everything I had to say.'

'You mean you're not going to recommend that your people let him have some modern tanks?'

'Oh, I'll recommend it. He sure needs them, from what I saw, and he didn't strike me as the kind of guy who'd give them up without a fight. But I can't recommend sending them through the Mediterranean. That browned him off a bit, because he's planning a big offensive for this summer. But there you go, he has his job to do and I have mine.'

Lonsdale gazed at her, admiringly. 'Are you as tough as you pretend?'

'Only in business matters. But say, you say you're only a rear-admiral. What's the next step up?'

'Vice.'

'Now that sounds interesting. When do you get to be in charge of vice?'

Lonsdale smiled; he guessed she was pulling his leg. 'Probably the day before I retire. They do that to boost your pension, you see.'

'Yeah. And when do you get to be a sir?'

'Probably never.'

'Oh, hell! That's a shame. Now tell me, how're things here?'

'Ah . . . what things?'

'Jimmy, you damned well know what things.'

'Hm. Well, she's taking it as well as can be expected.'

'Who?'

'Both of them really. I mean, they have each other to lean on, and the baby to think about. In the circumstances, that's probably fortunate.' He frowned. 'I suppose you don't know what I'm talking about.'

'I know exactly what you're talking about. My flight stopped at both Malta and Gibraltar. It's all the chat. And in Alexandria.'

'Ah. Then you know—'

'That Duncan didn't come back. But something cropped up just before I left Alex. Seems they received a radio message from some guy calling himself Tito. Ever heard of him?'

'Tito? Do you know, that rings a bell.'

'Seems he's a Yugoslav guerrilla.'

'That's the chap. Bit of a bad egg. He's a Communist.'

'Well, I guess he's a good egg right this minute. He, or his people, signalled that they had some English sailors with them, in the mountains or wherever it is they hang out, and asked for a plane to be sent to get them out.'

Lonsdale stared at her. 'You serious?'

'Cross my heart and hope to die.'

'Did he name these people?'

'Not so far as I know.'

'And when was this message received?'

'The day before I left Alex.'

The admiral shook his head. 'Then it can't be any of our people. The raid was three weeks ago. He wouldn't have waited that long to try to get them out.'

'You don't know that,' Rebecca argued. 'Those guys are fighting a guerrilla war, right? They're not sitting in a comfortable headquarters somewhere surrounded by equipment and secretaries. They'd have to be on the move all the time, dismantling their equipment, taking it somewhere, setting it up again . . .'

Lonsdale had been thinking. 'How do you know all this, anyway? About the radio message from Tito?'

'I make friends,' Rebecca said modestly. 'So you don't think it could be some of Duncan's lot?'

'I very much doubt it. I mean, apart from the time factor, Duncan is a lord. Surely this fellow Tito would have reported the presence of a peer of the realm.'

'Like you said, he's a Communist. Maybe things like peers of the realm don't register.'

'Hm. Are they sending a plane?'

'I reckon they're gonna try. It's not gonna be easy. Seems they've been flying some materiel in to these people, Partisans or whatever.'

'I think they're called Chetniks.'

'There's some chat about that, whether they're the same

or two separate groups. Anyway, the point is, sending stuff
in is risky enough, but that only has to be dropped. Now
they're being asked to put a plane down. That means a piece
of level ground, not overlooked by the enemy.'

'Hm. Yes. Well, all we can do is wait and see if they can
get them out, and who they are.'

'You don't think Kristin would be interested?'

'Perhaps, if we knew it was Duncan.'

'What do you mean, perhaps? He's her son!'

'Rebecca, we don't know that it's him. We don't even
know if these people are from Duncan's boat. Three MTBs
were lost on that operation. We don't even know if they're
off an MTB. We lost a sub in the Adriatic just over a month
ago. They could be survivors from that.'

'But there's a chance—'

'And you would like me to go rushing off to Kristin to
tell her there's a chance, a *chance* that Duncan may have
survived. What about the other fifty wives and mothers who
have been informed that their sons and husbands are missing
believed dead?'

'Well—'

'Listen to me. Kristin took the news as I would have
expected her to, on the chin. As I believe Alison also took
the news. After three weeks they will have come to terms
with the situation. Now we have to sit it out until we learn
just who these three people are. In the Navy, we do not
speculate, nor attempt to look at life through rose-coloured
spectacles. We deal in facts and realities. We cannot afford
to deal in anything else.'

He paused for breath, and also because of the way in which
Rebecca was looking at him.

'You know what,' she said. 'You have a problem. How
long have you been in this navy of yours?'

'I was a cadet at the age of sixteen.'

'And how old are you now?'

'I'm fifty-one.'

'Thirty-five fucking years, if you'll pardon my French.
You've become atrophied. Rigid from the neck up. I bet if
you lost your rule book you wouldn't be sure if it was right
to clean your teeth first thing every morning.'

'Rebecca, please.'

Rebecca stood up. 'Tell me what was left after Pandora opened her box and let all the evils known to mankind escape.'

'Ah . . .'

'Only one thing remained,' she said. 'Hope.' She went to the door. 'I'll see you around. Maybe.'

'Rebecca! Where are you going?'

'I'm not a member of your navy, Jimmy.' She closed the door behind herself.

Lucifer bounded along the path, barking vigorously. It was a brilliant early spring morning, and the rabbits were out in force.

'What do you suppose he would do?' Kristin asked, 'If he actually caught one?' She pushed the pram, while Alison walked beside her. They took a walk together every day, as they did most things together, sat in Kristin's sitting room every evening drinking quietly together.

They did not reminisce, because all their recent memories were shared. As for the future . . . but it had to be faced, sometime.

'He would probably have a heart attack,' Alison said. 'Kristin, I've been thinking.'

'Is that necessary?'

'It's been three weeks. We have to . . . well . . . about Duncan.'

Kristin turned her head, sharply.

'Baby Duncan.'

'He seems fine to me.'

'He is fine. But we have to . . . well, shouldn't we be putting his name down for school? I suppose you want him to go to Eton.'

'That's where Duncan went. I don't know if it did him any good.'

'Well, I suppose it taught him to be a gentleman.'

'A fate worse than death,' Kristin remarked. 'Oh, shit! I shouldn't have said that, should I?'

'No, you shouldn't,' Alison agreed.

'Do you think they, well, died together?'

It was the first time she had actually spoken about the tragedy for three weeks. And obviously she was thinking at least as much about Jamie as about Duncan.

Alison squeezed her hand.

'I'd like to think that,' Kristin mused. 'They did so much, in life, together. There's so much . . . I put petrol in the Bentley, yesterday. For the first time since . . . well, I hadn't seen the Gorings in all that time.'

'How are they taking it?'

'Tim looked so dreadful. What could I say? Do you know, I gave him a hug. I thought he was going to faint. But we were virtually related, by sex if not marriage.'

'Yes,' Alison agreed. 'I never told you, but I telephoned Barbara Parsons.'

'Were she and Cooper that close?'

'I think they were. But of course, as there had been nothing official, she hadn't been officially informed.'

'And how did she take it?'

'She wept a bit.'

'Poor kid. What the hell is that?'

They had come in sight of the house.

'It looks like a taxi,' Alison suggested.

'Shit! Who the hell . . .'

Lucifer had started barking again at the sight of the strange car, and Harry opened the door for them.

'Who is it, and where?' Kristin inquired.

'It's the American lady, milady. Mrs Strong. You remember—'

'Of course I remember,' Kristin cried and ran into the house, nearly falling over Lucifer. 'Rebecca! Where are you?'

'Here,' Rebecca said from the top of the stairs. 'Your man said you wouldn't mind.'

'Mind?' Kristin ran up the stairs to embrace her. 'It's so lovely to see you. Alison –' she looked back down the stairs – 'oh, she's taken Duncan up to change. She'll be along in a minute. Have you had a drink?'

'I helped myself to your Bristol Cream.'

'I'll join you.' She poured, topped Rebecca's glass. 'So, you're on your way home. Has it been a successful trip?'

'It had its ups and downs.'

'I'll say.'

'But on the whole, successful. It's certainly broadened my horizons.'

'Which is never a bad thing. Are you seeing Jimmy?'

'I have seen Jimmy.'

'Ah. First things first. How are you progressing?'

'We are not progressing.'

'What? What happened. I thought—'

'So did I. Well, perhaps. But I discovered, somewhat belatedly, that he already has a wife.'

'What? The bastard! And he proposed marriage to me?'

'This isn't actually a woman. It's a uniform.'

Kristin sat down. 'When did you find that out?'

'Yesterday morning.'

'Well, then, you probably had a lucky escape.'

'We fell out,' Rebecca said, 'because I felt I had something to tell you, and he didn't think I should.'

'I see. Well . . .'

'Let's wait for Alison. Oh, here she is. Come and sit down, Alison. Oh, and Kristin, you had better give her a drink.'

Kristin raised her eyebrows; the only person who normally gave orders in her house was herself. But she obeyed.

'Now sit down as well,' Rebecca commanded. 'And listen.'

Kristin and Alison were with Tim and Mary Goring at the station to greet the train when it arrived. Admiral Lonsdale was also there. As the news that the returning men were indeed Duncan and two of his crew had been received a month previously, he had got over any embarrassment about refusing to put them in the picture immediately, but he was clearly somewhat apprehensive at finding himself in such close proximity to Kristin. However, she smiled at him. 'Well, Jimmy, no doom and gloom today, eh?'

'Well, of course, it's a joyous occasion. But you do understand . . .' He looked anxiously as Alison.

'Here we go again,' Kristin said. 'Yes, we do know. The important thing is that he, they, are alive.'

'They're here,' Alison announced.

The train stopped. Duncan was first off, carefully placing his crutches and being assisted by two porters, and by Jamie.

Both were wearing new uniforms and looked very smart. Wilson had already departed for his London home.

Alison never said a word, just put both arms round him for a hug, then pulled her head back to peer at him. His face was unmarked, but it had aged. She kissed him, and looked past him at Jamie, and now did speak. 'Welcome home, Mr Goring. Welcome home.' In contrast to Duncan, he seemed quite unaffected by his ordeal. 'We'll look after him now,' she said.

'Yes, milady.' He was embraced by his mother, while his father shook his hand.

'Duncan!' Kristin hugged her son in turn. 'Oh, Duncan!'

'Duncan,' Lonsdale said, shaking his hand. 'It is good to have you back.'

'I'm afraid not immediately, sir. The quacks tell me it's going to take at least six months for this broken knee to knit, and then probably another six months of rehab.'

'That is the best news I have heard in a long time,' Alison said. 'With respect, Admiral. It means he'll be able to spend some time with his son, for a while.'

'No one will begrudge him that. There'll be a ship waiting for him as soon as he's ready. But you will be able to attend the investiture, eh? The Victoria Cross, what?'

'Ah,' Duncan said. 'It's very good of you to recommend me, sir. But I don't really deserve it. All I did was carry out my orders, as did everyone else in the flotilla. What about Beattie, and Wilcox, not to mention their crews? And my own people. Rawlings. Cooper. My God, Cooper. Has anyone told Second Officer Parsons?''

'Ah,' Lonsdale said. 'Probably not. I mean, they weren't related, or even officially engaged.'

'I told her,' Alison said.

Duncan hugged her.

'And they're all going to be recognized, posthumously,' the admiral said. 'And Linton, of course.'

'Thank God he got back,' Duncan said. 'If anyone was going to cop it, I would have said it would be him.'

'But you were the leader.'

'Yes, sir. But I did nothing over and above the call of duty. Engine-Artificer Goring did that.'

'What?'

'Sir?' Jamie gasped.

'When I was laid out by the blast, sir,' Duncan said, 'And the ship was in a sinking condition, Goring took command, and took both Cook Wilson and me to safety, under the very eyes of the enemy. He saved our lives, sir.'

'Good Heavens! Well, of course his action must be recognized.'

'With respect, sir,' Jamie said. 'I was saving my own life as well.'

'That's what they all say,' Kristin declared. She grasped Jamie's hand, and Alison watched the private message that passed between their eyes and their fingers. 'You saved my son's life and you deserve every possible recognition for that.' She released him and shook Tim's hand in turn then embraced Mary. 'You must be very proud of your son. Now I think we had better be getting my son home. For someone with only one working leg he's been standing around far too long.' She held out her hand. 'It's been nice meeting you again, Admiral Lonsdale.'

Lonsdale flushed. 'Lady Eversham . . . Kristin . . . may I call, to make sure that Duncan is getting on all right?'

'I'm sure Alison and Duncan will be very happy to see you, Admiral. And Lucifer, of course.'

She got behind the wheel of the Bentley, while Alison helped Duncan into the back seat and sat beside him. 'That was a bit rough on the poor chap,' Alison said.

'I think I was very polite,' Kristin countered.

'Have I missed something?' Duncan asked.

'Only that I am no longer engaged. Alison will explain it all to you.'

'Don't you think you should do that?' Alison asked.

'You know all the facts. Anyway . . .' She drove into the yard of Eversham House. 'I know you both have an awful lot to talk about. And to do. I assume you lunched on the train, Duncan?'

'Yes, I did.'

'Then I will leave you to it. I will see you later. Alison, just make sure that Lucifer doesn't knock him over.'

'Mother, there is absolutely no necessity for you to go off. We all have a lot to talk about.'

'I know, my darling boy. And we will, this evening. But you and Alison need to be alone for a while. We'll have our chat this evening. And I have something to do.'

'What have you got to do that is so urgent?'

'Well, do you know,' Kristin said. 'What with everything that has been happening, I haven't checked *Kristin* out, oh, since before Christmas. I really must go and make sure that she's all right. I'll see you later.' She engaged gear and drove away before he could protest further.

He looked at Alison. 'What on earth . . .? What does she suppose can possibly have happened to the yacht?'

Alison helped him towards the front door. 'Don't worry about it. Checking out *Kristin* is her hobby.'